I'll Stand By You

By

Wendy Kathryn Owen

Please enjoy with my very best wishes

Copyright © 2017 Wendy Kathryn Owen

ISBN: 978-0-244-94650-0

All rights reserved, including the right to reproduce this book, or portions thereof in any form. No part of this text may be reproduced, transmitted, downloaded, decompiled, reverse engineered, or stored, in any form or introduced into any information storage and retrieval system, in any form or by any means, whether electronic or mechanical without the express written permission of the author.

This is a work of fiction. Names and characters are the product of the author's imagination and any resemblance to actual persons, living or dead, is entirely coincidental.

PublishNation
www.publishnation.co.uk

1

"Do you want this table pushed back against the wall Love?" Tom Mortimer asked his wife, as he hefted the last of the leather upholstered dining room chairs through to the lounge.

"Mmmm.....please" Emily mumbled through a mouthful of the white chocolate she was supposed to be grating over the raspberry cheesecake, "and can you extend it right out for me too please." She added, trying to inject a little more appreciation into her voice.

She'd been a bit sharp with Tom a couple of times this morning. It really wasn't his fault that they had a house full of guests arriving in just over an hour, and she simply wasn't in the mood for entertaining today. She'd woken up feeling heavy limbed and lethargic, as though she was going down with something, and had been all fingers and thumbs ever since.

So far, she'd managed to burn her wrist on the oven shelf, over-cook the spuds for the potato salad, and produce a coffee and walnut cake that had a great deal in common with the leaning tower of Pisa.

They'd found the solid old table amongst a load of tatty house clearance junk, during a Sunday afternoon mooch at Church Stretton antiques market. Emily had instantly known it would look perfect in the enormous, kitchen/dining/family room they'd created by extending the full width of the house. This well-lit, south facing space had quickly become the hub of the house, the room that the family, and their many visitors, always gravitated to.

The catches had become really stiff over the last few years, and Emily had already wasted more than enough time struggling to open a jar of mayonnaise, before eventually admitting defeat and handing it over to Tom.

The grip in her right hand was deteriorating rapidly, becoming almost as useless as the left, and Emily's frustration showed as she watched her husband deftly remove the lid with one easy twist.

As Tom released the metal hooks, and slid the two ends of the table apart to reveal the panel beneath, Emily wondered why someone hadn't yet come up with some equally ingenious way of expanding a fridge. She'd been kneeling on the floor, playing Jenga with dishes of food for at least five minutes now, but no matter how carefully she stacked the contents, she could not create space for the Greek salad or the cheesecake she'd just finished decorating.

She and Tom were usually really laid back about hosting this type of impromptu get-together, and Emily had no idea why she seemed to be making such heavy weather of everything today.

Making people feel welcome in their home was something the two of them had a real flare for. They'd been taught well, shown by a pair of experts, that there was a great deal more to good hospitality than simply plying people with their own body weight in food.

Tom's solidly reliable, completely un-flappable mother, Helen, had taken the young Emily under her protective wing soon after the wedding. The older woman had quickly made it clear, that in her opinion, there were just two rules to stress free entertaining; do sufficient prep to make it look effortless on the day, and only accept offers of help from people who would genuinely get stuck in, rather than stand about getting in your way.

Emily adored her mother-in-law, and this deep abiding affection, shone from her striking amber-flecked hazel eyes, as she fondly recalled the first meal she'd prepared for her new family, more than twenty years ago. She'd been so keen to impress back then, leaping up and down from the table like a jack-in-the-box.

"Why don't you stay put for a bit now Emily." Helen had eventually urged her flushed, harassed looking daughter-in-law. "Tom and I will clear the table and make the coffee won't we love?" She'd stated firmly, fixing her recently married eldest boy with the sort of pointed look that only a mother of grown up sons is capable of delivering.

"I don't think you're going to fit anything else in there Em..." Tom brought his wife's trip down memory lane to an abrupt halt as he came to stand behind her. An indulgent smile softened the square features he'd inherited from his father, as he noted the dogged determination in the set of her jaw. He'd never been the sort of bloke, who was comfortable with flowery words or soppy gestures, but he'd fallen really hard for Emily within weeks of meeting her.

Despite the passing of the years, he was still fascinated by the irrepressible positivity she radiated, and her somewhat rose-tinted view of the world.

"Shall I get the cool box out of the garage for the overflow?" He offered diplomatically, having ascertained in one quick glance, that no matter how much Emily kept jiggling things around, there simply wasn't enough room for the mountain of food she was trying to cram into the already packed fridge.

Though Emily supplied much of their teams' general knowledge during the regular pub quizzes held at 'The Compasses', and produced far more obscure answers than him whenever they watched pointless together, she would be the first to admit that practicality was not one of her strong points.

Tom always experienced a rather cave-man like sense of pride whenever Emily, or the kids, turned to him, assuming that 'Mr fix-it' would be able to put right whatever it was they were struggling with. It wasn't just the uncanny physical likeness he'd inherited from his father; he shared his rather old fashioned values too, particularly when it came to his family.

"Why didn't I think of that?" Emily grinned sheepishly before closing the over-stuffed fridge and standing up.

Keeping her gaze averted, she leaned heavily into the circle of her husbands' arms as she came upright. They shared the kind of intimacy that allowed communication without words to be a common occurrence. Tom had always been able to read her like a book as she'd never been much good at subterfuge. Just about every thought she had, no matter how fleeting, radiated from the huge expressive eyes that dominated her elfin features and it was getting harder and harder to hide these recurrent light-headed spells from him...

"I suppose I'll be finding some weird and wonderful combinations in my lunch box for the next few days then?" He teased, before dropping a light kiss on the mop of strawberry blonde curls that barely reached his chest.

This deeply private comfortable familiarity had been built over years of affectionate banter, the reassuring touch of a hand, or a glance that conveyed a thousand words. They never felt compelled to make empty promises, or put on showy public displays of togetherness for other people's benefit. This was the first time in more than twenty years, that Emily had ever consciously kept something hidden from her husband, and she was finding the necessity to do so increasingly uncomfortable.

She wasn't being deliberately deceitful- just a little economical with the truth ... Dr Evanson had emphatically assured her that all these little health niggles 'were only to be expected at her age' so there really didn't seem to be any point in whinging to Tom about every new symptom. She knew plenty of women who seemed to have their own seat in the waiting room at the local medical practice, and she had no intention of swelling their ranks.

Most of the entertaining they did these days tended to be pretty low-key. None of their friends were the type of people to look down their nose, find her wanting, if things weren't up to scratch today because she wasn't quite firing on all cylinders.

Of course it had been very different when the kids were young. Their social life had been as rigidly orchestrated as the rest of the week back then. Precious 'date nights' had been shoe-horned in around Josh and Holly's after-school activities, and Helen and Mike's availability to babysit.

On those rare occasions that they had thrown a party, Emily had spent weeks agonising over the perfect mix of people, convinced that the entire evening was doomed to be an unmitigated disaster, if just one of the 'golden couples' proved to be unavailable.

The entire pace of their lives had shifted again recently, and they were revelling in rediscovering a more spontaneous way of life. It was hard to believe that Josh was already half way through his second year of Marine Biology, at Bangor University, and Holly was all set to follow him in September, to study Creative Writing. Where had the years gone?

The two of them had been snuggled up together on one of the oversized squashy sofas, watching the news, yesterday evening. Before their favourite weather girl, Shefali Oza, had finished delivering the unseasonably warm forecast, with her trademark endearing enthusiasm, Emily was already planning how to make the most of the sunshine.

"Shall we see if anyone is free to come round for a bit of lunch - we could call it a slightly belated birthday do?" She mused, blurting out her thoughts exactly the way they entered her head, just as she always did when she was with Tom.

"Don't forget Rachel and Martin are in London this weekend, so Mum and Dad have got the twins." Tom's eyes never left the screen for a moment as he reminded Emily of his youngest sisters' tenth anniversary celebrations.

"I was thinking of inviting a few friends round, rather than the family..." Emily went on, nudging him with her foot to gain his full attention. What was it about men and televisions? Her friends all moaned about the fact that their other halves practically climbed into the set, if you attempted to have a conversation with them while the flaming thing was still switched on.

The Mortimer family get-together to celebrate Tom's forty-fifth birthday, had taken place last weekend. Helen and Mike had been in their element as always, bustling round, taking care of all their children's, and grandchildren's, needs.

Emily enjoyed spending time with each and every member of Tom's close knit tactile family. They couldn't be any more different than her button-downed parents, and extremely distant unmarried sister. Though she loved the way they'd swept her up, drawn her in, and made her feel like one of their own, that didn't blind her to the fact that they could be somewhat overwhelming on mass to the uninitiated.

She generally found social events tended to work better if she separated friends and relatives. Everyone was able to relax then, safe in the knowledge that they wouldn't be required to make the sort of stilted surface chitchat most of us dread.

Despite the rather short notice, once they'd switched the telly off so Tom could focus on the job properly, the majority of the people they'd rung last night had all accepted their invitations.

They had a pretty eclectic mix of friends between them, and this circle was constantly being extended, due chiefly to Emily's penchant for collecting people- especially anybody in need of a bit of 'fixing'!

Like most easy going blokes who'd been married a long time, Tom tended to opt for the quiet life more often than not these days. He rarely made waves, only putting his foot down occasionally- usually when Emily's soft nature, and apparent inability to set clear boundaries, resulted in their home no longer feeling like their own.

"You're going to have to have a word with Joyce Em." He'd snapped just a few days ago, following another interminable visit from their no longer quite so new neighbour. She'd taken to calling in unannounced at all hours of the day and night, outstaying her welcome by several hours every time. "It's beginning to feel like we should be charging her bed and board." He'd added firmly, determined to nip the situation in the bud. They'd been here a few times before... especially where Emily's oldest friend Frances Carrington was concerned...

Fran had stepped on Tom's toes many times over the years, particularly so when her husband had left her, about ten years ago. She'd monopolised Emily's time to such an extent, that Tom had been made to feel like the outsider in his own home. He'd endured weeks of being relegated to the kitchen while Fran wept theatrically in the lounge, and grown accustomed to being left to his own devices at the weekends, whenever Emily was expected to drop everything and go running.

Of course he'd been supportive, to a point, but there was a limit to what any bloke was prepared to put up with in his own home. Who Emily chose to spend her time with, was of course entirely her business, but this particular friendship had always puzzled him.

You'd be hard pressed to find two people with more diametrically opposed outlooks to life if you tried. Emily always seemed to be so weighed down after a few hours in Fran's company too, but, he'd resigned himself years ago to the fact, that, the complex nature of women's friendships went way beyond simple male logic...

2

Standing in front of a full length mirror, in a bra that had seen better days and a pair of control pants, was never likely to be a particularly bright idea, even on the very best of days, and today was definitely not shaping up to be one of those.

The brilliant sunshine pouring in through the window behind her was acting like a spotlight, illuminating every lumpy bumpy bit of Frances Carrington's cellulite, not to mention her burgeoning love handles, in brutally harsh detail.

Fran cursed aloud as she threw another reject onto the growing pile of clothing on the bedroom floor. Life could be so hellishly unfair sometimes. Why was it that some women, specifically women like her best mate Emily, could get away with eating like the proverbial horse yet never put on an ounce of weight? She only had to glance at a chocolate biscuit in order to start piling on a few extra pounds.

"It's just a casual lunch." She assured her reflection, repeating the words in exactly the same cajoling tone that Emily had used yesterday evening on the phone. Talking to your self became inevitable when you spent as much time in your own company as Fran did.

The problem was, the Mortimer's definition of casual, was a long way removed from hers. Every event they hosted was guaranteed to be as irritatingly perfect as the last- a bit like Emily's life really. This 'impromptu little get-together', though supposedly being organised at the last minute, would no doubt prove to be equally flawless.

They were always the commensurate hosts, radiating warmth wherever they went, darting around, drawing everyone in as they sprinkled a little magic into each and every conversation. Fran had been sheltering beneath Emily's seemingly endless supply of positivity for years, always hoping that a little smidgen might eventually rub off on her one day...

"All the girls are coming, and it won't be the same without you..." Emily had persisted, when the lengthening silence conveyed Fran's inclination to decline more succinctly than any words. No matter how hard Emily kept trying to peddle that particular little white lie, they both knew it wasn't true. The 'girls' in question were all Emily's friends, not hers, and not one of them would give a damn whether she was there or not.

They were all connected through their husbands, kids, jobs, or gym memberships, and as Fran was single, unemployed, allergic to exercise, and lived on the wrong side of town, she was acutely aware that they merely tolerated her by varying degrees, for Emily's sake.

Fran stuck her head back into the wardrobe again, rummaging into the far corners, desperately hoping to discover some long forgotten item that might miraculously disguise the fact that she'd gained at least another half stone in the last couple of months.

Like so many women, she always seemed to struggle more with her weight during the winter months. She started hibernating almost as soon as the clocks went back in October, and then spent way too much time slumped in front of the telly, scoffing junk food, washed down with a great deal more wine than was good for her.

Struggling to hold back the familiar sting of tears, which seemed to be spilling over at the slightest provocation lately, Fran finally faced facts.

This disproportionate fuss she was making over what to wear was just a smoke screen, her classic form of defence- transference. She'd perfected the art of whittling away over something inane, in order to avoid looking at the real issue, years ago.

It wasn't just this bit of added girth around her middle that was causing her to have such a complete meltdown. The clothes strewn all around the bedroom were just another indication of how close to the edge she was sailing right now.

She'd been hanging on by her fingernails for weeks, was in imminent danger of spiralling out of control again, falling back into the all consuming pit of despair that constantly beckoned her.

Fran had been on the verge of depression enough times to recognise the signs by now, to know when she was approaching the point of no return. The empty days stretching ahead of her were once again becoming an oppressive weight she could no longer carry. On and off antidepressants since her twenties, she'd been referred to enough councillors and read so many self-help books, that she could predict what the latest therapist was likely to say before they had even opened their mouth.

Though the statistics for mental illness were bandied about so much more freely these days, in Fran's experience, the stigma and ignorance hadn't changed a bit. Unless someone had actually suffered with anxiety or depression themselves, they simply didn't get it, couldn't understand why you didn't just 'get a grip' or 'pull your self together'.

Fran was sorely tempted to text Emily and take the cowards way out, claiming a tummy upset or other easily trumped-up minor illness, but she knew Emily was watching her like a hawk. She'd already cancelled their plans a number of times in the last few weeks.

Her oldest friend knew her well, understood, at least in part, what an almighty effort it took to leave the house once she started to feel as low as this.

They'd been friends since their teens, had begun trading the unvarnished versions of their crappy childhoods from the outset, so consequently, Emily was one of the few people Fran allowed in, permitted to see the softer side hidden beneath her many protective layers.

Emily had always been able to see through her camouflage. She wasn't fooled by the bubbly mask Fran fixed in place, along with an extra layer of make-up, to convince the world she was 'fine', when all she really wanted to do was crawl back into bed and pull the duvet over her head.

Emily was the only friend who seemed to sense when she needed someone to be a bit pushy, to cajole and encourage her, give her a much needed kick up the backside, before she became too firmly locked into the downward spiral.

Living in this hyper-sensitive state, where every perceived criticism hurt so acutely was draining enough, but fighting the urge to closet herself away in an isolated bubble of self protection, despite the fact that she was drowning in her own company, was beyond exhausting.

"You could bring Scarlett with you if she'd like to come?" Emily had pushed, when Fran eventually responded with the kind of unenthusiastic candour only permitted between very old friends.

"Scarlie is at Simon's all weekend." Fran snapped, dismissing the suggestion in a clipped tone that implied Emily should have remembered this. "Zoe is taking her shopping again, but then of course, she can afford to bribe my daughter with new clothes can't she?" Fran's voice had become even more querulous as she prepared to off load.

The words tumbling over themselves to be heard were laced with years of long-held resentments. "It's so unfair." She fumed. "Zoe is the one who took her father away from her, yet my impressionable thirteen year old daughter seems intent on putting the stupid cow up on some sort of pedestal now. I'm left looking like the wicked witch, if I so much as dare to suggest that she might like to stay at home and keep her mother company once in a while."

"Well that settles it then Fran..." Emily cut in quickly, "if Scarlett is staying at Simon's, there is absolutely nothing to stop you coming over and enjoying the sunshine with us...you don't want to be stuck in on your own all day do you...?" Though they'd been friends for well over two decades, this was about as close as Emily dared go in expressing her concerns. The last thing she wanted to do right now was put Fran on the defensive by making any accusations. "There will be one or two other people coming by themselves..." she pressed on quickly, feeling as though she were walking on egg shells. A single word out of place seemed to be enough to set Fran off on another one of her tirades at the moment.

She really did try to be sympathetic to her friend's plight, and understood to some extent, why Fran had become so depressingly myopic about being on her own since turning forty. Secretly though, Emily couldn't help wondering how she ever thought she was going to remedy the situation, by sitting at home licking her wounds, rehashing the past, and staring into an empty wine glass all day.

"Tom can come and pick you up if you like?" She offered brightly, playing her trump card, in a last ditch attempt to get Fran onboard and get off the phone. She really hadn't got time to listen to another long winded rant about how unfair life was- how Emily had so much while Fran had so little. When Fran really got the bit between her teeth, she could bend Emily's ear for hours, and she still had a fair amount of organising to do if this last minute party was actually going to go ahead.

These warped life comparison were rolled out at pretty regular intervals, so Emily had learned to turn a bit of a deaf ear most of the time. As the characteristics bestowed on us by old friends, were almost impossible to shake off, she generally found it easier to ignore, rather than challenge, the sweeping assumptions that Fran so often made about her apparently charmed life.

Though it had been more than twenty five years ago, Fran still carried a deep rooted sense of injustice over the way their first employer had treated the two young girls so differently...

Emily had just completed a government funded training scheme, and been offered a permanent position, when Fran joined the same well known high street Travel Agency. Unfortunately, a year later, when Fran came to the end of the programme, the manager had decided to let her go.

It was Fran's unshakable belief that this decision had lain down the cornerstone for the future. The way she saw it, the good stuff always fell into Emily's lap, while she fought for the leftovers. Of course it had never once occurred to Fran that her volatile disposition simply hadn't been suited to Customer Service.

Over the course of a year, Emily had proved to be an uncomplicated people pleaser, whereas Fran had shown herself to be a truly mercurial Gemini, full of life one minute, then opposed to every word spoken to her the next.

Emily was growing increasingly aware, that her attempts to redress the balance, by indulging her oldest friend a little more often than was healthy for either of them, had contributed to the rather unattractive sense of entitlement that Fran frequently displayed towards her.

"I'll have a think about it and text you later." Fran begrudgingly conceded once it became evident that Emily wasn't about to be fobbed off. "I can always get Dad to drop me off if I do decide to come." She added, hedging her bets. Neither of them had remotely considered the possibility of Fran driving herself- they both knew that as far as she was concerned, there was absolutely no point in going to a party if you couldn't have a drink.

Fran had begun questioning the wisdom of her decision, almost as soon as she'd fired off the text to Emily this morning. Plastering on her party face really didn't hold much appeal right now. It was tough enough, even when she was on good form, not to feel a bit out of place amongst Emily's smart, intelligent friends. They all seemed to possess that air of knowing they belonged, so no matter how hard Emily worked to break the ice for her, there was no way to disguise the fact that Fran was the sad looser who'd arrived on her own again.

Wouldn't spending the afternoon surrounded by successful cosy couples just rub her nose in her own failings right now? Unfortunately though, she didn't exactly have a plethora of other invitations to choose from. The most exciting things on the calendar these days tended to be appointments with her dentist, doctor or hairdresser.

She'd fully expected the financial and emotional fall out when Simon had left her, but nobody had warned her that her social life would dry up instantly too, almost before the ink was dry on the decree nisi!

Whenever the 'girls' deigned to include her on a night out, they spent the entire evening punctuating every other sentence with the word 'husband'. Every time they shared another conspiratorial gripe about their partners, they effectively excluded her, reminded her that she was an outsider now, a second class citizen.

It hadn't taken long for the stark realities to hit home, for Fran to become acquainted with the fact that entire swathes of her former life were reserved exclusively for couples. Nobody really wanted the spare part that upset table plans, or horror of horrors, committed the seemingly unforgiveable social faux pas of having a laugh with someone else's husband. How frail some of those apparently perfect marriages must have been, to feel so easily threatened.

Retrieving one of the very first outfits she'd flung onto the pile on the floor, Fran squared her shoulders and lifted her gaze, recoiling slightly from the utter desolation in the topaz coloured almond eyes, staring back at her from the mirror.

'You are just as good as anyone else there." She assured herself firmly, tossing back the waist-length chestnut hair she considered to be her crowning glory. She really hadn't got time to stand here dithering in her underwear any longer. Her dad would be here to pick her up in about an hour, and she really had got her work cut out today if she hoped to inject some sort of glow, into the sallow winter complexion reflected back at her.

You didn't keep John Lord, head teacher extraordinaire, waiting- unless you wanted to be made to feel like one of his wayward pupils. Fran could really do without having to endure one of his monotonous lectures throughout the twenty minute journey round the by-pass.

"There is never any excuse for being late Frances." He would mutter sanctimoniously, tapping his watch impatiently with his long piano player fingers, whenever his habitually tardy eldest daughter upset his schedule. "It shows a complete lack of consideration, especially when I'm going out of my way to give you a lift." He'd chastise her, fixing her with the same steely grey glare he'd been using to put the fear of God into his pupils for decades. He always addressed Frances, and her sister Christina by their full names, and would visibly shudder whenever anybody used one of the more familiar shortenings within his hearing.

Pulling on a pair of black jeggings, that had just about enough give in them to accommodate her expanding backside, Fran covered the worst of her lumps and bumps with a colourful, loose fitting chiffon blouse. She drained what was left of the huge glass of red wine she'd poured to give her self a little Dutch courage, then, pulled her make up bag purposefully towards her.

Nobody at the party this afternoon, with the exception of the host, would have the faintest idea what this was costing her. The passing of each year was taking its toll, and it was getting harder and harder to transform her self from, fat frumpy despondent Fran, into bright bubby laugh a minute Fran; the Fran that everyone would expect to be the life and soul of the party...

3

Glancing out of the kitchen window again, Emily was pleased to find that Shefali had actually been a little cautious with her forecast! The cloudless sky was now a squint inducing cobalt blue, and the midday temperature had climbed to almost twenty, a degree or two warmer than expected and a rare treat for late March.

"Do you need me to do anything else in here now Love, or shall I go and fetch the garden chairs and table out of the garage?" Tom asked right on cue, as though he had just read her mind.

"I was just thinking exactly the same thing!" Emily smiled, the warmth in her eyes now conveying genuine appreciation. "We might be tempting fate by fetching them out this early in the year though ... the garden could be covered in snow again by this time next week!"

One of the great advantages of having been married twenty three years was this ability to work together, to see what needed to be done and get on with it without having to be asked. They'd had plenty of practice pulling together as a team working on their home. Having poured so much effort into the house, over such a prolonged period of time, Emily could never envisage either of them ever wanting to live anywhere else.

Studying the substantial property now, it was almost impossible to visualise the dilapidated little cottage that had stood here originally. The only redeeming feature that the aptly named 'Betley End' had been able to lay claim to back then, was the stunning location; and that, according to the gospel of Phil and Kirsty, was the only aspect of a house that you could never change.

It had taken a massive injection of financial and practical help, from Brian and Helen, just to make the place habitable initially. Then, after several extensions to their original mortgage, they'd eventually created this idyllic home, tucked right at the bottom of a very private lane. Anybody visiting them for the first time, was always slightly taken aback to find themselves turning off one of the main routes through the village, onto an un-adopted gravel track.

Bayston Hill lay three miles south of the county town of Shrewsbury, and was surrounded by the lush rolling countryside associated with this part of Shropshire, so close to the Welsh border. It was a village that had been earmarked for development in the 70's, thus creating two distinctly separate residential areas either side of the A49.

To the East, the village green was still surrounded by the original old cottages, though the majority had been extended and improved many times over the years. To the West, pockets of terraced cottages, Victorian Semi's and grand old villas had all been encased by different phases of modern estate housing. Despite the vigorous protests of the local council, and continuous campaigning by a hard core group of local residents, exclusive cul-de-sacs of 'executive style' homes still sprung up from time to time, on the outer perimeters of the village, which now boasted the facilities and population of a small town.

The dozen of so houses situated in Betley Lane, all had south facing gardens with open aspects, but the slope of the field directly behind them, affected the magnificence of the view afforded to each property.

Set at the very far end of the lane- hence the apt name that they had chosen to keep- Emily and Tom's house really did stand in pole position, a fact that had been pointed out to them on numerous occasions. On a clear day, it appeared as though you could actually walk across the fields to Ragleth or Lawley, the two most dominant peaks of the Stretton Hills. In reality the picture postcard town of Church Stretton and the surrounding valleys, always so popular with visiting tourists, were about ten miles away.

"You are so lucky to live here," Was the sort of comment the Mortimer's had learnt to receive graciously, when generally delivered with an envious sigh, "Most people would give their right arm to wake up to a view like that every morning."

Although Emily would readily agree that she and Tom were very fortunate to live in such a totally private spot, yet be so close to all the local amenities, when other people admired their home, they had absolutely no idea how much time and effort had been ploughed into achieving this idyll.

Emily had never bought into the concept of people being born lucky- or otherwise. There was no getting away from the fact that she had had a pretty rubbish start in life- had definitely been at the back of the queue when nurturing parents were being doled out- but the last couple of decades had more than made up for that as far as she was concerned.

She was perfectly willing to accept that she and Tom had been decidedly fortunate, but lucky implied that they had had no part in shaping their destiny, that everything had just dropped into their laps as if by magic, and she deeply resented that implication.

Weren't the majority of peoples lives' made up of a series of phases? Inevitably, there were those egregious periods that couldn't pass quickly enough, times when you had to dig deep and just plough on through. These lows were often followed by immense highs, like falling in love or discovering you were pregnant- times when you were so acutely aware of the fragility of your good fortune, you were almost afraid to enjoy it in case the bubble burst and life came crashing down around you.

During her teens Emily had been full of adolescent angst, only too keen to trade bitter childhood resentments with anyone who would listen. Throughout her twenties, her entire focus had shifted to creating the type of strong family unit that she had never known. She had been unashamedly fixated on ensuring that her children grew up as secure in her and Tom's love, as he and his brothers and sisters were in their parents'.

In her thirties, like so many working mums, Emily had struggled to keep all the balls up in the air, but she'd eventually learnt to stop striving for some illusive ideal of perfection, and finally begun to appreciate all the things she did have. One of the many fridge magnets she'd collected over the years- the one that always sat in pride of place- expressed this sentiment perfectly, 'learn to want what you have, rather than have what you want!'

It might just seem like a clever play on words, but it resonated deeply with Emily. We can all fall into the trap of comparing the inside of our own life, with the outside of other people's.

At forty two, Emily would consider herself to be in a quietly content stage- maybe that wasn't the most dynamic way to describe her life, or her aspirations, and probably not the wisest phrase to bandy about at her forthcoming annual appraisal, but in all honesty, this phase could last forever as far as she was concerned...

She enjoyed her job as a Senior Travel Consultant for a local independent agency (most of the time anyway), had a husband she still fancied (except when he left his toenail clippings on the bedroom carpet) a few incredibly loyal mates, and two grown up children whose company she thoroughly enjoyed. Without wishing to sound smug, apart from these niggling health issues, she was pretty happy with her lot, especially when she compared her own lifestyle to some of the other girls'-particularly her oldest friend Fran's empty days.

Like the majority of women, Emily's friendship group consisted of a couple of close dependable confidantes, a few fun but slightly flaky social butterflies, and of course the obligatory drama queen- Fran- who she seemed to have been bailing out of trouble ever since they'd first met in their teens.

It struck Emily as so inordinately sad, that, as she grew steadily more comfortable in her own skin with every passing year, Fran's inner confidence seemed to be ebbing away, leaving her constantly at odds with herself and the world around her...As she stacked the dishwasher, Emily chewed thoughtfully at her bottom lip, praying that Fran would be in slightly better spirits today, that she wouldn't place a huge dampener on the afternoon by turning up in full 'woe-is-me' mode...

Now her thoughts had turned full circle, back to the imminent arrival of their guests, Emily stole a quick glance at her watch and was pleased to see that they still had at least half an hour or so before anyone was likely to turn up- just enough time for a quick cuppa in the garden before she switched into full hostess mode.

A good dose of this glorious sunshine might be just what she needed to shake off the throat infection that was still plaguing her despite two lots of antibiotics. Everyone kept moaning about what a long cold winter it had been so she was probably just a bit run down...maybe it was time to start planning their next holiday?

As she flicked the switch on the kettle, Emily tapped on the kitchen window and made the universal sign for a drink. She could have staked a months' salary on Tom's response, and sure enough, when he turned to face her, she received the customary lop-sided grin and thumbs-up...

4

Helen and Mike Mortimer were making the most of the glorious spring sunshine too, basking in the first real warmth of the year. They were sitting side by side on one of the many grassy banks in Cardingmill Valley, watching their four year old twin granddaughters damning the stream, carrying out the operation as meticulously as all their children, and older grandchildren, had done before them.

"Well the Met Office certainly got the forecast right today." Helen sighed contentedly, raising her chin a fraction higher to feel the benefit of the long awaited rays on her face. February had been such a dismal month.

"Do you think I ought to put some cream on the girls Mike?" She asked, the question rendered entirely rhetorical by the fact that she was already rummaging around in the cavernous depths of her trusty old bag, the bag that had been going everywhere with them for years.

Grandma's canvas elephant bag was legendary! There wasn't an item any child could possibly require, that hadn't been plucked from one of its many pockets over the years. Sure enough, even this early in the year, Helen was prepared for every eventuality, and quickly found the Ambre Solaire she was searching for.

Mike smiled indulgently as he watched his wife fussing over the girls. Supermarket own brands had always been perfectly adequate for their own kids, but he understood why Helen was so cautious, treating these precious little ones as though they were made of porcelain. He was always acutely aware that their grandchildren were only ever on loan to them too, that they had to be handed back at the end of the day, and even something as minor as a grazed knee could make you feel grossly negligent.

"You love your children, but you fall *in love* with your grandchildren." Helen often quoted the little ditty she'd come across soon after Josh, the first of their seven grandchildren, had stolen her heart more than twenty years ago. Of course it wasn't the sort of thing a bloke of his generation was comfortable voicing, but he knew he could be equally over protective at times.

Mike continued to study his wife from behind his sunglasses, a tenderness he'd never been good at articulating, softening the square features inherited by their eldest son. Though a lot of people would consider their set up to be a bit on the old fashioned side, it suited them both down to the ground- he definitely had no cause for complaint.

He'd always appreciated the benefits of having a stay-at-home wife, a wife who'd happily lavished her time and attention on him and the kids, and of course, latterly their grandkids.

Helen didn't just slap the cream on willy-nilly. She diligently protected every exposed millimetre of the girls' necks and faces, the only bits of their bodies that weren't covered by their identical long sleeved pink tops and spotty leggings. Most of the other kids seemed to be running round in shorts, or summer dresses, but they had learnt the hard way that even on the very hottest of summer days, it always felt a degree or two cooler here in the valley due to the permanent breeze that ran the length of it.

This part of Shropshire was about an hour and a half's drive from the Welsh coast, or The Wirral, so local families tended to use Cardingmill, Inwood, or Batch valleys, as a substitute for the beach on sunny days. Even this early in the year, several multi generational groups had already staked their claim on the favoured spots, by the time they'd arrived a couple of hours ago.

He watched Helen clean her hands with a wet wipe, before rejoining him on the plastic backed tartan picnic blanket- another family heirloom, like the bag.

They continued to watch the twins in companionable silence, fascinated, as always, by the way the two little girls worked so incredibly effectively together. While Lucy gathered the biggest rocks she could find to block the flow of the water, Lauren shored up the gaps with smaller stones. They had operated like this since the time they could first sit up, always tackling any task as a team, two halves of the same whole.

Helen's close friends all thought she'd taken leave of her senses, volunteering to look after the twins when their youngest daughter Rachel went back to work part time.

"I don't know how you think you're going to find the energy to cope with two of them, on consecutive days." Her childhood friend Karen had warned her, expressing her concerns in her usual forthright manner, "I'm absolutely shattered by the time Calum goes home, and I only have him occasionally during the school holidays!" She'd gone on, worried that her extraordinarily generous friend really was biting off more than she could chew this time.

None of them were getting any younger after all, and it seemed to Karen as if Helen had been saddled with one or other of her grandchildren for far too many years now. As far as Helen and Mike had been concerned, there had never been the faintest shadow of doubt over who would care for the twins.

Their youngest two, Anna and Rachel, had still been living at home, when Tom and Emily had presented them with their first grandson over twenty years ago. Consequently, they'd seemed to sail effortlessly from one generation of children to the next.

Despite the joy her own four babies had brought her, nothing had prepared Helen for the overwhelming sense of adoration she'd felt, when Josh, had been placed in her arms for the first time.

She and Mike had been signing up for various stints of child care ever since Emily first went back to work. She'd never viewed taking care of the youngsters to be a chore, and had been only too wiling to help each of their kids out in this way, saving them from the exorbitant costs of child care. Of course she did tire far more easily now, and some days did feel decidedly longer than others – particularly when it was wet- but the rewards were absolutely priceless.

She'd always been at her happiest when surrounded by little ones, and she couldn't help noticing how much more hands on and mellow Mike was with their grandchildren.

Like the majority of couples of their generation, they'd carved out pretty clear roles for themselves from the beginning of their marriage. Mike had been the provider, working all hours in the early years, to turn the small building company he'd inherited from his father, into the well respected, thriving family business it was today. Never one to blow his own trumpet, Helen would never forget how puffed up with pride he'd been when, first Tom, and then Jack, had chosen to follow him into the business.

Mike had taken such good care of her- protected her in many ways- and Helen knew she was very fortunate. She had never had to push a heavy mower, or climb a ladder in her life, as Mike took on all the practical jobs. He never interfered in her domain either. He'd probably struggle to set the washing machine correctly, or iron a shirt, and as for the Aga, well that still remained as bigger mystery to him now as the day they had bought it!

It was all so very different for this younger generation, Helen mused. In the majority of households now, both parents worked, and the child care and chores seemed to be divided up between them. Helen was never quite sure if she envied or pitied her daughters, and daughter-in-laws, their so called freedom. As far as she could see, this apparent progress came at a huge cost.

With out a shadow of doubt, life had been far simpler back then. Quite a lot of women had done a bit of this or that for pin money, but nobody had called it a career, tried to kid them selves that they could have it all. Both sexes had instinctively known what was expected of them, and very few kids had been shipped out for half the week, the way so many of them seemed to be now.

The girls always seemed to be under such immense pressure all the time, juggling far too many balls. Of course they were all independent adults in their thirties and forties now, with children of their own, but Helen still found herself worrying about one or other of them most of the time... Emily was the one occupying her thoughts currently...

As she recalled the previous weekends' birthday celebrations, a frown puckered her relatively unlined, unadorned face- apart from a touch of pale pink lippy she'd never been one to bother much with make up. She had been keeping a close eye on Emily throughout day, and was absolutely convinced that something wasn't quite right with the poor girl.

"Did you notice how washed out Emily was looking today?" She'd asked Mike when everybody had left, and they were putting away the spare chairs, restoring the house to normal.

"Umm... I suppose she did look a bit peaky now you come to mention it... she seemed to be coughing a fair bit too didn't she? I expect she's probably just going down with this bug that's doing the rounds." Mike had reassured her.

"She barely ate a thing Mike, and to be honest with you I'm getting a bit worried about her. She hasn't been right since Christmas has she? I wonder if she's been overdoing things at work...." Helen pondered. Emily was such a tiny little dot of a thing compared to her strapping brood, so she did have a tendency to be a little over protective at times.

Despite the fact that Tom had been just twenty-one when they'd announced their engagement, she and Mike had never had a moments doubt that Emily was the one for their oldest boy. She loved the bones of him, had grown him, softened the selfish edges of youth and encouraged him to be everything he could be. They honestly couldn't have asked for a better daughter-in-law, and it was unlike Emily to be so withdrawn.

"Talking about overdoing things... "Mike had interrupted her concerned musings, "Seeing as you've been running round, looking after everyone else all day, why don't you go and put your feet up for a bit? I'll finish up in here, and then go and make us both a nice cuppa. We're not spring chickens anymore you know love." He chuckled softly.

"Well thanks for that...!" Helen laughed, "are you trying to tell me I'm past it Michael Mortimer!" she teased, knowing full well that her husband only ever had her best interests at heart. She must be looking a bit worn out too, if Mike was volunteering to put the kettle on, instead of waiting for her to get round to it as usual.

Helen made her way through to the snug, where they spent the majority of their time when it was just the two of them. Before she'd even sat down she was already planning the best way to engineer a quiet word with Tom. Perhaps he could persuade Emily to go back to the doctor again, just to be on the safe side?

She really wasn't one for making a fuss, but her gut instincts rarely ever let her down, particularly where her family were concerned, and she just couldn't seem to shake off this niggling sense of unease...

5

If Helen could see her daughter-in-law right now, her concerns would be multiplying dramatically.

The mega watt smile Emily had kept glued to her face all afternoon was doing little to disguise the fact that her dull, tired eyes, seemed to have sunk into their sockets. The dark smudges beneath them were only serving to emphasise how totally devoid of colour she'd become in the last couple of hours.

Rather than the much needed boost she'd been hoping for, a few hours in the sunshine and a couple of glasses of white wine, had left her feeling even more leaden and headachy.

Thankfully, one or two couples had just started making noises about leaving soon, as thoughts inevitably turned to the ritual Sunday evening preparations for the week ahead. Though she was doing her level best to hide how exhausted she felt, Emily couldn't wait for everyone to go home, and leave her in peace.

She usually enjoyed any opportunity to catch up with friends, but today it had all seemed like such hard work. The first hour or so hadn't been too bad, but by about three o'clock, waves of fatigue the like of which she had never known before, had begun to wash over her, leaving her feeling utterly drained. As virtually every conversation she'd taken part in had ended with a choking fit, her voice had become noticeably husky too.

Emily scanned the garden searching for Tom, hoping to catch his eye and subtly indicate that she'd like to start winding things down. She watched the last inch of beer swilling around in the bottom of his glass, as he recounted yet another of the referee's apparent shortcomings during yesterdays match at the Greenhouse Meadow.

Growing up in such a large family, Tom had learnt from a very early age that there was always room for more than one opinion. Even when it came to his precious football, he never felt the need to verbally batter anybody into submission.

"They were completely robbed. The ref should have been carrying a white stick if he couldn't see that penalty at the end of the first half."Mark's rather more impassioned pleas rose above the general mummer of voices, as he continued to pore over the numerous injustices that had been heaped on their beloved Shrews.

"It was a pretty close call." Ben chipped in diplomatically. A life long Manchester City supporter, impartiality allowed him to be particularly magnanimous on this occasion, as his team were already sitting at the top of their league; and looking pretty untouchable if they maintained their current form.

Before she'd moved within hearing distance of these fervent exchanges, Emily could have predicted the subject under debate. Whenever these three men got together, it was never very long before the beautiful game became the dominant topic of conversation.

Tom was a typical man's man. He worked in a particularly male dominated industry, and loved his footy and a pint, which generally enabled him to strike up a conversation with the majority of blokes he encountered socially, pretty effortlessly. He had immediately declared Ben and Mark (Kath and Jess's respective husband's) to be "sound", from the very first time the three couples had gone out together.

Emily had met kath and Jess at Banatynes, when the health club first opened at Meole Brace, which was a mere five minute drive from Bayston Hill. Their friendship had developed pretty rapidly, no doubt due, in part, to the fact that their partners had all hit it off so famously too.

Despite the many differences in their lifestyles and personalities, they'd fallen into the habit of meeting for coffee, after the Pilates class they attended on Thursday evenings. They each added their own indefinable little something to the mix that worked so incredibly well. Eight years down the line, Emily was really thankful that Kath and Jess had become such an integral part of her life. She treasured the easy undemanding friendship they offered.

Though closest in age, Jess and Emily could not be more physically unalike- a classic case of little and large. Emily, a very petite size eight, with extraordinarily expressive almond eyes, and hands that whirled away like a wind turbine in a gale whenever she spoke, selected the majority of her trade mark eclectic layers from White Stuff or Fat Face.

Career orientated advertising executive Jess, was professional chic personified. With her glossy angled bob and willowy limbs, she was one of those ladies whose legs appeared to be pretty much the same width from ankle to thigh. Twice a year, she would queue at five in the morning, for the Next sale.

Almost a decade older than the other two- and resigned to the fact that she would always be a few sizes larger- Kath possessed a regal timeless grace, that afforded her a classic style of her own, while keeping the local branches of M&S and Debenhams in business.

They never pretended life was perfect, and had each faced their own trials. Despite being under constant pressure from unachievable targets and cutbacks, Jess always managed to remain upbeat. Kath, who had faced the worst kind of loss any parent could imagine with humbling dignity, would be the first to tell you that 'shit happened' and you simply had to get on with it.

Self sufficient from a very early age (through necessity rather than choice), Emily had grown accustomed to being the listener, rather than the listened to. Though we all subconsciously adjust a little to fulfil the expectations of those around us, she'd been shocked by how readily she'd opened up to the girls, voicing her unfiltered thoughts in much the same way as she'd previously only ever allowed her self to do with Tom.

They shared the frustrations of life with absolute candour, but although their time together was regularly peppered with black humour- generally supplied by straight talking Jess- they rarely slipped into maudlin rehashing of the past.

Emily sighed heavily. The pity party currently being conducted at the far end of the garden was becoming impossible to ignore any longer. Now that the numbers were beginning to thin out, Fran's querulous tone was carrying increasingly shrilly over the general hubbub. Emily had already noticed several of the remaining guests casting uneasy glances in her direction.

No matter how many times Emily told herself that Fran was an adult, who was perfectly capable of taking care of her self, she habitually slipped back into the role of guardian angel, surreptitiously watching over her friend, poised to dive in and defuse any potentially embarrassing flash points.

Fran could never claim to have been blessed with a great deal of tact, even when she was stone cold sober, but the moment she got a few drinks inside her, she was ready to take on the world, convinced that everyone one was against her, including Emily whenever she was obliged to intervene.

It was an awful thing to have to admit about one of your oldest friends, but since she'd turned forty last year, Fran had become a bit of a nightmare to be seen out with, as she kept getting noticed for all the wrong reasons. Wherever they went out now, it felt as though Fran was desperately trying to prove something. She genuinely seemed to believe that if she drank harder and laughed louder, she could actually hold back the years and convince everyone, including herself, that she was still fun, still 'up for it'.

Emily's colleague Rita was currently embroiled in a very acrimonious divorce, so it didn't require a great deal of brain power to work out the gist of the plaintive grumblings being exchanged between the two women - what was that old saying about misery attracting misery?

Emily knew it wasn't fair to place the blame for the gulf that seemed to be opening up between them entirely at Fran's door. She was the one who had changed the most, bore little resemblance to the desperately unhappy, bitter young woman Fran had befriended all those years ago. Fran still clung firmly to the belief that she knew the 'real Emily' better than anyone else though.

As teenage colleagues, they'd shared far too many alcohol fuelled evenings, comparing childhood hurts and resentments, almost competing for the title of most damaged victim. The difference was that Emily had moved on, put the past behind her and tried to ensure an entirely different upbringing for her own children. Fran still paraded the scars like a badge of honour, habitually blaming anyone or anything else, for the mistakes she was now carrying over into the next generation, unwittingly inflicting on poor Scarlett.

Emily cut this recurrent train of thought off abruptly, feeling horribly disloyal. She simply wasn't the type of person to drift away from an old friend, just because their lives were no longer quite so in sync.

She really had taken her eye off the ball lately though, and judging by the amount of wine Fran had been pouring down her neck all afternoon, she was in a much worse place than Emily had realised. She was just going to have to dig deep, push on through the weight of her own exhaustion and find a diplomatic way to bring the afternoon to a close, before things started to get really ugly...

"Do you think that this might be a good time to hide the booze?" Jess dead panned, studying her friends ghostly pallor with concern. Her sherry coloured eyes narrowed with distaste as she turned to follow her host's gaze.

"Mmmm...I was just wondering if Fran's dad is coming back to pick her up, or if I should try and organise a lift for her?" Emily mused, conscious that neither she, or Tom, could possibly drive anybody anywhere at the moment, as they'd both had a couple of drinks, "I've got an appointment with the client from hell first thing tomorrow morning, so I could really do without this turning into a late night session." She confided wearily.

Emily worked for the only independent Travel Agency in Shrewsbury, and the thought of Graham Fletcher marching through the doors, before she'd even had time for a coffee, was hardly likely to get her week off to the best start. Graham Fletcher was one of those bombastic, vertically challenged bully's, who'd obviously 'been something' in his field before he retired, and still remained crammed full of his own importance more than a decade later.

Emily had been with the Agency, which specialised in luxury travel, for many years. She was perfectly accustomed to dealing with his type, and rather enjoyed the challenge of proving men like him wrong, when her uniform, slight build and mop of unruly curls, prompted them to underestimate both her age and ability.

The very first time she'd served this particular client and his long suffering wife, there had been something about him that had got right under her skin, making it harder than ever to maintain the professional but friendly service she usually prided herself on. She supposed she must be doing something right though, because despite all his nit-picking, first world gripes, he did keep coming back.

To the majority of people, Emily's comment about avoiding a late night might appear rather ludicrous as it was barely five o'clock, but Jess was privy to the way this somewhat one-sided friendship tended to work. She was familiar with how one of Fran's maudlin drunk sessions could drag on, if Emily allowed her to get the bit between her teeth.

The accepted protocols that everyone else had managed to adhere to today, had totally eluded Fran as usual. She'd turned up over an hour late, and would presume it was fine to stay long after everyone else had gone, claiming that she'd barely had a moment to talk to her 'best friend' properly.

The poor-me, down-trodden divorcee mantle was being milked for all it was worth right now, so Emily would definitely be in for a lengthy ear bashing is she didn't manage to bundle her off home soon. Half the women Jess knew were divorced, yet the majority of them managed to live full and happy lives, but to hear Fran banging on you would think she was the only woman who had ever suffered the indignity.

Jess really struggled to understand why anybody would choose to stay at home all day, moaning about how boring her life was, while relying on the generosity of the state, and her ex husband, to support her. Why couldn't Fran just get off her backside and start earning an honest living like everyone else had to?

"Ben and I will be leaving in a few minutes, so we could run Fran home if you like?" Kath offered, catching the tail end of the conversation as she joined them.

Kath always tended to suggest slightly less sledge-hammer like solutions than Jess. Though she and Emily both knew Jess to be a true and loyal friend, they were acutely aware that she didn't suffer fools gladly or mince her words, and she had never tried to disguise the fact that she didn't exactly hold Fran in the highest esteem.

"Thanks Kath, but it hardly seems fair to ask you to drive right across the other side of town...?" Emily wavered. Kath was offering her the perfect way out of this sticky situation, but it was always far too easy to take advantage of her generous nature.

"Actually, I could do with nipping over to the twenty four hour Tesco for a few bits and bobs." She assured Emily easily. Her lovely caring friend seemed to possess this wonderful knack of making it sound like you were doing her a favour, whenever she was putting her self out for you.

"Perhaps I should just let them enjoy themselves for a little while longer, then call a taxi? It's not as though either of them can come to much harm in my garden- no matter how much they have to drink." Emily shrugged her narrow shoulders, her entire demeanour conveying a distinct lack of enthusiasm. "They probably think I'm a boring old fart, having nursed a mug of tea most of the afternoon." She laughed, mocking herself. It was a well known fact amongst their circle that Emily was a real light weight- a couple of glasses of white and she was done whatever the occasion.

"I'd rather look like a boring old fart than a lush." Jess cut in dryly, shaking the perfect curtain of her shiny chestnut hair back into place with the slightest flick of her head. She rolled her subtly made-up eyes dramatically "I'm sure Fran was half cut before she even got here." She went on, making no attempt to disguise her disapproval of a lifestyle that seemed to be so entirely without purpose.

"Mmmm... I think you're probably right... she's obviously going through another rough patch ...." Emily put in defensively, the age old burden of guilt she carried automatically resurfacing. She had so much to be thankful for, whereas Fran seemed to have precious little in her life right now...

As Emily continued to procrastinate, dithering over Kath's kind offer, she watched Tom casually sauntering over to that end of the garden with a couple of his mates in tow.

Within a matter of moments, as if by magic, Fran and Rita had been whisked away amidst a flurry of goodbyes, and a sense of calm settled over the garden once again...

The sheer relief on Emily's face and the gratitude in her weary eyes, conveyed so much more than the heartfelt "thank you" she mouthed in the direction of her intuitive husband.

She simply hadn't been up to the task of tip-toeing around Fran's inebriated histrionics- not today. Once the last few guests had gone, she was going to go and have a bit of a lie down as she was really struggling to stay on her feet right now...

6

Fran stumbled through the front door and slammed it forcefully behind her. She had just been utterly humiliated and she was absolutely seething. Who on earth did Tom think he was ordering her and Rita about in such a highhanded manner, hustling them away like a couple of batty old aunts who'd been on the sherry?

Did he have the slightest idea what it had cost her just to show her face at their stupid party, and this was the thanks she got? She still couldn't believe that Tom had dumped her onto one of his friends like that, offloading her like a piece of abandoned luggage, as soon as her presence was no longer required.

Everybody saw Tom as such an easy going, laid back, affable sort of bloke, and the majority of the time he was- until you upset his precious Emily. Fran had learnt the hard way, that on those rare occasions when Tom did draw a line in the sand, you crossed it at your peril.

It was supposed to have been a party- a late celebration of his birthday for goodness sake- and it wasn't as though she and Rita had been doing anything wrong, behaving particularly outrageously. They'd simply been making the most of the rare opportunity to compare notes with a kindred spirit. It had been so refreshing to meet somebody who wasn't already neatly paired off, who didn't adopt that patronising pseudo-sympathetic head tilt, before asking how you were.

Fran had been aware of Emily hovering anxiously for some time before Tom had eventually pounced, obviously worrying about them lowering the tone of her twee little garden party. Just because Emily had never been much of a drinker, that didn't give her the right, to be so damned judgmental. She always prided herself on being the consummate host, yet standing there radiating disapproval from every pore, she'd started to make her and Rita feel about as welcome as a couple of gate-crashers. What really rankled the most, was, that instead of just coming over and having a quiet word her self, Emily had obviously fluttered her eye lashes helplessly at Tom, and then stood back while he did her dirty work for her.

One minute, she and Rita had been enthusiastically planning a proper night out together (one without a mug of tea in sight.) and the next, Tom had strolled over, and in his most casual, amiable chap way, begun engineering lifts, foisting her onto one of his mates, a guy she'd barely spoken to before, simply because he lived on the same side of town as her- albeit in a far more salubrious area.

Still bristling with indignation, Fran grabbed a half full bottle of red from the kitchen work surface and poured the entire contents into an oversized wine glass, before going in search of the remote. She could never abide silence if she was in the house on her own. From the moment she woke up, until the time she went back to sleep, the television or radio was her constant companion, offering some vital background noise to drown out the monotonous hum of the fridge or tick of the wall clock, both of which seemed to reverberate off the walls and bore straight into her skull.

Leaving the French windows open, she grabbed the folded lounger from the corner of the dilapidated lean-to that was supposed to pass as a conservatory, and stepped out into the sunshine. The one redeeming factor of this postage stamp sized lawn was that, it caught all the afternoon and evening sun, and as sunlight was often the only pick-me-up available to her, Fran tried to grab every precious drop of it that she could.

She had really been looking forward to having a proper catch up with Emily, once everyone else had gone. She'd barely had a chance to exchange more than a word or two with her all afternoon, as she had spent the entire time in cosy little huddles with one or other of her cronies.

Fran had never been able to work out why someone as bubbly as Emily, chose to spend so much of her time with a woman as middle-aged and boring as Kath, but at least she did smile once in a while- unlike Jess who was just a stuck-up cow... people like her hadn't got a clue what it was like, always having to rob Peter to pay Paul every month, the way she'd had to for the last ten years.

Brandishing their exclusive health club memberships, and National Trust cards, they occupied an entirely different world to the one Fran was had been forced to inhabit. She would bet her bottom dollar that Jess had never tried to eek out a paltry bit of birthday money in somewhere as cheap and cheerful as Primark.

Fran deeply resented the air of barely disguised disdain that always seemed to emanate from just beneath Jess's slightly turned up nose whenever their paths crossed. Being subjected to any form of disapproval had always been like a red rag to a bull as far as Fran was concerned, goading her into behaving just a little more outrageously.

She'd been exactly the same at school. The more a teacher got on her case, branding her as trouble, the more she played up, particularly so in the first couple of years after her mother had walked out, and left her and her younger sister Chrissie, with nothing but their father's vague efforts to guide them through their formative years.

As soon as Fran settled on the lounger and closed her eyes, fragments of the day began to whirl away behind her eyelids like some sort of demented kaleidoscopic slide show. It was the thought of facing these horrendous lows when she got back that made her so reluctant to go out in the first place.

It had taken so much effort to paint on her face today, to don the role of good old Fran, and the only thanks she'd received was to be placed in the care of some poor unsuspecting responsible adult, like an out of control teenager who didn't know her own limits.

Admittedly Tom's mate, James, had been incredibly gracious, but she'd still felt as though she'd been well and truly foisted on him.

James Marsden was one of those rare people who seemed to match their chosen profession to perfection. A great big bear of a man, who radiated outdoor pursuits from every pore, on the few occasions when their paths had crossed previously, Fran had come to the conclusion that he was probably more at home with the animals he treated than in a social setting. Apart from the fact that their daughters were in the same class at The Grange, and they were both divorced, they had precisely nothing else in common.

With his dirty-blonde hair and puppy dog eyes, he wasn't remotely her type, and yet today, when he'd taken her arm so solicitously, and held the car door open for her until she was safely buckled in , she'd felt deliciously waif like beside him. Flicking back the long dark hair, which with the help of nice and easy (and some dramatic brow reshaping) accentuated her slight resemblance to Corrie's Carla Connor, she'd began to assess James in a very different light.

No longer lost in the crowd, he'd chatted away surprisingly easily in the car, and appeared to be genuinely interested in everything she had to say. As the journey progressed, Fran found herself regretting her choice of comfortable old underwear as she contemplated the probability of being cuddled up against his large protective body. The prospect of some totally unexpected male company suddenly seemed a whole lot more attractive than returning to the cold empty house alone, as usual.

Was she starting to loose her touch? Was forty one really past it, because by the time they had pulled up outside her front door it was blatantly obvious that she'd read the signs all wrong, and that there was absolutely no point in inviting James in for 'coffee'. She sighed again as she recalled the way he'd so very politely but firmly dismissed her.

"It was really good to meet you properly today Fran." James had begun the second the car came to a standstill, leaving the engine running. "I'll keep an eye out for you at the next school event...perhaps we can keep each other company?" he'd added in the same friendly, but totally immune to her charms manner he'd been adopting throughout the journey.

She'd stumbled out of the car muttering some vague response, feeling utterly mortified that her attempts to flirt with him had failed so dismally. She'd made a right tit of herself, and still ended up with this oppressive mantle of loneliness wrapping it's self around her as soon as she walked through the front door, destroying any pleasure she might have experienced in a nanosecond.

She hadn't been about to admit to James that he had as much chance of running into her at a school event, as he had of bumping into the queen. She always left that kind of thing to Simon and Zoe, as any contact with Scarlett's teachers, just brought back memories of her own school days, and she could do without being reminded of all the times she'd been written off as one of life's failures.

Zoe revelled in every opportunity to discuss Scarlett's academic prowess with her fellow professionals, playing the doting second wife and step-mother to the hilt. Perhaps if Zoe had suffered such a horrendously long labour, followed by months of post natal depression, she'd be less inclined to look down her rather long nose, at what she considered to be, Fran's many failings as a mother.

Fran's full mouth, still outlined with the smudged remains of her bright coral lipstick, narrowed into a bitter grimace as she took out her favourite weapon and polished it... Zoe might have robbed Fran of her husband, stolen the lifestyle that had belonged to her, but the one thing the oh-so-perfect Zoe would never be able to do was give Simon another child...

7

Emily snuggled in against Tom's solid chest to get warm, as soon as he slipped his arms around her. It may have felt like a summer's day earlier, but the moment the sun set, the temperature had begun to plummet dramatically.

Emily loved being cuddled up together in their super king sized bed, cocooned in the privacy of the dark, sharing their innermost thoughts, with the sort of intimacy that ran far deeper than the physical kind. This probably stemmed from when the kids were very young, and the bedroom had become their sanctuary- the one place they actually got to finish a conversation.

Comparing notes after one of their parties, exchanging interesting titbits as they filled in the blanks regarding anything juicy the other one might have missed, was almost the best bit.

For such a total 'bloke'- a proper mans' man- Tom had an uncanny knack of homing in on any subtle undercurrents, and enjoying a good old gossip with Emily about them afterwards.

"So what did you make of Sean's new partner Tina?" He murmured against her forehead, moving his darkly shadowed jaw fractionally, in order to avoid a mouthful of curls.

"I didn't really get a chance to do more than scratch the surface with her to be honest, but she seemed nice enough." Emily replied candidly. They had both been incredibly fond of Sean's wife Judy, and though she hated to admit it, even to herself, Emily had found it really difficult to suppress the resentment she felt over someone else being here in her friend's place. To cover this somewhat uncharitable reaction, she'd gone out of her way to ensure that Tina had felt welcomed into their home, introducing her to several people she thought she might have something in common with, but she knew it was going to take a while to get used to being around this couple in the first flush of new love. She sincerely hoped that neither of them had noticed that she'd almost called the poor woman Judy at one point.

Like the majority of their piers, Sean and Judy were a few years older than them. Even so, Sean was still far too young to spend the rest of his life on his own, and Emily had absolutely no doubts, that someone as generous as Judy would have wanted him to start building a new life for himself, as soon as possible. Though in many ways her passing still felt so raw, it was well over a year since the inspirationally gutsy lady had lost her valiant fight with breast cancer.

The shape of their social circle had been steadily altering over the last few years. Several couples who had appeared to be head over heels in their twenties, found they no longer had any common interests by the time they'd reached their forties. Emily and Tom had witnessed a couple of solid looking marriages start to crumble, once the children that had been gluing them together for years flew the nest.

"It was really good catching up with James this afternoon." Tom put in, as though reading her mind. "I thought he seemed to be in pretty good shape too?"

"Mmmm...."Emily had always harboured a soft spot for the softly spoken gentle giant, who instantly made you feel like you could trust him with your life- or certainly the life of your pets anyway. Grace- his somewhat inaptly named wife- had walked out on him several years ago, and unfortunately, as was so often the case, they had seen relatively little of him since.

"He did look really well didn't he?" Emily readily agreed. She and Tom had been steadfastly refusing to entertain the ugly rumours that had started to circulate a while ago, and they were emphatically sure that he hadn't touched a drop of anything stronger than orange juice today- they would never have asked him to drive Fran home otherwise.

"I do feel a bit bad about the way we dumped Fran on him though Tom- she had had a hell of a lot to drink and you did kind of back him into a corner." Emily sighed, rolling her eyes dramatically, despite the fact that her husband couldn't actually see her in the dark.

Her exasperation was aimed entirely at herself, not Tom. She wasn't about to pretend that she had been anything other than relieved when he'd stepped in and taken charge of the situation.

She'd achieved precisely nothing by hovering ineffectually, while desperately willing Fran to take the hint and tone things down a bit. Why did some friendships have to be so flaming complicated?

She and Fran had spent more than two decades psychoanalysing each others lives in minute detail, so why was it that Emily still found it so hard to just say what she really thought whenever Fran stepped on her toes. She could be such a pathetic wimp sometimes. Was she frightened of hurting Fran's feelings- or just scared of incurring her wrath?

Emily began to rub her left arm absentmindedly as she rolled on to her back, staying nestled against Tom's side, her head resting on his shoulder. The heavy aching numbness had been getting progressively worse for quite a while now- especially when she was tired- and the pins and needles were really bothering her this evening.

"Do you think I should have rung Fran and made sure she got home Ok?" Emily asked, pushing back the duvet and sitting up again. She'd been yawning her head off an hour or two ago, yet now she was finally lying down she just couldn't seem to get comfortable.

Tom's snort of laughter expressed his thoughts on the subject far more succinctly than any words could have done.

"Come off it Em...you're not seriously telling me you're remotely worried about her virtue. I'd be more inclined to text James and make sure he got home in one piece." Tom had given up trying to work out why his wife kept this totally one sided friendship going years ago. The way he saw it, Fran was never going to change, and Emily would just keep running herself ragged trying to 'fix' her.

Tom did have a point, Emily conceded ruefully. Their love lives were yet another area in which she and Fran had always sat on completely opposite sides of the fence.

Emily had been a fairly innocent nineteen when she met Tom, so apart from the usual fooling around he'd been her only serious boyfriend. They'd married a year later and had Josh and Holly in quick succession, yet she could honestly say she had never regretted settling down so young. It might sound a bit cheesy, but Tom really was her soul mate. Though it was unrealistic to expect to still be love's young dream after more than twenty years together, they did still actively seek each others company.

Fran, on the other hand, had always maintained that there was absolutely nothing wrong with one night stands. She seemed to have made a habit of keeping several guys dangling at the same time, and had only ever fallen for one type- players who couldn't keep it zipped. She hadn't married until she was almost thirty, and although Simon had been the only guy who had ever shown her a modicum of respect, in hindsight it was clear to see that the relationship had been doomed from the beginning.

Emily fidgeted incessantly, annoyed to find that now she was finally tucked up in bed, she really couldn't settle. What was the point of lying here mulling over the past, harking back to that brief period when she and Fran had started to share an entirely different kind of friendship, a friendship that had been so much more ...equal?

Tom and Simon had got on really well, so the two couples had enjoyed some fabulous times together, but on closer inspection, the writing had probably been on the wall, even in those early days.

Fresh out of yet another abusive relationship, with the big 'Three O' looming just around the corner, Fran had met Simon on line and married him less than six months later. Scarlett arrived within the year, but after the initial honeymoon period, Fran had soon baulked at the humdrum routine of a new mum. Despite all the support Emily had tried to give her, she'd spiralled further and further into the black pit of post natal depression. It had broken Emily's heart to witness her friend rejecting both her husband, and the beautiful little girl she simply didn't seem capable of bonding with...

Fran still seemed to hold Simon entirely responsible for the breakdown of their marriage. The way she saw it, he'd abandoned her- just like her mother had- but Emily had witnessed more than enough of the goings on in that house, to know that most blokes would have been out the door, long before Simon had finally thrown in the towel...He was a decent bloke and nobody could say he hadn't tried his level best to make the marriage work, for Scarlett's sake...

"Is your arm bothering you again Em?" Tom cut into this routine trip down memory lane that always seemed to follow a few hours spent with Fran.

"Mmmm....a bit," She hedged, dragging her thoughts away from the pointless rerunning of what couldn't be changed. She lay back down, snuggling up close to Tom again as she registered the familiar concern in his voice. "It's probably just because I've been tapping away at the keyboard a lot this week, dealing with a load of long-winded email enquiries..." She reassured him quickly.

"You promised you'd go back to the doctor if it got any worse." He reminded her, not for the first time.

"But if it is carpel tunnel everyone says it's best to leave it as long as possible before having it operated on." Emily insisted, just as she had each time he'd tried to raise the issue of her health lately. "How come I couldn't seem to stop yawning earlier on, but now I'm in bed, I'm not at all sleepy." She switched the subject deftly, her tone blatantly suggestive.

"Well seeing as I'm wide awake now too...?" Tom picked up her cue, just as she'd known he would...

"That'll be all those brownies you scoffed keeping you awake." Emily giggled, recalling the way his crestfallen face had lit up when she'd shown him her secret stash hidden in the kitchen, as soon as the plate on the table had emptied. Mel's brownies were divine and she was never allowed to arrive at one of their parties without a batch.

Emily couldn't help smiling to herself as her husband began to move his hands expertly down her body - talk about double standards. If Tom got into bed after she had settled down for the night, he'd be lucky if he got a chaste peck on the cheek and a curt good night, whereas Mr every-ready, given the slightest bit of encouragement, was always more than happy to oblige.

8

Sinking back into the deep lavender scented bath, until only her face remained above water, Emily closed her eyes and inhaled deeply. She could honestly say she had never felt so drained, so utterly strung out in her entire life.

She'd arrived home just over an hour ago, having spent the week on a luxury river cruise, sailing down the Po. In theory, the trip should have been absolute bliss, compared to some of the more intensively packed educational trips she'd taken in the past.

Unfortunately, the cruise had managed to get off to the worst possible start, and that had set the tone for the rest of the week. The entire journey had been plagued with glitches from the moment the group had begun to assemble at Gatwick airport.

Miscommunications over the V I P door-to-door pick-ups, resulted in several members of the party (including the guy holding all the boarding passes), arriving at the meeting point over an hour late. After an egregiously chaotic check in, and equally stressful dash through security, they'd just about made it to the gate before the aircraft doors closed. By the time Emily realised that nobody had bothered to pre-order a gluten free meal on the flight for her, she was really beginning to wish she'd never agreed to come.

A five AM pick up, before the long journey down to Gatwick, and nothing for lunch except the Crimbles macaroon in her bag, and a box of grossly overpriced hand cut crisps, hadn't exactly put her in the right frame of mind to get acquainted with the group of random strangers, she would be spending the next week with- not to mention the complete fruit loop sitting next to her, who'd apparently been assigned to share her cabin.

When, after a very long wait in the arrivals hall in Venice, it became evident that two of the cases were not going to appear on the conveyer belt, tempers had really started to fray. Though the two ladies facing a week on a cruise with nothing but the contents of their handbags, and the clothes they stood up in were justifiably distraught, instead of showing a modicum of sympathy, the rest of the group had become visibly impatient as completion of the necessary paperwork added to the delay.

It had been a very subdued bunch of Travel Agents who'd eventually sat down to dinner that first evening, and the wonder of their location, moored just a mere stroll from the Grand Canal, was entirely lost on them.

By their very nature, these educational trips always had an element of 'big brother' about them. The inevitable personality clashes generally started to emerge a few days into the trip, but with this particular group, they'd seemed to be evident right from the very first day.

To make matters worse, despite the maitre d' guiding her through the menu with patronisingly unctuous ostentation, and emphatically assuring her that her selections were gluten free, she'd spent most of the night in the bathroom, which hadn't been the most fortuitous way to ingratiate herself with her decidedly weird roommate Paula.

Emily had come down to the dining room the next morning, as white as a sheet, and tried to explain the situation as delicately as possible to their group leader Scott, before heading straight back to bed.

By the afternoon, feeling brave enough to leave the ship (as long as she stayed in close proximity to anywhere likely to have a loo), Emily had wandered quite happily through the myriad little alleyways and bridges that linked the canals. She'd taken endless pictures of the flower bedecked, crumbling buildings, reflected in the slightly murky waters of the lagoon.

The possibility of being taken short on the long minibus journey to Bologna the following day, was a risk she hadn't been prepared to take, so she'd spent another day, equally as content in her own company, sauntering round the beautifully un-commercial, authentically Italian harbour town of Chioggia, which, like Venice, was built over several islands, but without the hoards of tourists.

By the time Emily felt confident enough to travel on a bus again, and rejoined the others, for a visit to an exquisite Italian summer palace, two very separate camps seemed to have been formed. Emily had never understood why some people chose to make life so difficult for themselves? A trip like this was such a flaming privilege. The beautiful cabins they'd been allocated were costing the paying guests onboard around three thousand pounds each, so why couldn't this bunch of free loading agents just swallow their differences for a few days? Without a shadow of doubt, she'd drawn the shortest straw when it came to roommates, but what was the point of being unpleasant about it. She and Paula would never have to clap eyes on each other again once the cruise was over.

Though a born mediator, Emily had been struggling far too much with her own issues, to assume that particular role during this trip. The combined effects of the unusually high April temperatures, that disastrous first night, and the continuous lack of sleep due to Paula's incessant snoring, had left her feeling worryingly light headed and completely washed out. She was pretty certain the other members of the group had written her off as a right misery- not to mention a raging hypochondriac.

She'd barely touched a drop of the all-inclusive, free flowing wine or beer served with lunch and dinner, and had been the first to head back to her cabin every evening. She would definitely not be rating this as one of her best educational trips, and in all honesty, if things didn't start to improve dramatically now she was back home, she really was going to have bite the bullet and make another appointment at the surgery...

Emily sighed as she leant forward to pull out the plug. Because the symptoms were all so vague, she knew it was very likely that Doctor Evanson would make her feel like she was wasting his time again. He'd been so quick to attribute the growing list of niggles to her age last time...assuring her that her concerns were almost certainly hormone related...

By the time the Holby credits began to role an hour or so later, Emily's jangled nerves had been soothed by the long soak in the bath, followed by an hour sprawled in front of the telly, catching up on her weekly dose of hospital tittle-tattle. She was just hauling herself up from the sofa, preparing to sleep the clock round, when the shrill ring of the land line jerked her out of her lethargy.

She was sorely tempted to just let the machine pick up, but after a quick glance at caller display she realised it would probably be simpler to just take the call. Fran rarely left a message. If she wanted to speak to you, she would just keep trying- over and over again.

"Hi stranger- Caught you at last." Was it just because she was so tired that Fran's accusatory tone immediately set her stretched nerves on edge again? Emily drew in a long slow calming breath, preparing to dig deep. She really wasn't in the mood to deal with Fran at full throttle right now, so she would just have to keep the call as brief as possible.

"Yeah...sorry... things have been a bit mad lately" Emily began instantly on the back foot, not sure exactly what it was that she was supposed to be apologising for. "Tom said you'd rung a couple of times while I've been away so I was going to give you a ring tomorrow. I've not long got in, and just had a long soak in the bath, before having an early night." She paused meaningfully knowing that anyone else would take this less than subtle hint, wish her good night and promise to phone back another time, but as oblivious as always, Fran just ploughed on.

"Oh yeah... it must have been really tough getting pampered on an all expenses paid luxury cruise the whole week." Though she knew this was supposed to be an attempt at humour, Emily picked up the all too familiar undertone of jealousy that laced Fran's words. The age old resentments always resurfaced when anything came Emily's way courtesy of her job.

Most people tended to assume, that because Emily had always worked in the travel industry, it had been a conscious, chosen career path. The reality couldn't be further from the truth. She'd actually wanted to be a teacher, but her father, like so many men of his generation, thought women were destined to work in shops or offices- until they got married.

Despite the constant upheavals of an army education, Emily had obtained very respectable GCSE grades, but her father had still refused to entertain the idea of sixth form and university. The local secretarial college was the route he had planned for his bright daughter, and you generally didn't argue with Major Brian Sanderson.

Emily's rebellion had come as something of a surprise- as much to herself as her parents- but if she couldn't teach, she wasn't about to waste two years studying something she had absolutely no interest in pursuing. In the same week that she been offered the apprenticeship, she'd also been interviewed by a florist, and an estate agent, and sometimes found herself wondering how life might have turned out if she'd made a different choice.

"I haven't seen you for ages, so, I was wondering if you are free tomorrow evening?" Fran went on, "Maybe we could get a Chinese... you could get Tom to drop you off, rather than drive, then we can relax and have a proper catch up."

"Tomorrow...." Emily hedged, an unintentional edge of froideur creeping into her voice. She'd been carefully dodging invitations to go over and 'relax' for quite a while now as the last few times she'd been over to Fran's house to 'catch up properly', her friend had put away a staggering amount of booze making the experience a far from enjoyable one . There was a limit to how many times you could listen to the same mendacious rehashing of the past.

Though she had no right to try and police Fran's drinking, Emily had vowed not to do anything to encourage it, following that cringingly awkward scene at the end of Tom's birthday party a few weeks ago.

In their teens, and early twenties, a couple of bottles of plonk had regularly fuelled a good old pity party. They'd revelled in the opportunity to put the world to rights, trading resentments, as they slated their respective parents' many shortcomings.

Emily looked back on that period of her life as a right of passage, the phase of hating your parents that the majority of young people go through. Surely though, by your early forties you really ought to have moved on, accepted that not everybody was cut out to nurture children? Fran was still clinging onto the hurts and rejections like a security blanket, as though she drew some sort of perverse pleasure from the pain.

"I can't tomorrow Fran." Emily proceeded, with caution, as she was really keen to wrap this conversation up and get off the phone now before things turned ugly, "Its Mel's birthday on Monday, so a few of us are going to The Peach Tree..."

She wasn't actually lying she consoled herself, just being slightly economical with the truth- she really was meeting the girls tomorrow but at lunchtime. Having just got back home after a full week away, Emily understandably wanted to spend the rest of the day with Tom, but she knew how well that was likely to go down. Distorting the facts slightly seemed like the most tactful option, until it dawned on her that she'd just told Fran that she and her friends were all going out, but she hadn't been invited.

Though Kath and Jess were willing to include Fran in their plans occasionally, Mel was not so accommodating. It was fascinating watching the way your friends interacted with each, and to say that Mel and Fran didn't hit it off was the understatement of the century.

"Oh right..." the fact that she'd been excluded was left dangling between them for a few moments, as Fran obviously waited to see if the situation was about to be rectified. When it became obvious that an invitation was not forthcoming, she tried again, "How about Sunday then? It's supposed to be sunny all day so we could have a BBQ....

"We're going over to Bangor to see Josh on Sunday and Tom's lined up a couple of properties for us to have a look. Now that Holly is definitely settled on going there too, it seems pretty stupid to pay out two lots of exorbitant rent, when property is so cheap in Wales. Tom thinks we ought to buy something he can do up, and then rent out one of the rooms, to help pay the mortgage, then, the kids won't have to take on so much debt-"

"Isn't the whole point of university to learn how to cope on your own? Won't you just be making life far too cushy for them yet again?" Fran cut in, her tone really sharp now- Josh and Holly were far too mollycoddled in her opinion. "Scarlett certainly won't have anyone paying all her bills for her- that's if I can even afford to send her to university." she added bitterly, wondering why life always had to be so damned unfair. Everything had always dropped into Emily's lap so effortlessly, and now it looked as though her kids were about to be given a ridiculously easy ride too. Meanwhile, she and Scarlett would have to go on fighting their corner every day for a few crumbs, just to survive.

Emily bit her lip as she endured the familiar litany, about how she had Tom to provide everything for her and the kids, while Fran struggled on alone... It was getting harder and harder not to bite back lately, to point out that if people like her and Tom didn't pay their taxes, there would be no benefits for Fran to claim, and that instead of relying so heavily on Simons' generosity, she could try getting off her flaming backside and working for a living like everyone else did. Scarlett was such an amazingly independent thirteen-year-old, so there was absolutely no excuse for Fran to stay at home any longer.

"I'm going to let you go now Fran..." Emily cut in, aware that her patience seemed to be wearing thinner and thinner at the moment." I'll get back to you about meeting up when my brain is back in gear...have a good weekend....bye."

She hung up quickly, knowing that if she didn't get off the phone soon they really were in danger of having one of their rare fall outs. Maybe it was because she'd been feeling so dreadfully run down recently, but she really hadn't got the energy to tiptoe around another of Fran's confrontational outbursts tonight. She applied absolutely no filter between her brain and her tongue most of the time, just opened her mouth and let the words spew out, no matter how much they might wound.

Emily knew it was pointless wishing their relationship could be different...more honest...equal...that she could share her worries with Fran, the way she did with the girls... It was never going to happen. They'd become friends such a long time ago, when they'd both been incredibly angry young women, yet looking back, even then, they'd had very different ways of dealing with the crap life had thrown at them.

Fran seemed to have spent her entire life in conflict, thriving on the endless dramas, whilst Emily had grown up avoiding confrontation at all costs, and that, in a nutshell, was the problem. The dye had been so well and truly cast, that no matter how many times Emily resolved to be more a little more assertive, treat Fran the same way she did everyone else, she still trod the line of least resistance, pussy footing around Fran's unacceptably abrasive outbursts, simply because it was less hassle than actually dealing with them head on...perhaps it was time to start manning-up a bit, for Fran's sake as much as her own?

9

Fran stood gaping at the phone for a few seconds before slamming it back down on the base. She couldn't believe that Emily had actually just hung up on her.

The niggling feeling that her oldest friend was slowly drifting away from her was becoming impossible to ignore now. She'd only seen Emily once since that dreadful party a few weeks ago, and that had just been a rushed trip to the cinema as she hadn't even had time to go for a drink afterwards.

What on earth had gotten into Emily recently? She no longer seemed to be anywhere near as involved in Fran's life. They hadn't spent any real quality time together recently. When was the last time they'd had a few drinks, been able to relax and have a good old catch up, putting the world to rights the way they used to? Emily always seemed to be fobbing her off now, claiming to be too busy for anything other than a quick trip to the pictures or a coffee.

Fran poured herself another large glass of red, as she went back over the call again from start to finish. She analysed every word, poring over the tiny details, examining each perceived slight, as she wrestled with this latest snub, which had come at a time when she could have really used a bit of support.

She'd had another massive row with Simon over the weekend, when he'd started lecturing her about feeding Scarlett more healthily, telling her he was unhappy with the amount of weight their daughter had been piling on lately. She'd really lost the plot when he'd gone on and on about the importance of feeding their daughter a better diet, when it was obvious it was just her hormones kicking in- did he have the faintest idea how much fresh fruit and vegetables cost. Then, just to cap her week off nicely, her dad had started banging on again about the money she'd borrowed from him, to get herself through Christmas.

Neither of them seemed to have the faintest idea how hard she was finding it to make ends meet lately, how tough it was struggling to get by on your own. She'd always did her very best to eek out the little money she had, constantly robbing Peter to pay Paul, yet instead of getting an atom of encouragement or praise, all she ever got was constant criticism.

It was just like being back at school again. No matter how much effort she made it was always going to be a case of 'could do better'. Nothing she did was ever going to meet the exacting standards demanded by John Lord- head-teacher extraordinaire.

She'd been desperate to run everything by Emily this evening, bring her up to date, so they could have a proper catch up tomorrow night, but Emily had blown her out spectacularly again...

It had been obvious from the minute she'd answered the call that she couldn't wait to get off the phone, yet, it would appear, she hadn't been too exhausted to arrange to go out with Mel the moment she was back in the country.

Pleading exhaustion every time she got back from another one of these all expenses paid jaunts really did rub salt in the wound- everyone knew familiarisation trips were just a complete skive...a free holiday.

Why was life so bloody unfair? Princess Emily had always had everything offered to her on a plate, ever since she'd known her. She had a fabulous home, and was always travelling to exotic destinations courtesy of her job. Married to someone like Tom, she would never know the misery of lying awake worrying about how you were going to pay the bills, the way Fran often did.

Josh and Holly seemed to have sailed through the awkward teen years without causing their parents much hassle, and now Tom had come up with this preposterous idea of buying a house for them. What planet did they actually live on?

Someone needed to point out that the kids would be far better off living in halls, like the rest of the students in their year, learning how to take a few of the knocks that life would inevitably throw at them.. Emily's determination to make sure they received everything she had missed meant the precious little darlings had already been wrapped in cotton wool for far too long, in Fran's opinion. They gave the impression of being such a perfect, squeaky clean family they ought to audition for their own version of The Waltons.

Fran's mouth twisted wryly as she remembered all those nights she and Emily had sat up, trading the grim details of their own less than idyllic childhoods. She wondered how much her adoring in-laws, and top drawer friends, knew about her background- about the real Emily? The bitterly unhappy, screwed-up girl she'd got to know over twenty years ago, tended to be well and truly brushed out of sight these days.

For a short time, while she'd been married to Simon, Fran had had a taste of Emily's current lifestyle, been permitted entrance to the inner sanctum, granted honorary membership to the dinner party club, but even before the paperwork was finalised, the invitations had stopped arriving. She'd very quickly learnt that a spare woman, a pariah that might pounce on someone's precious husband was about as welcome at one of their get-togethers as a dose of the clap.

Not surprisingly, Mel had been the first one to show her true colours. Fran had met her sort many times before. She almost felt sorry for these plain women, punching way above their weight, married to guys with a permanently roving eye. They clearly felt the need to eliminate any threat, as they clung on to their husbands for dear life.

Fran tipped what was left of the second bottle of wine into her glass, allowing the tears of self pity that inevitably followed one of her rages to flow. Scarlie was staying over at Simon's yet again this weekend- no doubt being fed mung beans and lentils by the oh so virtuous Zoe- so she was on her own for the next couple of days, with absolutely nothing to look forward to now Emily had blown her out so spectacularly.

There was absolutely no point in trying to get to sleep while all the old hurts were pushing their way to the surface, clamouring to be aired afresh, yet sleep was fast becoming the only escape she had from this swirling mass of despair her life seemed to be descending into again.

As she shook a couple of sleeping tablets out of the bottle into the palm of her hand, she paused, staring down at the brightly coloured capsules intently for a few seconds, wondering, not for the first time, just how many more she would need to tip out, in order to avoid waking up to face another pointless day...

10

"Morning sleepy head..." Tom smiled indulgently as he placed a steaming mug of tea on the bed-side cabinet beside Emily. There was something so endearingly childlike about the way his wife slept, with her arms above her head and her pale auburn hair splayed across the pillow. Their super king sized bed merely added to the Alice-in-wonderland effect.

"Feeling any better?" He asked softly, watching intently as Emily sat up cautiously, her movements still appearing very tentative to him.

"Mmmm... all I needed was a good nights' sleep." Emily assured him quickly, meeting his lips with the merest brush of her own. Her throat still felt like sandpaper this morning, and she was horribly conscious that her breath was probably far from sweet.

She swung her legs over the side of the bed, waiting for the dizziness to pass, before she attempted to stand. Despite the ready assurances she'd just offered Tom, she actually felt like hell, even though she'd been in bed a good twelve hours.

Lost in her own thoughts as she waited for the room to stop spinning, Emily failed to notice the hurt in Tom's eyes, or how quickly he left the room. The brief pre-occupied peck she'd just offered him was just another rejection as far as he was concerned, a further indication of the distance that seemed to be opening up between them daily.

Until recently, he'd been a hundred percent certain that Emily treasured the easy intimacy they shared as much as he did, the mutual trust that went way beyond mere sex. They had always been so attuned to each others moods...needs... but recently, Emily always seemed too tired ...too distracted... even for a cuddle...

As Emily glanced at the bed side clock, she was annoyed to discover that half the morning had already gone. They were due at her in-laws in just over an hour for a BBQ for the twins' birthdays. Usually, she looked forward to the regular Mortimer family gatherings. Whenever Tom, Jack, and their younger sisters Anna and

Rachel got together, with all their partners and children in tow, any occasion was guaranteed to be a pretty lively affair, but today, as she headed for the shower, Emily was finding it hard to summon up any enthusiasm.

She'd been back from the cruise a couple of weeks now, but in all honesty, she still didn't feel right. These peculiar flu like days when her balance and coordination felt so worryingly out of sync, were becoming far too regular. She was really struggling to cope with any social gatherings that involved eating, as she kept choking on her food, or in the middle of every conversation.

It was getting harder and harder to hide her problems at work too, and that was becoming a major concern. She'd resorted to keeping a large glass of water by her desk to stem the embarrassing coughing fits, and one of her colleagues, who sang in a choir, had recommended something called 'Vocalzone' to protect her voice. She kept a packet of the revolting black pastilles with her all the time now, because a sales person who couldn't talk wasn't really a lot of use to anyone.

A couple of hours later, reclining in a sumptuously padded garden chair, Emily felt horribly churlish about her earlier reluctance to be with Tom's family today. With her eyes half closed, she was lapping up the May Day sunshine, allowing the ebb and flow of the conversation to drift around her as it moved effortlessly from Holly, and her cousin Ben's fast approaching A-levels, to Rachel and Martin's Easter holiday in Florida with the Twins.

Lucy and Lauren, had been babbling away non-stop, about all the wonderful adventures in the theme parks, but from their glowing account, it sounded as though Rachel and Martin had definitely enjoyed the second week on the Gulf Coast, a great deal more.

"The villa was like something out of a celebrity magazine." Rachel enthused, her bright blue eyes shining as she passed around the photos "look at that view over the lake and golf course. Emily really did us proud as always." Her tone was full of warmth as she turned towards her eldest brothers' wife.

"We're already talking about going back next Easter Emily, but we're thinking of spending the whole two weeks in Bradenton this time?" Martin continued. "It was so lovely not to hear another English voice- to feel like we were part of a real American community. The beaches on Anna Maria Island and Long Boat key, rivalled anything we've seen in the Caribbean, and even though it was Easter, we often had miles and miles of pure white sand to ourselves. That Miaka state park you recommended was amazing. We did an airboat trip and the gators were coming up everywhere." The two girls immediately ran off giggling, as their dad formed a snapping motion with his arms, and began chasing them round the enormous garden.

Looking at the house now, it was hard to believe it had once been two very modest semi-detached rural cottages. Mike and Helen had started their married life in the left hand side, but as both their family and the building company had grown, they'd grabbed the chance to snap up the adjoining property as soon as it came on the market. Having altered and enlarged the cottages in several phases to accommodate their growing brood of children, and grandchildren, they now had a substantial property sitting in the centre of a sizable plot of land.

Emily continued to coast along on the back of the easy flowing banter, as Anna and Joel's teenagers, Calum and Claire, wryly contrasted their own modest Easter break in a caravan in Wales to their cousins' luxury holiday.

Though she'd managed to cope with a fair amount of salad and chicken, Emily had been surreptitiously slipping bits of her chop to Poppy, Mike's very happy to oblige rescue dog, whenever she thought no one was looking. She'd realised that the pork was just going to stick in her throat when she'd accepted it, but she'd been acutely aware of her mother-in-law keeping a beady eye on her while she'd been selecting her food.

Even on a good day, when she was absolutely ravenous, Emily always struggled to cope with the enormous portions served in this house, but since her appetite had become so sorely depleted recently, she hardly seemed to make a dent in the mountain of food heaped onto her plate.

Each time she'd seen her mother-in-law over the last few weeks, after enveloping her in one of her customary bone crushing hugs,

Helen would step back and ask, "Have you lost some more weight Emily?" as she scrutinised her from head to toe.

She had actually only lost about half a stone, which in the grand scheme of things hardly seemed worth worrying about, but when you'd never weighed much more than about eight stone, that represented a full dress size, and all her clothes were starting to visibly hang on her.

It had taken a few years for Emily to get used to being part of such a close knit family, a family in which someone always noticed if you were ill, or just not quite on form, and then followed through with support. Initially, she'd found the way the Mortimer's lived a bit claustrophobic. The way they were all so intensely immersed in each others lives, with Helen always bustling away at the centre of everything, couldn't be further removed from the family life she'd known.

She and her older sister Joanna had resigned themselves long ago to the fact that some people simply weren't cut out to be parents. They'd learnt to live with Anne and Brian's 'out of sight out of mind' approach to their offspring. They both settled for the stilted restaurant meals, arranged a couple of times a year, whenever Joanna was back in the country, accepting that nothing was ever likely to change so this was as good as it was going to get.

Used to the girls being away at boarding school throughout term time, their parents had pretty much left them to their own devices during the school holidays too. Major Brian Sanderson had firmly believed that children should be seen and not heard, and any misdemeanours had always been harshly punished. Though both girls had been on the receiving end of some pretty heavy handed discipline, they were both pragmatic enough to accept that it had been a different era back then...

Just like the floodgate of historical abuse prosecutions, against so many household names, in the wake of the Jimmy Saville scandal, Emily couldn't help feeling it was rather unfair to judge what had been acceptable parenting in the seventies and eighties, by today's standards... society had changed significantly since then.

As Emily sat in the sunshine idly musing over the contrasts between the two families, she had no idea that her concerned mother-in-law was currently in the kitchen cross examining Tom about her...

"I've been watching Emily slipping most of the food on her plate to the dog all afternoon Tom, and she's still nursing the same glass of wine your dad gave her when she arrived." Helen's observations were voiced succinctly as she came straight to the point in her usual forthright manner.

"She's never really been much of a drinker Mum, and Dad did pile everyone's plates up..." Tom pointed out reasonably.

"I know that Tom, but it isn't just the fact that she's eating so little and loosing weight that's worrying me so much... it's more that she seems to have just lost her spark lately....surely you must have noticed what I mean?" She sighed in exasperation as she folded her arms across her ample chest, preparing to stand her ground. She loved her son dearly but like most men, he tended to plod on in his own little world without noticing what was going on right under his nose sometimes. Since Christmas, she and Mike had been growing increasingly alarmed about Emily, and Helen was determined to find out what was going on today.

"Has she been back to the doctor at all... she still hasn't got rid of that awful cough she had at Christmas has she?" Helen persisted.

"Yeah... Dr Evanson gave her a second lot of antibiotics and did a load of blood tests and a chest x-ray but they all came back fine." Tom explained patiently, knowing how fond his mum was of Emily, that it was only her deep affection for his wife that was making her sound so brusque.

"But she obviously isn't fine is she?" Helen continued, determined to push her point home. They were incredibly fortunate that all their children's partners had blended into the family so smoothly. Of course she'd never admit the fact to another living soul, but despite her monumental efforts to never show an atom of favouritism, Emily had somehow snuck her way into a special place in her heart, and she was genuinely worried about the girl. Maybe it was because her daughter-in-law's family had proved themselves to be so utterly useless, or just because she was such a delicate little thing, compared to her healthy brood, but Helen always felt compelled to protect her, to mother her.

It wasn't as though the poor girl could rely on her own mother to take care of her. How any woman could show so little interest in her children, or grandchildren, was beyond Helen whose entire life had always revolved around her family.

"I did suggest that she ought to go back to the surgery again Mum, but she's not keen... apparently when she went back for the results, Dr Evanson just went on about the start of...you know... women's stuff."

Helen struggled to suppress the laughter that bubbled up at her son's obvious discomfort. Her eldest son might be Forty four and well over six foot tall, but right now, he looked like a naughty school boy, as he shuffled his feet awkwardly on the tiled kitchen floor, and avoided his mothers' eyes.

"I take it we're talking about an early menopause?" She put in succinctly helping him out.

"Hmmm ...."

"Well I don't see how that would explain the weight loss or the choking....I really think she ought to go back and see the doctor again Tom, and maybe this time you should go with her?

His mother was only voicing the thoughts that had been whirring away in his own head recently, and she didn't know half of what he'd seen since Emily had got back from the cruise- he wasn't stupid- Emily had obviously been trying to hide things from him for a while... when they got home, he was going to sit her down and have a proper chat about his concerns... all of them...maybe it was selfish, but he missed his warm, funny, vibrant wife and he wanted her back.

Even if it was all down to hormones, then surely they could try HRT or something, not just plod on like this, living half a life?...No. His mum was right- as usual. They would make an appointment for her day off on Wednesday and he would go with her this time. Like most blokes he knew he was pretty good at burying his head in the sand at times, but they'd both been playing the 'ignore it and it'll go away' game for far too long already.

11

The rain skittering across the conservatory roof finally broke the suffocating silence, bringing Tom out of his trance like state. Though he still had Emily's hand firmly gripped within his own, he couldn't think of a single word of comfort, that didn't sound like the tired old clichéd platitudes you'd trot out to a friend or neighbour... don't cross any bridges...the great strides in medical research...how the C word no longer meant an automatic death sentence...

They had been sat here for a good ten minutes now, nursing untouched mugs of tea, but he still couldn't get his head around what had just taken place at the surgery. He knew Emily wouldn't want to listen to a load of well intended promises about how everything was going to be OK- and who the hell was he to be offering her those kind of assurances right now anyway?

When Emily did eventually speak, it was clear that instead of focussing on her own fears, as he had so selfishly been doing, her first priority, as always, was the kids.

"How much do you think we should tell Josh and Holly Tom?" She asked him simply, her beautiful dancing eyes completely dull, her voice conveying about the same level of emotion as if she were discussing her next dental appointment. The ramifications of the scene that had just unfolded in the consulting room were obviously as surreal to her, as they were to him.

Tom swallowed hard, struggling to force any words past the weight of emotion constricting his throat.

"Well... I think we will have to tell them that you have been referred to a specialist love..." He began, doing his level best to just focus on this one thing she was asking of him, in order to stop his own feelings of panic spiralling out of control.

"Mmmm... but at this stage I don't think we need to mention anything about this two week rule thing do we? I can't see the point of scaring them until we know if it's..." Emily trailed off, leaving the sentence hanging awkwardly between them. She wasn't remotely ready to verbalize the word that had been ricocheting around her head for the last half hour...that would make it too real and at the moment it still just felt like they were caught up in a bad nightmare...

"That makes perfect sense to me Em." Tom tried to inject a level of positivity he was far from feeling into his words, before he carried on, "Let's just wait and see if the tests doctor Evanson has arranged all come back clear." He tried to hold her gaze, assuring her that this would be the case with an encouraging lop-sided grin, but despite his best efforts it wobbled horribly out of control, and ended up more of a grimace.

There was absolutely nothing to be gained by allowing them selves to start thinking the worst yet... but cancer... Just hearing the word had made his blood run cold, so goodness only knows what was going on inside Emily's head right now. Nothing had prepared either of them for the sudden change of direction the appointment had taken, but thank God he had listened to his mum and been with her.

Just as he'd promised he would, as soon as they'd got home from the BBQ, he'd sat Emily down and started asking some very direct questions, making it clear from the outset that he had no intention of being fobbed off again. Though he'd actually been reeling from the shock of just how much Emily had managed to hide from him, he'd immediately started to write everything down, so that when they saw the doctor, they'd be fully prepared, and not find them selves being led off down any blind alleys.

Dr Evanson had been running a bit late, and Tom had watched Emily growing visibly anxious as they sat in the waiting room. When they were eventually summoned through to his room, and the doctor began asking in depth questions relating to the list of symptoms they'd compiled, she'd struggled with her replies as she'd kept choking in the middle of so many sentences. After carefully examining her throat, he'd asked a barrage of further questions about her general health, looking towards Tom several times to seek confirmation or embellishment.

Fully anticipating another course of antibiotics, they were both mildly surprised when the doctor suggested referring her to a specialist, who would be able to look much further down her throat.

"Obviously at this stage I don't want to alarm you, and I'm not suggesting that there IS necessarily anything sinister going on, but there is a set of markers- red flags if you like- that a GP looks for, so I wouldn't be doing my job properly if I didn't refer you under the two week rule Emily." He'd explained gently.

"What does that mean exactly?" Tom had asked, frowning slightly when he saw the colour instantly draining from his wife's face.

Emily knew all about the two week rule, as Judy had been referred under the same scheme when she'd first found a lump, but she remained silent, concentrating on just breathing deeply and letting the doctor fill Tom in.

"If a GP suspects that cancer may be present then the patient is guaranteed an appointment with a consultant within two weeks of being referred." Dr Evanson explained levelly.

"Cancer?" The word itself seemed to rasp on Tom's tongue. He blinked several times as the slighter man across the other side of the desk momentarily slipped out of focus.

"Like I said at this stage it really is just a precaution." The doctor's tone remained reassuringly neutral as he went on to explain the procedure that would take place, at the appointment with the specialist.

"Mr Shah will probably perform something called a Laryngoscopy, which is basically just a small camera that enables him to see much further down the throat than I can."

Stumbling out of the surgery into the bright sunshine, Tom had found himself praying that they wouldn't bump into anyone they knew as they walked home. Why on earth hadn't he brought the car down? He had never felt so ill equipped...so utterly useless...such a total bloke, in his entire life...

Emily needed his support more than ever before, and he had absolutely no idea how he was supposed to offer it, because right at this moment he couldn't seem to get past the fear that he might actually loose her. As she'd tucked her hand through his arm, he'd squeezed it close to him, hoping that the old saying about actions speaking louder than words was in fact true.

Jack had always been the one with the gift of the gab, while he was your archetypical mans' man, retreating into his cave at the first sign of trouble. He could only pray that just this once, he'd be able to dig really deep, and discover his very well hidden feminine side, because he was damn well going to need it now if he was going to be of any use to Emily...

12

Fran's morning hadn't exactly worked out quite the way she'd been expecting it to either, but instead of turning to the good old traditional cuppa for comfort, like Emily, Fran sought solace in a hefty measure of vodka.

The rage that had been surging through her when she'd stormed out of her fathers' house, a short while ago, was already turning to panic. Where on earth was she going to find the spending money she needed for her holiday now?

Every spring, for the last few years, she'd taken Scarlie to see her grandmother in Majorca during the May half term. Her Mum always offered some money towards the flights, and found them somewhere to stay, and her Dad gave her a few hundred quid spending money. She had been on the verge of persuading him to do the same again this year, when Sarah had stuck her great big oar in.

"We have already told you that your father is retiring at the end of this school year Frances." Her step-mother had cut in firmly, the moment Fran came to the end of her well rehearsed 'just one last time' speech.

"But I only need to borrow a couple of hundred and obviously I'll pay you back as soon as I can." Fran persisted, a belligerent edge creeping into her voice, as the deep-rooted resentment she harboured towards her step-mother quickly roe to the surface.

"The way you've paid back the money you 'borrowed' for the car, or before that, to help you out over Christmas?" Sarah's voice remained perfectly civil, but her body language, as she planted her feet a little more firmly on the green swirly lounge carpet, made it clear she was preparing to do battle.

Sarah often found herself wondering if things might have been different between her and Frances if she'd stood her ground a little more from the start, but when she first became involved with John, her head had been full of romantic notions. She'd envisaged herself as the fun young step-mum, cum friend, that his poor abandoned daughters would soon learn to adore.

Ten year old Chrissie had been like a sponge, soaking up every last drop of her eager new step-mothers' enthusiastic nurturing, and Sarah had been incredibly blessed by the close bond they had formed. Her children, Imogen and Daniel, had called her Nan from the moment they could talk, and she loved them as dearly as if they were her own flesh and blood.

Frances, at thirteen, had been something more of a challenge to say the least, laying the gauntlet down from the first disastrous meal. Foolishly, she and John had opted for the line of least resistance, made allowances for her adolescent outbursts, optimistically assuring themselves that things were bound to improve given time. Despite Sarah's not inconsiderable efforts, hostilities had merely intensified after the quiet marriage ceremony.

Having met Angie Lord just once, at a family funeral, Sarah had quickly identified the source of Frances' abrasive attitude, but that wisdom had done little to protect her from the unadulterated hatred she'd had to live with.

Sarah had endured years of increasingly spiteful manipulations, as John's eldest daughter never missed an opportunity to usurp her, to make her feel like the outsider in her new home- a home that would always belong to John and the girls as far as Frances was concerned.

"I didn't realise you were keeping a tab Sarah...You'll be charging me interest next." Fran practically spat the words at the woman who had been a thorn in her side for far too long. Who the hell did Sarah think she was, trying to dictate how much of her fathers' money she was entitled to?

"There is no need for sarcasm Frances. We are simply pointing out that things will have to change once your dad only has his pension coming in." Her step daughter always made this great big palaver about taking Scarlett to see her 'real grandmother' ever spring, but Sarah knew that poor Scarlett had actually come to dread this annual trip.

A week in the Spanish sunshine, with plenty of free-flowing booze, courtesy of her mothers' bar, may seem like heaven on earth to Frances, but her freckled, fair skinned, introverted and painfully self-aware teenage daughter, wasn't comfortable with either the heat, or the Palma Nova lifestyle.

"We- I notice you're the one doing all the talking as usual Sarah? What do you think dad? Are you really going to deny me and Scarlett the chance of a decent holiday? It's the only thing I have to look forward to all year-"

"And maybe that is the real problem here Frances?" John's voice changed immediately, an edge of wariness creeping in as he finally broached the crux of the matter, the elephant in the room they'd been tip-toeing around for far too long. "Sarah and I have been growing very concerned about you lately... we are really worried about you spending a week in that sort of environment just now..." He cleared his throat and shuffled his feet awkwardly before hurrying on "We both feel you need to look at how much you are drinking ... start cutting back a bit... maybe then we could help you out with a little holiday later on in the year, perhaps somewhere that's a bit more family orientated-"

"That sounds suspiciously like blackmail to me dad?" Fran cut in scathingly, refusing to be lectured, as though she were one of his delinquent pupils. "So I like a few drinks." She snapped "Perhaps if you had to struggle to get by the way I do, you'd want to blot out the misery once in a while." Fran could hear her voice rising hysterically as she defended herself.

"But it's not just once in a while anymore is it..." having come this far John was not about to back down now. "Sarah and I couldn't help noticing the amount of bottles in your recycling box when we dropped Scarlett off the other evening and we-"

"Are you actually telling me you've been snooping around my bins now?" Fran exclaimed, incandescent with rage by this point.

"Now you're just being melodramatic Frances. It's impossible to talk to you when you get like this- your mother was exactly the same." Reluctantly accepting that it would be pointless to try and pursue the conversation now, John closed the subject down before tempers really flared, just as he'd done so many times throughout his first marriage.

"Talk-" Fran shrieked back at him. "Don't you mean dictate? Just because I asked to borrow a few quid, that doesn't give you the right to tell me how to run my life? No wonder mum left you. She probably just wanted to have a bit of fun instead of leaving her money squirreled away under the mattress." As her voice continued to rise, becoming ever-more shrill, Fran knew she was being grossly unfair, lashing out indiscriminately, but she always found it impossible to rein her temper in once she got started.

Angie lord had walked out on her long suffering husband and daughters, to set up a bar in Spain with her gym instructor. The toy boy had only lasted a year or so, but the new lifestyle had remained permanent.

Angie would be sixty this year, and despite some cosmetic work, and the host of expensive potions lining her bathroom shelves, three decades of over exposure to the sun and late nights running the bar, had taken their toll. Fran used to be proud of her mothers' dramatic individual style outside the school gates (that is on the few occasions she actually remembered to turn up), but these days, the raven black hair and heavily made up eyes still turned heads, but for all the wrong reasons. She was turning into a caricature, morphing into Lesley Joseph... but not in a good way.

Fran was painfully aware that when she lost control and shot her mouth off, she sounded exactly like her mother. She was never going to forget the shrill tone of her mother's voice reverberating through the floorboards, as she cowered upstairs with her hands over her ears, trying to block out the vile profanities her mother had regularly hurled at her dad. Fran had vowed to never marry a man who allowed him self to be walked over like that. She'd make sure that, when the time came, she'd find herself a real man...

After storming out of her father's house, she'd spent the journey home reassuring herself that he'd soon come round if she just kept her distance for a bit...it was a tactic that had always worked in the past...despite his many failings as a father, her dad was undeniably very fond of his grandchildren...

As soon as she'd knocked back the vodka, Fran picked up an unopened bottle of red from the cluttered work surface and took it through to the equally untidy lounge. She picked up the remote and flicked despondently through the channels, eventually settling on Loose Women. A good rant at Janet Street-Porter was exactly what she needed right now.

She poured almost half the bottle into a mug, and then sat with her hands clasped around the comforting ruby liquid, in much the same way as most people would nurse a mug of sweet tea when in shock.

If she could just get through the next few hours, she could pour her heart out to Emily later, filling her in on her step-mothers' latest attempt to do her out of what was rightfully hers. Emily understood how much she needed this half term break in the sun, how desperately low she got in the winter...she'd text her in a bit...see if perhaps she could come over a bit earlier instead of meeting at the pictures...maybe they could cancel the film all together and just have a proper girly catch up instead...

It was several hours before her daughters' key in the door and cheerful greeting, brought Fran out of her comatose state on the sofa.

"What time is it?" She rasped, attempting to sit up without moving her head. The dull ache that started as soon as she opened her eyes was already turning into a pounding drum beat.

"Just after seven" Scarlett answered warily, the lovely warm glow she'd been feeling fading instantly now that she was back home. She'd smelt the booze and cigarette smoke as soon as she'd opened the front door, so had a pretty good idea how the next few minutes were going to play out... whatever the problem was, it somehow always ended up being her fault...

"Where the hell have you been until now?" Fran snapped, as it dawned on her that she was running way to late to meet Emily now. "You should have been home hours ago."

"I told you last night that I was going to Izzie's to do my homework, and that her mum had invited me to stay for tea." Scarlett reminded her mother, careful to keep her tone placatory.

As soon as she'd walked though the door of her friends' big old Victorian house she'd been greeted by the smell of fresh baking. The moment they'd settled themselves in the vast, airy conservatory, Mrs Roberts had brought mugs of hot chocolate, topped with whipped cream, and a plate of melt-in-the-mouth flapjacks.

When Mr Roberts got home a couple of hours later they'd all sat around the big kitchen table, and Scarlett had enjoyed the home made cottage pie almost as much as the easy, affectionate banter. She turned away from her mother, her cheeks flaming, as she recalled the way Charlie- Izzie's older brother- had caught her eye as he tried to include her in the teasing.

He was in his first year at sixth form, and obviously way out of her league, but he was sooo fit. She couldn't wait to get up to her room and start recording every little detail about him in her diary, while it was still fresh in her mind.

"Right....Well if you've already eaten there is no point cooking so I'm going to go to bed as I feel really rough. Can you ring Emily for me? I'm supposed to be meeting her at eight." Fran really couldn't face the thought of being interrogated by Emily, after the grilling she'd already had from her dad.

Scarlett scowled at her mothers' retreating back as she left the room, her freckled nose wrinkling distastefully. If only she had the guts to tell her mother to do her own dirty work. She was always letting people down at the last minute like this, but Scarlett had learnt from a very young age that it was always best to just obey instructions, no matter how unjust, in order to avoid one of those brutally cruel, unpredictable outbursts that could just come out of nowhere. She had gotten off incredibly lightly so far this evening so, sighing resignedly, she reached for the phone to do her mothers' bidding.

"Hi Emily... It's Scarlett." She greeted her honorary aunt warmly, despite her reluctance to make her mothers' excuses for her.

"Hi love. How are you? Is everything alright?" Emily's concern for the quiet studious girl was immediate. Having been robbed of her childhood, Scarlett already possessed a maturity that was way beyond her years.

"I'm absolutely fine thanks. Mum has asked me to give you a ring though as has had to go to bed, so she won't be able to meet you later." Scarlett always offered the minimum information required in these situations to avoid having to tell any lies.

"Oh right...tell her that's fine... I really wasn't very bothered about seeing the film anyway." Emily accepted the let down with more than her usual grace. She was so immensely relieved that she hadn't got to go out now after all, that she hadn't got to go through the motions, try to pretend that everything was perfectly normal for the rest of the evening.

As Holly was working at Pizza Hut until ten, she and Tom could ditch the fake smiles they'd been offering each other all afternoon and start to talk properly.

She wasn't about to let him retreat into his man cave. Neither of them knew what the next couple of weeks would throw at them, but they had to be able to share whatever they were thinking with honesty, instead of trying to protect each other by keeping their fears hidden away inside.

As she chatted to Scarlett for a little while about school, and her forthcoming holiday, it didn't occur to either of them to discuss the nature of Fran's 'illness' The euphemism had been used so many times over the years, that once Emily had satisfied herself that Scarlett was safe she left well alone.

13

"Hi Em... How are you doing?" Fran didn't pause before ploughing straight on. She never expected an answer to this habitual greeting. "Sorry I had to cancel the pictures on Wednesday...I spent most of yesterday in bed, but I'm feeling loads better now, so we can go and see the film one night next week?"

It had pretty much rained incessantly yesterday, so Fran hadn't seen any point in bothering to get dressed. She'd stayed snuggled under the duvet, channel hopping through episodes of Location Location Location, A Place In The Sun, and Escape To The Country, drooling over the properties the couples on each of the shows dismissed so haughtily.

She'd spent the entire day brooding over all the times Sarah had come between her and her father. No matter how hard the stupid cow tried to push her away, Fran was never going to let her win.

She had been on to Sarah from the beginning- seen her for the calculating gold digger she was. Of course her younger sister was way too naive to see what was right under her nose, and simply dismissed her concerns whenever Fran tried to enlist her support. Chrissie might have been taken in by Sarah, but Fran had never been fooled by the doting second wife and step-mother routine. All she cared about was getting her hands on the house and their Dad's investments.

"I've just been looking at the forecast for tomorrow, and it's supposed to be really warm, so I thought we could have a casual lunch in the garden?" Fran suggested eagerly. She was really keen to run Sarah's latest attempt to do her out of what was rightfully hers past Emily. She was also hoping her best friend might help her out a bit too- it wasn't as though she couldn't afford it, a couple of hundred quid was nothing to Emily.

Emily hesitated for a moment, straight-jacketed by the frightfully English politeness that prevented her from voicing an honest response. Knowing Fran, a 'casual' lunch in the garden, would still involve alcohol, and she really wasn't sure she could cope with Fran in full on inebriated mode at the moment.

Her head was all over the place. Goodness knows how she'd managed to get through work the last few days. She'd come really close to telling Mrs Ashton to get a life, as the vacuous woman had wittered on, endlessly regurgitating every minor detail of her recent holiday. The hotel decor hadn't been to her taste, and the Portuguese food had naturally been inedible, but then, there was always a list of things that weren't up to scratch wherever she went. Why the simpering woman ever bothered to leave the country was beyond Emily. She'd be far happier eating fish and chips on the pier in Bournemouth.

Emily quickly ran through her options as she couldn't keep fobbing Fran off indefinitely. Even if the appointment with the consultant did come through in the next few days, there would presumable still be a bit of a wait before they got any results.

Though nobody would ever describe Fran as a domestic goddess, on the odd occasions she did make the effort to cook, the food was fine and always beautifully presented on an assortment of surprisingly good table wear, dug from the depths of her bulging cupboards. Emily had grown accustomed to opening the doors in the cramped kitchen very cautiously, in order to avoid anything falling out on top of her.

Tom was involved in a squash tournament most of the weekend - he'd offered to pull out but Emily had insisted they should try and carry on as normally as possible- so the next couple of days stretched ahead of her, with nothing more exciting than some gardening or housework to occupy her. She had half arranged to go for a walk with kath tomorrow, but she was having second thoughts, realising that her astute friend would pick up on the fact that something was wrong immediately. Emily always found it impossible to hide anything from the wise old owl, who, seemed to possess radar like antennae that homed in on any worries.

While her nerves were in such a raw state, a couple of hours in Fran's company might prove to be exactly the kind of antidote she needed? She always had to push up a gear to cope with her scatty friend's butterfly mind, and Fran would be far too immersed in her own issues to notice if Emily was a bit distracted. Fran's self absorption would actually provide Emily with a place to hide from her own fears for a while.

The moment Emily arrived at Fran's house the following day it was obvious that the goal posts had been moved yet again. She really just wanted to turn tail and run for home.

"It's a bit too windy to sit out, so I thought we'd go for a cheap two for one at The White Horse instead- you don't mind driving do you Em?" Fran launched straight in the moment she opened the front door, grabbing her bag and putting on her shoes, before Emily had even had a chance to respond.

Emily felt her hackles rising. It was the innate sense of entitlement that grated on her already stretched nerves, the automatic assumption that Emily would naturally jump to do her bidding. It was partly her own fault- she had taken on the role of chauffeur years ago, in order to avoid being left waiting for goodness knows how long, before Fran eventually showed up claiming to have 'lost track of time'

"Why don't we go somewhere this side of town?" Emily dug deep as she strove to find a compromise, without letting her irritation show. "It seems a bit daft for me to spend an hour driving back up and down the by-pass, to go somewhere that's only a few minutes from my own house."

"Oh right...I didn't realise you were in a rush." Fran conceded begrudgingly, just about resisting the urge to mutter 'just for a change' under her breath.

Emily studiously ignored the sarcastic tone as she racked her befuddled brain for an alternative. "How about the Two Henry's?" She suggested, trying to inject a smidgen of enthusiasm into her voice.

"I really don't like it there Em. The Staff all look down their noses at you. The last time me and Pippa went there, the waitress was really off with us, and when we tried to complain to the manager, he was absolutely useless.

Emily could just picture the scene, envisaging the pair of them deriding the poor girl serving them, if they'd both been drinking. She'd only met the delightful Pippa a couple of times and that was more than enough for her thank you. The loud brash older woman had an enormous bust that was constantly on display, and a cloud of white candy floss that was supposed to pass as hair. She didn't just have a chip on her shoulder she had a dirty great boulder permanently welded to it.

"What about the Red Lion then? I'm pretty sure they do two-for-ten meals every day?" It was also dimly lit and quiet, Emily added silently to herself, and that was always a crucial factor to take into account when eating out with Fran. She was one of those people who invariably found something wrong with her food, and wasn't happy until the entire restaurant had heard about it.

Just as Emily had predicted, a short while later, when Fran cut into her lamb, she wasn't happy with the way it had been cooked. Emily began to wish the floor would open up and swallow her when the poor young lad that had served them, was summoned back to the table in an imperious tone that must have carried all the way out to the car park.

The way Fran over enunciated each word as she made her complaint, merely confirmed Emily's earlier suspicions- Fran had clearly had a few before she'd picked her up.

As she set about demolishing her replacement meal, Fran was still regaling the occupants of the next table with her views on how low standards had slipped. Thankfully, she did lower her voice fractionally before suddenly changing direction, and filling Emily in on her step-mothers latest attempts to do her out of what she considered to be rightfully hers.

"Dad has always helped me out with a bit of spending money every year." She finished, ending the frequently aired monologue about her stepmothers' campaign to disinherit her and her sister.

"But if your dad is retiring this year, perhaps they simply can't afford to help you out anymore Fran?" Emily observed, striving to be the voice of reason as usual.

"So how come they have just booked a Caribbean cruise...you of all people know how much that will have cost them." Fran put in triumphantly, her point proven in her eyes. "Sarah was the one doing all the talking, as usual, and you know how much that woman hates me."

"Oh come on...She doesn't hate you she just-

"You weren't there Em. It's ok for you. You've got a husband to pay all your bills, and you're in the perfect position to find all the best holidays. You've no idea how hard it is for me to swallow my pride and rely on handouts all the time."

Emily took a deep breath. She was finding it increasingly hard to swallow the urge to point out, that, if people like her and Tom didn't pay their taxes there would be no 'handouts' for her to live on.

"Have you thought anymore about looking for work now that Scarlett is so independent?" This was an old chestnut, but Emily really felt that a job wouldn't just fix Fran's finances, it would give her some much needed purpose, stop her from staring into an empty wine glass all day as she constantly raked over the past.

As Fran weaved her way to the toilets, obviously avoiding taking part in that particular conversation, Emily took the opportunity to catch the waiters' eye and ask for the bill. She'd had more than enough of sitting in this gloomy pub watching the sun pouring in through the windows. She simply didn't have the patience to cope with Fran's warped view of the world today no matter how sorry she might feel for her. All she wanted to do was go home, have a nice cuppa, and then take her self off for a good long walk. A bit of fresh air, and the oh so familiar but still stunning views from Lyth hill, would lift her spirits and help put everything back into some kind of perspective, while she waited for this damned appointment to be over. Even if the results were not good, at least they would know what they were dealing with. It was the waiting, the uncertainty that was so hard to live with.

"You always see everything as so black and white don't you Em." Fran began as soon as she slumped back into her seat.

'Here we go' Emily thought as she slipped a generous tip to the waiter, when he returned with her change. It was obviously time to make a sharp exit before things got too embarrassing. She had noticed the disapproving looks being cast their way every time Fran's voice rose above the general hubbub.

"Everything has always gone so perfectly for you hasn't it? Tom has always earned enough for you to be able to choose whether to work or not, and you have a job you love. Most of us aren't quite as lucky as you with your orderly little life."

Just for a second Emily was tempted to give it back with both barrels, and the words that formed in her head very nearly tripped off her tongue 'Yeah my life is a real bundle of laughs right now. I'm waiting for an appointment to see if I have cancer- it doesn't get much better than that does it?'

She had to suppress an almost hysterical urge to laugh out loud as she imagined the stunned silence that would follow that particular gem, but of course, she remained silent. She'd resigned herself long ago to the fact that this would always be a rather one sided friendship, and that wasn't likely to change any time soon, whatever the outcome of her appointment.

Emily helped Fran into her jacket, and then took her firmly by the arm, inwardly fuming about all the inaccurate assumptions she continually made about her life. She was always making her out to be a spoilt little princess, when the truth of the matter was she and Tom had worked damn hard to attain the comfortable life style they now shared.

"It's obvious that Sarah is trying to cut me and Chrissie out of dad's life so she can get her hands on the house and all his shares." Fran was practically shouting now as she staggered across the car park, clutching Emily's arm for support.

"Fran they've been married for almost thirty years, she's his wife so it IS all hers already." Emily had been down this road so many times before, but when Fran worked herself up into this sort of state there really was no reasoning with her. She was permanently locked in the past, so immersed in a misery of her own making that she truly believed her own propaganda.

"They had the cheek to say that I'm out of control...that I have to cut back my drinking if I want their help...they were telling me what to do as though I'm a child."

Fran was really ranting now, but Emily just let it wash over her as she helped her into the passenger seat, wondering if she truly believed she was in control right now? Had she even noticed that

Emily had picked up the entire bill again, just to get out of the place as quickly as possible?

Emily knew she was on a pretty short fuse herself today and understandably so, but she couldn't help agreeing with John and Sarah's new tough love approach. Fran really did have to learn that she couldn't just keep borrowing money from people, never stopping to think about how she was ever going to pay it all back.

After dropping Fran off and making some black coffee, Emily beat a hasty retreat as there was absolutely no point in staying now Fran had gone past the point of listening. She'd wasted too many hours in the past, offering solutions that had been consigned to oblivion before she'd even walked out the door.

These last few days had brutally hammered home the fragility of life, making it incredibly frustrating for Emily to watch someone she cared about so deeply throwing away far too many precious years...

14

Throughout the drive home, Emily's thoughts ran round in circles, as she searched for where she had gone wrong. What could she have done differently to avoid being placed in such an awkward position? It was all well and good making grand statements, vowing never to be manoeuvred into a similar situation again, but how was she supposed to enforce this when Fran invariably moved the goal posts at the very last minute?

Had she got the guts to clearly elucidate her stance, to spell out the fact that she simply didn't want to be around Fran if she'd been drinking?

As she pulled off the narrow lane on to their gravelled drive, she was surprised to find Tom's car already parked in front of the double garage. As soon as he started to explain how he'd been knocked out in the first round, Emily found herself wondering if that was because his heart simply hadn't been in it, or a deliberate ploy on his part? Either way, she hadn't taken much persuading when he'd suggested that they head out towards Church Stretton to make the most of what was left of the gorgeous mid May afternoon. A bit of quality time together would do them both a world of good right now.

After making the tight turn by the twee little village hall in All Stretton, they left the car at the base of Batch Valley, and then started to climb steadily, following the path of the stream until the track began to level out again. By the time they reached the flatter ground, and were enjoying the panoramic views from the top of The Long Mynd, they were talking far more openly without the strained wariness of the last few days.

Emily always found something very therapeutic about letting her thoughts flow freely in rhythm with her feet. Over the years, their mutual love of walking had taken the heat out of many of the inevitable disagreements that surfaced from time to time, within any healthy marriage.

As neither of them had been in a hurry to bring the afternoon to an end, they'd decided to stop at The Fox in Ryton, for a bite to eat in the huge south facing gardens with breathtaking views towards the hills they'd just been walking. As they began tucking into the hearty platefuls of pub grub, Emily felt relaxed enough to share the new sense of calm that had washed over her...the sort of gut instinct...that had been growing throughout the last couple of days.

"Ever since they took my tonsils out- what would that be- ten years ago...? I've been loosing my voice whenever I get a really bad cold, so I'm fairly sure it'll turn out to be something pretty minor again Tom." She began.

"Well I don't think Mr Shah can put your tonsils back in again Em." Tom laughed, feeling much less agitated now than he had at any time since they'd walked out of the surgery on Wednesday. Sitting here in the sunshine, he was inclined to agree with Emily. It was hard to imagine that there could be anything too sinister wrong with her.

As he stretched his legs out in front of him and lifted his face up to feel the warmth of the sun, he acknowledged that he should have just pulled out of the tournament this weekend and let one of the reserves take his place. He had been next to useless from the first game, but at least being kicked out so early meant he and Emily had been able to share this much needed time on their own, free from the constant interruptions of family life...they'd really managed to clear the air a bit this afternoon and get back on the same page.

They spent all day Sunday just pottering about, easy in each others company again as they worked in the garden, and then Emily had cooked a roast for when Holly got back from her shift at Pizza Hut...seemingly, just an ordinary Sunday...

Though Emily had been diligently practising every cliché in the book...one day at a time... not crossing any bridges until you got to them, etc, she'd still been asked several times if she was alright. One of the biggest drawbacks of working with the same bunch of people for so long, is how well they all get to know you. If, like Emily, you were one of the bubbly members of staff who generally kept the energy level up, you couldn't get away with having a quiet day without it being commented on.

By the time Friday arrived, and there had still been no word from the hospital, Tom began to chaff against Emily's calm sense that all would be well and started nagging her again, urging her to call the surgery and find out what was going on.

"The referral could have got lost in the system, or the letter offering you an appointment might have gone astray. Our post does go to Betley Villa instead of Betley End sometimes." He'd pointed out, visibly frustrated by this seemingly endless wait.

"I'll leave it until Monday, and if there is still nothing in the post by then I'll give the surgery a ring on Tuesday" Emily promised, refusing to allow his anxiety to rub off on her.

Apart from a rather sticky moment the other evening with Holly, she was managing to keep her head down and just plod on. They had been at Bannatynes, revelling in having the Jacuzzi all to themselves, when Holly suddenly changed the subject without any warning.

"What do you think the specialist is planning to do this time Mum?" The question had come so totally out of the blue that it had caught Emily off guard, and with her daughters' face just inches from her own, there had been no where to hide.

"Dr Evanson says Mr Shah will probably want to put a tiny camera down my throat so he can have a look at the larynx and see what is causing the problems." She offered truthfully.

"But what are they are actually looking for?" Holly persisted.

Emily swallowed hard. She wouldn't lie to her daughter. Holly was eighteen, a young woman about to leave for university in a few months, but she didn't want to frighten her unnecessarily either.

"I think they just want to check that there is no blockage of any sort causing the choking." She answered honestly, praying that Holly wouldn't ask what kind of blockage. This was a bit like when the kids were still being bathed together, and had started to question why they were different.

She and Tom had agreed to always answer every question directly, without the silly euphemisms of their parents' generation, but even then, they'd only ever told them what they felt they were ready to cope with, and all she could do now was apply that same common sense.

Thankfully Holly had seemed satisfied with what she'd told her, and talk had quickly returned to the end of term prom, and the all important matter of the perfect dress which they were still searching for. Though she was an inch or two taller than her mother, Holly had inherited the same strawberry blonde curls, dancing hazel eyes, and tendency to speak with her hands flailing around, emphasising every point.

Whenever they spent time together, Emily was swept up in her daughter's exuberance for life, reverting about twenty years as they giggled away like a couple of teenagers. She'd lost count of the amount of times the two of them had been in absolute hysterics, practically crying with laughter, yet when they tried to explain what had set them off to Tom and Josh, they'd just shrug and look at them as if to say 'and?' .

Once that potentially sticky moment had passed her daughter's company had been just the tonic she'd needed as they'd moved leisurely between the loungers, the pool, the steam room and Jacuzzi, jabbering away about everything and nothing as usual.

When Emily eventually found the letter waiting on the doormat Monday evening, she'd felt strangely disconnected from it as she read it several times, as though trying to glean something extra hidden between the few typed lines.

Her appointment was at ten thirty on Wednesday 19th May. Mr Shah, or one of his team, would perform a laryngosocopy which was described as 'a slightly uncomfortable but painless procedure lasting no more than a few minutes'. Wednesday, the day after tomorrow, was exactly two weeks since her referral. At least it was her day off, so that was convenient, and she could easily tell Holly and Helen that she'd been offered a cancellation, at short notice, to explain the speed at which she was being seen.

Her mind automatically turned to the practicalities, rather than the possible consequences. She'd always been good at transference, had learnt from a very young age how to obsess about something minor, in order to avoid looking at the bigger issue.

Glancing at the calendar she noticed that she was supposed to be going to the pictures with Fran in the afternoon, but to be honest, it was just another inane Rom Com. She would simply bend the truth a little, and imply that the appointment was later in the day.

She fired off a text, in the hope of avoiding a lengthy call, but unsurprisingly, her phone rang a few minutes later, just as she was putting the potato wedges in the oven. With the phone jammed between her ear and her shoulder, she began cubing the pork and vegetables, and spearing them onto skewers, ready to pop under the grill.

"What hospital appointment is this?" Fran's opening line was delivered without preamble and as bluntly as usual.

"Didn't I mention it on Saturday?" Emily kept her tone studiously casual. "I'm seeing Mr Shah again...maybe he'll whip out my larynx or something this time." Her laughter sounded forced and tinny to her own ears.

"Oh right, nothing serious then...just your throat again? What time is the appointment, maybe we could just catch a later showing? I know it's a bit more expensive in the evening, but it'll still be two for one on a Wednesday." In reality the cost was totally academic as far as Fran was concerned, because Emily generally paid for the tickets anyway.

Emily bit her lip. To some extent, she only had herself to blame whenever she found herself in these tricky situations, as she so rarely confided in Fran about anything that really mattered, but she could be so obtuse at times, and didn't seem capable of taking a hint, no matter how heavy handed it was.

"I'd rather leave it for now Fran if you don't mind. We could be sitting round the hospital for hours as the doctor thinks the consultant will probably want to do some tests...put a camera down my throat."

"Oh right... OK...What about going after work tomorrow then? I really fancy seeing this film... you know I've always had a thing about George Clooney, and I could really use a laugh right now. Dad is still being really awkward about lending me this money, and the half term is only a couple of weeks away..." Fran left the sentence dangling meaningfully, wondering if she dare ask Emily outright if she could lend her the money. She really did want to see this film, but she'd also hoped to find a way to work the conversation round so that Emily might offer to loan her the money she needed, without her actually having to ask for it.

"I'll have a look at the calendar and get back to you Fran. I'm in the middle of cooking our meal right now..."

"But it finishes this weekend- "Fran broke off realising the line had already gone dead...

What on earth was the matter with Emily lately? Fran felt like she was continually being fobbed off at the moment. What with her dad, and her ex-husband on her case, she'd had the week from hell, and could really use a break from her own company- not to mention a couple of hours drooling over George.

Simon had had a right go at her for leaving Scarlett alone the other night...but it wasn't as though she'd gone out with the intention of being out all night for goodness sake. The party at Pippa's had just got a bit out of hand, and by the time she'd realised how late it was, it really hadn't seemed worth paying a ridiculous amount more for a taxi, when the rates would drop back down to daytime in another couple of hours. How was she supposed to have known that Scarlett would wake up feeling sick and call her dad at five in the morning....He would never have known about it if only she hadn't inadvertently left her phone on silent and missed all Scarlett's calls.

Simon had gone on and on about how much Scarlett needed her mother right now, but it sure as hell didn't feel that way- she hardly ever spent any time at home lately. She was either at his house, out shopping with Zoe, or at Izzie's with her domestic Goddess of a mother waiting on her hand and foot. When she was at home, she spent all her time in her room, no doubt scribbling away in that stupid diary she was always poring over.

Fran remembered how she used to do the same thing at thirteen, and wondered if Scarlett embellished every miniscule detail, about any boy who so much as looked at her. She hadn't kept a diary in years, but then it was bad enough having to live this dreary life. The last thing she wanted to do was record her misery.

The nearest thing she'd come to a bit of male attention recently, was a quick pizza with a guy who'd clearly found his stuffed crust more interesting than her.

She'd literally bumped into James again as she was backing out of Izzie's front door, having just dropped Scarlett off for yet another sleep-over.

"It seems like Sophie has a better social life than me these days." He laughed as they began comparing taxi duties for teenagers. "I'm just going to grab a pizza and watch a DVD...pretty sad for a Saturday night eh?" His tone was self deprecating, rather self pitying. "If you're not too busy do you fancy joining me for a quick bite to eat Fran?"

"Oh...that would be lovely James but I...er... rushed out with just my phone and keys." She improvised quickly, ashamed of the fact that she had to live like this. She was so strapped for cash, while she tried to come up with some spending money for the holiday that even a pizza was a luxury she couldn't afford at the moment.

"Don't worry about that, it's only a pizza Fran, and call me old fashioned, but as I invited you it should be my treat anyway." James responded easily.

More than happy to accept on that basis, Fran surreptitiously kicked her bag out of sight under the passenger seat, before following his car down to the retail park.

The way James pulled out her chair and recommended his favourites, you'd have thought they were dining in a proper restaurant, and although she knew if anyone else had done the same thing, she'd have probably have felt patronised, James had this way of turning the old fashioned courtesies into an endearing trait- he made her feel like a lady.

The conversation flowed just as easily as it had in the car, when he'd given her that lift home a few weeks ago (that is before she'd made a right tit of herself by trying to flirt with him) but this time, Fran was able to contribute somewhat more coherently as she sipped a very-berry smoothie.

When she thanked him as he settled the bill, he'd offered her another of those easy grins that totally transformed his face.

"Maybe you could buy me a hotdog at the school fete next Friday? I hate going to those things on my own..." He confessed.

Fran hadn't had the slightest intention of going, but it would be rather amusing to see the look on Simon and Zoe's faces, if she turned up with someone as respectable as the local vet in tow.

Despite the 'date' they'd arranged, the evening had ended on pretty much the same note as before. Always the perfect gentleman,

James waited until she was strapped into her car, before walking towards his own, but there hadn't been a flicker of anything other than friendliness in his eyes all evening.

This was entirely new territory to Fran, and it felt decidedly weird. She had never had a male friend who wasn't a boyfriend- not even back in her school days- and it was definitely going to take a bit of getting used to...

15

When Emily and Tom arrived the stipulated fifteen minutes before her appointment, the reception area was already heaving. Fortunately they didn't have to wait too long, before they were summoned through to the comparative quiet of the consulting room.

The rather dapper quietly spoken throat specialist, had barely altered in a decade, and though Emily knew he couldn't possibly remember her, Mr Shah's pleasant greeting clearly acknowledged the fact that he had treated her before.

When she was referred to him ten years ago, she'd been struck by his gentle unhurried approach, and he was just as courteous today, very different from the aptly named gynaecologist she'd been referred to in the early stages of her pregnancy with Josh- Blunt by name and blunt by nature.

His patronising manner had made her feel like she was wasting his precious time as he'd performed a cursory examination. He would probably face a law suit if he spoke to a patient in the same off hand manner today, treating her as though she were a piece of meat, rather than a human being with raging hormones. To be fair to the man though, his somewhat crude assessment of her nether regions, which could have come straight from an episode of Doc Martin, had proved to be entirely accurate. Despite her tiny frame, she'd delivered two eight pound babies with nothing more than a bit of gas and air.

Once Mr Shah had confirmed the symptoms she was experiencing, it was straight down to business. As he'd approached her with the long tube like apparatus, Emily had automatically opened her mouth, only to be told that it was actually going up her nose.

Just as advised in the leaflet, the sensation was strange and uncomfortable, but she was not in any pain as she concentrated on breathing as normally as possible. The procedure was over in a very short time and Mr Shah smiled reassuringly as he pronounced the verdict.

"That all looks perfectly healthy to me, Emily." He paused allowing his words to sink in a little before he continued. "It looks to me as though your symptoms are probably being caused by something called laryngopharyngeal reflux which is very easily treated."

"Reflux...as in acid..." Emily puckered her brow in confusion. "But I don't have any heartburn or indigestion or anything like that?" The relief that he hadn't found anything more sinister was so overwhelming that Emily was itching to get out of here and start processing it, but common sense urged her to make the most of this opportunity to find out what **was** causing all her problems. Though she didn't want to sound as though she was questioning the consultants' judgment in any way acid damage made no sense at all to her.

"It is often referred to as 'silent reflux' Emily for exactly that reason." Mr Shah explained patiently, passing her a leaflet which showed a diagram of the valve at the top of the oesophagus no longer doing its' job properly, and an explanation about the medication usually prescribed to prevent further damage, plus a list of foods to be avoided.

Just as they were preparing themselves to leave, Mr Shah looked up again from her file, where he'd been making notes in his meticulously neat handwriting.

"Just to be on the safe side though, I think it would be a good idea for me to take a closer look at your oesophagus, so I'm going to arrange a panendoscopy for you Emily." He continued.

Emily's heart sunk as Tom immediately asked "How long is she likely to have to wait for that?" They were supposed to be going away for a few days at the end of the month, and she really didn't want any doubts still hanging over them and spoiling it. Surely if it was this reflux thing then she could just start taking tablets to correct it straight away?

"A panendoscopy is performed in theatre under general anaesthetic. I think I may have a slot on my list tomorrow, so if you'd like to take a seat back in the waiting room for a few minutes, I'll make a couple of calls and see if I can find a bed to have you admitted tomorrow morning Emily."

They'd obediently trooped out of the consultant's room and resumed their places on the ugly rows of fixed plastic chairs in the waiting area in stunned silence. One minute they were being assured that it was likely to be a simple problem, and the next Mr Shah was arranging to have her admitted the next day.

"Would you like to come back through now Emily?" By the time they were summoned to his room once again a few minutes later, they still hadn't exchanged any actual words, just a few startled glances and a shell-shocked clasping of hands. "I've managed to find a bed for you, and as it is such a short procedure, I've made space on my list. If you can be at the head and neck ward for eight thirty tomorrow morning, they'll get you prepped for the last slot on my morning list. You are likely to have a very sore throat for a day or two afterwards, so you'll need to take a little time off work." He smiled benignly, handing her yet another leaflet about the exploratory operation he was going to perform and what she would need to bring with her, before he rose and shook both their hands.

Emily rang her office as soon as she got home, and Mike's stunned reaction gave her a pretty good indication of how hard it was going to be to explain this latest development to the kids and Helen. No matter how many times they reiterated Mr Shah's words, that it is was a precautionary procedure to confirm the diagnosis, the fact that he was admitting her the very next day did rather tell its own story.

When she told Tom she was going for a walk as soon as she'd finished on the phone, he didn't suggest joining her as he had a pretty good idea where she would be heading...

Emily never got involved in intellectual debates about religion because her simple, unshakable certainty that God was 'there' in everything she did probably wouldn't cut it, but from a fairly young age, she'd always offered her thoughts to him- prayed if that's what you wanted to call it. She did attend church sporadically, but on the rare occasion someone from the ministry team had prayed with her, she'd found her self wondering if they were actually talking to God or just trying to impress her with their clever words and bible knowledge.

At times like this, whenever she was in need of more strength than she could ever find in her own right, she headed up Lyth hill, to the wooden bench, half hidden in the bracken, with the most spectacular views of all the hills that surrounded Shrewsbury, protecting the county town from the worst of the elements in every direction.

The awe inspiring beauty of nature is where she always saw God's hand at work, and sitting in this secret place, she usually managed to get her worries back into some kind of manageable perspective. This was actually no different to any other problem in that it still came down to one simple question...when push came to shove, was her faith really strong enough to trust God implicitly. Stressing about tomorrow wouldn't change the outcome one iota, so as she sat there quietly with her thoughts, Emily simply prayed for a few more years as Holly and Josh still needed her...her job as their mother wasn't finished yet... she still had so much more to teach them...

While Tom unpacked the few bits and pieces Emily had been instructed to bring with her, and the cheerful matronly ward Sister who'd introduced herself as Barbara, double checked the paperwork, Emily kept glancing towards the bed opposite her. The young girl who had been brought in by ambulance seemed to be in a bad way, and was obviously in a great deal of pain.

"Tonsillitis!" The nurse confided sotto voice, noting Emily's concern. "Just watch what happens when she hasn't got an audience to play to though." She chuckled, good- naturedly.

Sure enough, once she had been settled into her bed, and the curtains either side of her had been pulled across, so she was no longer quite so visible, the girl immediately sat up and began texting.

"A bit of a regular is our flame haired prima-donna." Barbara confided, as she checked Emily's blood pressure.

In no time at all, Tom had been given a number to call after three o'clock, and she was on a trolley making her way down to theatre. Just as the double doors opened, she suddenly started to shake uncontrollably and apologised profusely for holding everybody up.

"Don't worry, everything has been sprung on you very quickly Emily. It'll just be a bit of shock." The pretty young theatre nurse, with the strong Yorkshire accent assured her easily, wrapping another blanket around her.

When she came round in the recovery room, the same thing happened again, and her body was practically convulsing as she shivered violently. Once again she was covered in several blankets and advised that it was not an unusual reaction. Just as the shakes finally subsided, and she was being offered a sip of water, Mr Shah re-appeared still in his cap and gown. Though she was still feeling pretty groggy she was perfectly capable of understanding that he was very happy with the results.

"I found a little tenderness in the oesophagus as expected, but there is absolutely nothing else to worry about. I'll write a prescription so we can get you started on lansoprazole immediately." He explained reassuringly.

As she thanked him for all he'd done Emily raised her eyes heavenwards and smiled, acknowledging the fact that she'd always been in the safest hands of all, before she slipped back off to sleep again...

16

It was still only three o'clock in the morning, and Emily was beginning to feel as though she had seen pretty much every single hour of this interminable night. The luminous red digits of the alarm clock pulsed back at her, mocking her, as they pressed home the fact that the loneliest hours definitely were the ones just before dawn.

Pulling the quilt firmly around her as she climbed back into bed again for the umpteenth time, Emily tried to draw in a little of Tom's body heat as she struggled to hold back the tears of self pity.

She'd really had a gut full of these sleepless nights now, and was finding it hard not to resent the fact that Tom could just lie there all night, completely oblivious to the fact that she was spending most of her time in the bathroom.

If the boot had been on the other foot, she'd have been wide awake in an instant, immediately sensing that something was wrong if Tom had been the one getting in and out of bed all night. She was sorely tempted to thrash around a bit until she woke him as she could desperately do with a cuddle, but of course he still had to get up for work in the morning- unlike her.

Her second sick-note was due to run out tomorrow, and she was clearly going to have to be signed off again. She dreaded the thought of having to ring work again as the 'meds disagreeing with her' was beginning to sound a bit lame, but she could hardly go into graphic detail with someone as old fashioned as Mike as he'd be absolutely mortified. He always looked as though he was about to spontaneously combust if one of the girls so much as mentioned a period pain while he was within earshot.

Emily had always maintained a decidedly 'glass half full' approach to life, and was generally inclined to make the best of every situation, but lying here in the dark, it was impossible to stop the hideously life intrusive side effects of the tablets from dragging her down.

A few weeks ago, when Mr Shah had given her the prescription, after the exploratory procedure he'd performed in theatre, she'd naively assumed that her problems were behind her, but now it seemed as though they were escalating, and at a terrifyingly rapid rate.

She'd been to and fro from the surgery so many times over these last few months, that, she was beginning to feel like she should have a chair in the waiting room, with her name on it. She was also beginning to get the distinct impression that Dr Evanson was secretly thinking 'not her again' every time he called her through to his consulting room.

After just a few days taking Lansoprazole, her light headedness had become so acute that she'd started to feel horrendously disorientated. On the odd days she had felt able to risk being away from the bathroom for long enough to get some much needed fresh air, she'd been leaning heavily on her mahogany walking stick. She usually only carried it as a deterrent against the increasing number of dogs whose owners seemed incapable of controlling them. The numbness in her feet wasn't helping either, as it made it incredibly hard to judge when she was making contact with the ground.

Doctor Evanson had been fairly sympathetic when she'd gone back to see him the first time, to explain that everything she ate seemed to be upsetting her stomach now. He'd listened patiently before assuring her that it would all settle down given a little more time.

"PPI's- proton pump inhibitors- do take a bit of getting used to Emily. They are suppressing the production of stomach acid, so it might take a little while for your digestive system to adjust. I can sign you off work for a couple of weeks if you're really struggling, but you really need to give them a chance." He'd stated firmly.

She'd left the surgery feeling thoroughly deflated, but resolved to try and eat as simple a diet as she possible could, in order to give the tablets a fair chance, as it sounded like she didn't really have much choice.

Two weeks later she'd had to make another appointment, as she'd lost an additional half stone and was beginning to look like death warmed up- or 'a bit rough' as Mel had so succinctly put it, when she'd popped in for a quick coffee.

"Perhaps Lansoprazole just doesn't suit you." The doctor had finally conceded. "Why don't we try something else?"

Emily had happily trooped over to the chemist to part with some more of her hard earned cash, only to find the effects of Omeprazole were even more life intrusive.

From the moment she'd started taking them she'd hardly been able to leave the house, so stuck at home all day she'd began doing a little research of her own. She'd soon come across numerous web sites and forums, and quickly gleaned, that, although PPI's worked perfectly well for some patients, a large percentage of people simply could not tolerate them, so had to be switched to some other form of medication.

Emily had printed off all this information, and armed with the facts this time, she'd made another appointment for tomorrow morning- or this morning, she corrected herself, glancing ruefully at the clock again.

She fully understood that acid blockers would not offer the same level of protection against any further damage to her oesophagus, but to be honest, she'd rather spend the rest of her life choking on her food, than spaced out and incontinent- not to mention unemployable if this carried on much longer.

She'd taken so much time off work, and cancelled so many plans with family and friends, that she'd become even more flaky than Fran recently. Thoughts of Fran reminded her that she still hadn't got round to returning her call...explained why she'd been pretty much off the radar these last few weeks. The message Fran had left, when she'd got back from visiting her mother, had been on the machine for a few days now.

Though she could always have a laugh about playing 'phone tag' with Mel, of her sister Joanna, who both lived such busy lives that she didn't get to touch base with them that often, if you didn't get back to Fran straight away, she always took umbrage... and they hadn't exactly parted on the best of terms after that awful meal either...she really must give her a call tomorrow...explain, at least in part, what was going on...

17

Fran was lying in bed staring incredulously at the clock too, but her reaction to the digits displayed was very different to Emily's. She couldn't believe she'd actually slept through until seven o'clock, without the aid of alcohol or sleeping tablets. For her this was nothing short of a miracle.

She'd been out with James most of the day again yesterday, and clearly, the combination of fresh air and exercise had done her a power of good. She'd been unable to keep her eyes open as she watched the news, and must have gone spark out almost as soon as her head had touched the pillow.

When James first suggested a midweek walk, to avoid the weekend crowds, she'd assumed he meant a leisurely little stroll somewhere like Ellesmere, not a two hour trek over Wenlock Edge. It was a good job she'd dug her trainers out from under the bed, and put on an old pair of jeans and a sweatshirt borrowed from Scarlett.

She would have been absolutely horrified if she'd been the same size as her mother at thirteen, but unlike Fran, Scarlett seemed to have accepted the curvy frame that nature had given her. Fran had spent the last few years trying to convince her self she was still a size twelve so consequently, she had a wardrobe full of clothes that didn't really fit her. Scarlett was always quoting Zoe, after another of their shopping trips. 'It's just a piece of material mum, it really doesn't matter what the label says as long as it fits properly'- of course that was easy to say if you had an athletic frame like Zoe.

Despite the fact that it had been many years since Fran had done any serious walking, she'd really enjoyed their day out. The scenery had been absolutely breathtaking, and the thought of a hearty pub lunch, washed down with a nice big glass of red, had been spurring her on the whole way.

Though the food in the cute little cafe in Much Wenlock had been absolutely delicious, it was hardly the type of lunch that Fran had been expecting. Perhaps James had been planning days out with his daughter for so long, he'd just fallen into the habit of choosing places that were child friendly?

Once they'd finished the wholesome home-cooked quiche, washed down with nothing more intoxicating than some locally produced elderflower cordial, they'd taken a stroll around the ruins of the old priory. Later on, deciding to make the most of the sunny afternoon, they'd stopped at the tea rooms, chatting away, perfectly comfortable in each others company, as they enjoyed the views from the sheltered terrace.

Fran had never felt so totally relaxed- released from any concern over her appearance. She felt under no pressure to constantly check her make up, or brush her hair. Though it was decidedly alien to her, she was beginning to enjoy spending time with a guy who was old fashioned enough to pull out her chair, open doors and insist on paying for everything, while seeming to expect nothing but her company in return.

This platonic friendship thing really did seem to require very little effort. She'd already found herself sharing things about her chequered past with James, that she would have never dreamed of revealing to a potential boyfriend.

It had been early evening by the time they'd eventually pulled up outside her house, but approaching the longest day of the year, there was still plenty of daylight left.

"If you don't need to rush off I could make us a bit of supper...my way of saying thank you for such a lovely day?"

The moment she'd issued the invitation, Fran had suddenly felt strangely coy about inviting James in. Though he'd picked her up from the house several times now, she'd always made sure she was ready to go. She hadn't actually been to his home yet, but she knew the area, and couldn't help thinking he was going to find her tiny two-up-two-down new build decidedly pokey in comparison, especially with all her clutter everywhere. She had never been particularly house-proud, but she'd really let things slide lately.

"That would be lovely Fran if you're sure, but don't feel you need to thank me, I've really enjoyed myself. A day out on your own is never the same somehow is it?" he'd responded easily, as though picking up on her doubts.

She'd mumbled her agreement, but in all honesty it would never have entered her head to try. She'd be far too self-conscious, acutely aware of all the hand holding couples and perfect families looking down their noses at the sad looser on her own.

Though James' big solid frame filled her little galley kitchen, she didn't feel at all crowded by him as he chopped the mushrooms, while she cut the chicken into strips and tossed it into the wok. There was something so still, so calming about his affirming presence- a bit like being with Emily's in some ways.

Their respective glasses weren't just half full, they were practically brimming over, and Fran knew she would definitely benefit from applying a good dollop of that positivity to her own life. Thinking of glasses, she wasn't being much of a host...

"Would you prefer red or white with the pasta?" She asked reaching into the cupboard above her head for a couple of glasses.

"Neither for me thanks..."

"You haven't tried my cooking yet. It might help to wash it down." Fran laughed as she poured the carbonara sauce into the wok from a jar. With her back turned towards him, she missed the look that crossed James' face as he studied her thoughtfully. "There should be some beer in the fridge if you don't drink wine?" The spatula being waved in that general direction was intended as an invitation for him to help him self.

There was no point in putting it off any longer. James had been here several times in the last couple of years, and he knew there was never a right time to slip something like this into the conversation, so he may as well just get it over with.

"Actually Fran I don't drink." He began quietly.

"Oh....right...I was beginning to wonder..." she responded frankly, feeling a little bit relieved. She'd begun to wonder if he'd been avoiding alcohol for her benefit. She had been completely off her face, when Tom had coerced him into giving her a lift home from Emily's a couple of months ago. She'd started to think he thought she had a problem. Dad's nagging was obviously getting to her- she was becoming totally paranoid.

"Is that for health reasons?" Fran asked, her curiosity manifesting itself as bluntly as usual as she heaped two generous helpings of the creamy pasta onto plates, and handed one to James.

"Umm...kind of...." He paused as they made their way through the lounge, and out to the postage stamp sized garden, only continuing once she'd put her plate down on the tiny bistro style table- he didn't want her to drop her meal after going to all the trouble of cooking it. "I'm a recovering alcoholic Fran." He spoke softly, waiting for the revulsion that usually followed this statement to flood her face.

"Oh right...."Fran stalled, subconsciously putting her wine glass back down on the table a little further away from him.

"Sorry...I know it's a bit of a shock...nobody ever knows quite how to react." They both ate in silence for a few moments, as he allowed her to process what he'd told her and form her own opinions. He didn't have to wait long, but her first question certainly took him by surprise.

"Do you mind talking about it?" She'd asked, her eyes holding his levelly, her tone completely without censure.

"No... Not at all...It's usually other people who want to change the subject- that's if they haven't already made a run for it!" he chuckled softly. "Fire away, ask whatever you want to."

And so she had... They'd sat in the garden until the light begun to fade, while he explained with absolute candour how a couple of whiskeys in the evenings, after his wife left, had escalated so rapidly. Though, at the lowest point, James's life must have been a living hell, at no point did Fran feel as though he was asking for her sympathy, and he gave every ounce of credit for his success to his sponsors.

"Fortunately, by the time I got to the point of carrying a water bottle filled with vodka, to steady my hands before operating, one of my colleagues had started to recognise the signs, as his wife is a recovering alcoholic too. He basically issued me with an ultimatum- get help or resign." He recalled with a grimace. "I won't pretend it was easy, but with the support of Keith, and the rest of the group, I've been dry for over three years now."

"But you still can't risk even one glass of wine?" Fran frowned, obviously puzzled.

"I'm in an entirely different place now, and would probably be absolutely fine Fran, but it's just not worth taking that chance when other people have invested so much time in me. I can't risk loosing access to my daughter again for the sake of a drink." He concluded sombrely.

Long after James had left, Fran stayed in the garden, nursing a mug of hot chocolate. So much of what he'd shared with her had really struck home, resonating uncomfortably deeply, and she had to admit that she was definitely guilty of using alcohol as a crutch to get by these days, rather than just enjoying a drink socially. Of course the big difference was that she could still cut back anytime she chose to... Couldn't she...?

18

Fran was merrily humming away to herself as she gave the lounge a quick tidy before Emily arrived. Every year, she came back from Majorca on a high, full of determination, brimming with resolutions, but this year, with James' support, rather than letting all those good intentions fade quicker than her tan, she'd managed to harness the feel good factor, and take some positive strides forward.

Now that James had shared his problems so openly with her, it was really easy to be honest with him, admit how much she struggled to get through the days. Having had the guts ripped out of his own life, he actually got it- understood why she used anti-depressants, or a few drinks, to take the edge of the utter despair that washed over her, especially during the winter months.

When he'd first broached the subject of voluntary work though, she'd raised her eyes in exasperation.

"How many times do you think I've heard that old chestnut James? What is the point? How is it going to change anything if I'm not even going to get paid?" The words tripped off her tongue automatically, as she'd repeated them so often to Emily, but James wasn't so easily thwarted.

He had calmly gone on to tell her about his friend Barbara, who managed a charity shop, and offered voluntary positions to people who had been out of work for some time (alcoholics in other words.) He'd gone on to describe how a number of the volunteers had successfully found paid employment, once they'd gained some current skills to put on their C V.

"Why don't I give her a ring and see if she's got any positions available?" Fran couldn't help smiling at the way James managed to make it sound like she would be applying for some high powered executive role, rather than just rummaging through peoples unwanted tat.

When she'd met Barbara Hughes a few days later, she'd interviewed her in exactly the same vein, as thoroughly as though she was being considered for a proper job.

That had been three weeks ago, and to her surprise, Fran was actually enjoying herself in the shop. As they were always so busy, the hours seemed to whizz by really quickly. Barbara had let her loose on the window displays for the first time yesterday, and she and Janet, the other volunteer she'd been working alongside, had been full of praise for her efforts, assuring her that she had a real flair for it.

It was finally beginning to feel like her life had actually turned a corner. Being at the shop a couple of days a week, and spending a fair amount of her free time out walking with James, she hadn't been drinking anywhere near as much recently, and was also sleeping so much more soundly.

She'd almost laughed out loud when she'd seen the look on her dad's face the other day, when he'd come round to see if he could find out what was causing her washing machine to make such an ominous clanking noise.

"The place looks great love." He'd complimented her straight away, his eagle eyes having no doubt already clocked the numerous bottles of Schloer in her recycling bin, as he'd waited for her to answer the door. She'd always got some in the fridge now for whenever James came round.

Though he always insisted it was fine by him if she wanted a glass of wine, she knew it was doing her good to cut down, besides which, she could always have a glass or two of red once he'd gone home if she wanted to, but to be honest, most nights she was more than ready for her bed now.

She glanced at her watch again, realising that as punctuality was practically her middle name, Emily would be here in a just a few minutes. Fran couldn't wait to see her reaction to the changes she'd made to the house and fill her in on all her latest news.

For the first time in years she actually felt proud to welcome someone into her home, OK, so it was still tiny- there was absolutely nothing she could do about that- but all the hard work she and James had put in last weekend had really paid off. The lounge looked like it had had a complete make over, and the best thing was, it had hardly cost any money at all- just a lot of elbow grease.

The yellowing paint work was now brilliant white, thanks to James's deft use of a brush and the gloss he'd apparently had 'lying around in his garage'. The chocolate brown throws, covering the old chintzy sofas, had been an amazing find, and although they wouldn't stand too closer inspection, artful draping ensured the flaws were tucked out of sight. The 'Wilkinson's own' sugared almond paint had gone on surprisingly well for the price, and getting rid of the tatty old rug that had been down since she moved in, and giving the laminate floor a good polish, had completed the transformation. By removing one of the units and turning the sofas to face each other, they'd succeeded in making the room appear so much larger too.

She loved the new, clean minimalistic lines, and though she and Emily were planning to head to 'The Range' for a mooch and a coffee this morning, she was only looking for a couple of statement pieces to finish the room, as she had no intention of filling every surface with all her twee bits of clutter again...

"Wow. This looks fabulous Fran. The room looks so much bigger." Emily enthused wide-eyed with approval a few minutes later, her admiration tinged with slight concern over how her friend had managed to achieve such a dramatic change, when just a few weeks ago she had been unable to find enough spending money to go on holiday. She could only hope that Fran's dad had stepped in to help after all, and she hadn't fallen prey to one of those awful pay day loan sharks you were always reading about in the papers.

As though reading her mind Fran took her on a guided tour, revealing all the money saving tricks she'd used as they moved around the room.

"I've been doing a couple of afternoons a week in the Heart Foundation shop all this month, and someone brought these throws in a couple of weeks ago. They were totally rank- absolutely reeking of cigarette smoke- the one even had a hole in it, but I thought it was worth risking a fiver to see if I could clean them up."

"You always had a good eye for that sort of thing." Emily complimented her warmly. "When you and Simon first moved into Brookfield Close I remember being really impressed with how quickly you made it your own."

"Yeah...." Fran mused wistfully. That felt like a different life time now, almost as though it had happened to someone else, but they had been really happy for a time when they'd first got married. "Simon was so impressed with how little I spent by furnishing the house with car boot and charity shop finds." She giggled, enjoying the rare pleasure of being able to recall a memory of that time without the accompanying surge of bitter resentment towards him and Zoe.

"Did you do all the painting yourself then?" Emily asked, admiring the neat brushwork on the gleaming skirting boards.

"I did the walls myself but...a friend... did the paintwork." Fran answered, looking away and quickly and changing the subject, though she had absolutely no idea why she had reacted so coyly. Why hadn't she just told Emily it was James? It wasn't as though they had anything to hide or be ashamed of?

Emily noted the tinge of colour that had flooded Fran's face. A 'friend'- that explained things! Whenever Fran turned over one of her new leaves, there was generally a man at the centre of it. Though she didn't want to rain on Fran's parade, she'd watched her friend coming up with schemes to totally transform her life, about as often as most people changed their bed sheets. The trouble was the good intentions generally lasted about as long as the smell of fresh laundry too.

Even if this new found positivity was to be as short lived as usual, Emily intended to make the most of it and enjoy what was shaping up to be a 'normal' drama free, couple of hours with her old friend. As Fran looped her arm through Emily's and they headed out towards her car, chattering away like in the old days, Emily felt a long absent rush of affection for this troubled woman, whom she had been subconsciously pushing away recently.

"Sorry I've been so rubbish at staying in touch lately." She apologised softly, as they both strapped themselves in. "I've been having a pretty rough time with the side effects of the medication I was given, and had to be signed off work for a few weeks."

She'd blushed to her roots when she'd attempted to make Dr Evanson understand exactly why she wasn't prepared to endure the life intrusive repercussions of Omeprazole any longer. She'd floundered around, searching for similar delicate phrasing when talking to Kath, who had never so much as belched in front of her in almost a decade, but sitting in the car with Fran, she explained the humiliation she'd endured in much the same way as she had to Jess. We all adopt a slightly different persona to suit our various friends' delicacies, and Fran and Jess had a lot more in common than either of them would care to admit. If they had something to say they'd both just spit it out with no preamble.

Jess had predictably rushed straight in with well intended advice, urging Emily to make an appointment with the lady doctor in the practise she always saw, as personally, she had never rated Dr Evanson much. Kath had of course responded entirely differently. She never rushed in to fill a silence and always thought carefully before offering any opinions.

"It got so bad at one point, I could barely leave the house, and whenever I did, I had to carry a spare pare of pants in my bag." Emily confided in Fran now, knowing she should probably have shared some of this with her weeks ago, "But it was when I had to rush into a field of crops, in the middle of a short walk, that I decided I'd had enough of living like an incontinent old woman."

Emily deliberately kept her tone light, playing down the utter mortification she'd been enduring for weeks. It was over now, and although she was still struggling with some other issues, her stomach had definitely begun to settle down within days of changing to Ranitidine.

"Oh Em...Why didn't you tell me...I had no idea it was that bad. You know I'm always here for you." Fran had looked horrified on her friends' behalf.

"I just sort of kept it to myself to be honest, as it's such a grim topic." Emily laughed, not looking for pity."Anyway let's change the subject. How was the holiday? You look really well so it must have done you good?"

"Oh it was fabulous Em." Fran jumped straight in full of enthusiasm, "Mum has met some new bloke." She rolled her eyes as if to say 'what's new' before carrying on, "and Roger rented this really lovely apartment in an exclusive private development for us- a bit of a step up from the flea pit we had last year."

"What's he like?" Emily was already imagining Angie with the usual toy boy in tow.

"A bit of a pot bellied Julio Iglesias lookalike, who sings in the local bars," Fran laughed, "but he seemed to treat mum like a princess, and at least he's nearer her age than mine."

"What about Scarlett- did she have a good time too?"

"Oh you know Scarlie. She spent the whole time sat under an umbrella with her nose in a book, or scribbling away in that damn diary that she seems to take everywhere with her these days." Fran grimaced.

"Well she's at that age now isn't she, where everything in life is all so intense and immediate." Emily pointed out astutely.

The two women began a trip down memory lane, laughing about the exploits they'd shared during the year they'd worked together at Thomas Cook. Fran had been so much more of a drama queen than her daughter was ever likely to be.

When Emily dropped Fran back at her house a couple of hours later, they hugged warmly before Fran got out of the car with her usual "love you to bits." parting.

Emily was still smiling as she pulled out of the parking area that served the little mews to the left, and courtyard to the right. This was such a claustrophobic way to build houses, all piled on top of each other, but to be fair Fran had got the tiny little house looking lovely inside now.

She'd noticed that the kitchen had obviously had a lick of paint, and been de-cluttered too. Maybe Fran really had turned a corner this time? She really hoped so. On days like this it was easy to remember why they'd become friends...when she was on form, Fran really lit up a room and was such good fun to be around...

19

As soon as she walked through the front door, Scarlett sensed that the period of calm was over. It was only ever a question of time. She sighed heavily, fixing the obligatory smile on her face before walking into the lounge.

Her mum was supposed to have been at 'work' this afternoon, so if she was sitting here drinking, she could be fairly certain that the stint in the charity shop was over too- had gone the same way all her mothers' other 'fresh starts' had. She'd have had some major bust up with one of the other volunteers, or perhaps a customer, but of course it would have been entirely the other persons' fault.

Scarlett had learnt never to question why she wasn't allowed to see her dad or granddad for a while, whenever her mother had fallen out with one of them. That was just the way she dealt with things- burying her head in the sand until it all blew over. It made little difference whether it was a member of the family, a friend, or one of the neighbours, who'd received a tongue lashing. Whenever her mother knew she'd over-stepped the mark, she'd hide herself away, claim to be ill for a few days, and then just carry on as though the argument had never happened.

"Hi Scarlie...come and sit down and talk to you're mum babe...we haven't had a proper catch up in ages have we?"

Scarlett had taught herself not to cringe whenever her mum used that naff shortening of her name, but she hated the ridiculous pet name even more- she was thirteen for goodness sake, and by no stretch of the imagination, was she the kind of girl you would ever call a 'babe'.

She threw her bag down on the table and reluctantly took a seat on the opposite sofa, studiously ignoring the fact that her mum had just hitched over to make room for her. Whenever her mum went all girly on her, wanting them to be best friends, a session could go on for hours. Scarlett was finding it increasingly difficult to hold her tongue and just agree with her mothers' warped view of the world lately, but if she actually started to express her opinions it would just prolong the agony.

She almost preferred her mother in her other drink mode. Then she would start hurling abuse at her the moment she walked through the door, laying into her for some imagined crime, like having forgotten to do a job she didn't even know she was supposed to have done. If she stayed quiet and just accepted the punishment, it was over much quicker and she could escape to her room.

Scarlett had grown accustomed to doing 'chores' from the moment she could walk and talk. She could quote her mothers' mantra that 'it was just the two of them now, so, they had to be able to rely on each other' off by heart, from a very early age. She'd heard it many times over the years- along with how much her mum had sacrificed for her. The way Scarlett saw it, her mum just got to sit around on her arse and moan all day, while dad and Zoe worked their butts off.

"So how was school today? Did my brain box have any tests?" Scarlett watched her mother tucking her feet up under her, preparing to bask in her daughter's success, as her own day had presumably been a complete disaster.

This was her standard opening line, and although Scarlett would love to just say 'fine' and go to her room, she'd learnt from experience, that it was generally less painful in the long run, if she just went into the well rehearsed prattle her mum wanted to hear, about how brilliantly she was doing.

"Well you certainly didn't get your brains from me." her mum responded as she always did, before launching into the mandatory trip down memory lane, the antics she'd got up to when she was Scarlett's age.

"Was Sophie in school today?" Fran eventually asked her tone overly casual.

Ah... that was it. She and James (she still found it really weird calling him that) had probably had some big fall out. This thing between her mother and Sophie's dad was kind of freaking her out, but at least her mum seemed to be a bit more chilled out and off her case whenever he was around. Despite the fact that he'd been here quite a few times now, mum was still insisting that they were just friends who enjoyed each others company, and to be fair he hadn't actually 'stayed over' at all yet. She could just imagine how cringingly gross that would feel- facing her best friends' dad over breakfast.

The walls in this house were so paper-thin, that whenever mum had had a 'guest' stay in the past, she'd had to shove her earphones in and turn the volume right up. Trying to get back to sleep with music thumping in her ears wasn't great, but it was a whole lot better than the alternative. At least when she'd been younger, noises coming from her mothers' room might have woken her up, but ignorance had spared her the indignity of knowing why.

"They're in Ireland." She informed her mother guardedly, wondering if this was going to end up being her fault simply because she had known and not mentioned it. "Her great-grandmother died at the weekend, so Sophie and her dad are staying until after the funeral."

"Oh right." Despite the sad nature of the news, Fran felt her spirits lift a little. At least that explained why she hadn't heard from James at all this week- why he hadn't been in touch to arrange something for his day off. She was a little bit surprised that he hadn't let her know that he was going though, but then, to be fair to him, it wasn't as though they were a couple and answerable to each other in that way.

She probably shouldn't be allowing herself to depend on James so heavily, but they had fallen into the habit of going out together a couple of times a week recently, and after the way she'd been treated in the shop yesterday, she'd been looking forward to a bit of sympathy.

Everything had been going so well while she'd been working along side Barbara, but then she'd asked Fran to do her a massive favour and change her afternoons, as someone was leaving. Hoping that this might lead to some paid work, as they seemed so pleased with her, she'd readily agreed, only to find her self stuck with a proper snooty cow, and still working for nothing.

Valerie was one of those patronising old bags who kept peering at you over the top of her glasses, like some battleaxe headmistress. She had made it perfectly clear from the outset that she didn't particularly like Fran, and had been giving her all the crap jobs to do. Yesterday she'd had the temerity to bawl her out for putting a pair of boots aside for herself, before they'd been priced and put on the shop floor. She'd put a few quid in the till for them, so it wasn't as though she'd been planning to nick the damn things, but Valerie had banged on and on about company policy, until in the end Fran had told her to stick the boots where the sun don't shine.

They'd spent the remainder of the day in stony silence, and unwilling to face the thought of working in that atmosphere again today, she'd phoned in sick- let the stupid cow cope on her own for the afternoon and see how she liked that. Hopefully, things would have all blown over by the time she was due in again next Thursday, and if not she'd just have to have a word with Barbara, get her to alter the rota again, so she worked with someone else.

Of course Fran knew exactly what Valerie's problem was- she'd met her type before. Though they were almost exactly the same age, Valerie's prim little bob and glasses made her look at least a decade older. Probably written off as middle-aged and invisible by the time she was thirty, she was obviously just riddled with jealousy.

"OK if I go up to my room now mum?" Scarlett spotted her chance to escape. "I've got a load of homework to do...you haven't forgotten I need a lift to Izzie's in the morning, and that I'll be sleeping over?"

"Ummm....Yeah sure..." knowing that James definitely wasn't going to be around for a few days, Fran was already busy thinking how best to fill her own empty weekend... she'd give Emily a ring in a bit...see if she fancied coming over...

As Scarlett headed up the stairs, carrying a huge bowl of cereal, Fran lent forward to pour herself another glass of wine, only to discover that there was just a dribble left in the bottle. She stumbled slightly as she got to her feet, knocking into the table and catching the trailing handle of Scarlett's bag with her bare foot, spilling the entire contents on to the floor.

She was about to yell for her daughter to come down and clear up her mess, when something caught her eye, immediately evoking memories of her own teenage years.

She smiled to herself as she looked at the brightly coloured highlighter pen doodles, clearly showing through several pages of the diary as it lay open on the floor. No doubt the artwork was framing the name of some spotty lad. Before shoving everything back in the bag, she quickly flicked to the decorated page, curious to know if it was one of the boys in her year.

As the words leapt up off the page, Fran was momentarily rocked back on her heels with shock. Her brain befuddled by the amount of alcohol she'd drank, it took a moment or two for the full implication of the words on the brightly coloured page to really sink in. For her to realise she was about to loose her trump card...

'GUESS WHO'S GONNA HAVE A BABY BROTHER OR SISTER FOR CHRISTMAS...........'

Looking more closely at the date as she read the rest of the page, Fran realised that Scarlett had been keeping this secret from her for weeks...

Simon and Zoe were having a baby? He must have had the vasectomy reversed or something? They had clearly sworn Scarlett to secrecy, until after the twelve week scan, and it would seem her daughter had been only too happy to be complicit in their conspiracy against her.

If Scarlett was capable of hiding something this huge, what other secrets was she keeping from her mother? Suddenly terrified that she didn't really have a clue what was going on in her daughters' life any more, she started scanning randomly through the pages searching for some reassurance.

Fran felt the bile rising in her throat as she flicked through page after page of Scarlett's meticulously neat hand-writing, learning exactly what her quiet, studious, seemingly amenable daughter really thought of her...

As the red mist closed over her she clambered to her feet, intending to yell at Scarlett to get down here right this minute, but the vividly clear memory of a similar scene stopped her dead in her tracks.

For a number of years now she'd been encouraging Scarlett to put her own clothes away, and clean her own room, in order to give her daughter some privacy and avoid exactly this kind of scenario from ever occurring. After all her moralising on the subject, how could she possibly tell her daughter that she'd just read her most private thoughts, had invaded Scarlett's privacy in exactly the same way her own mother had violated hers all those years ago.

It was evident that Scarlett already hated her. It would appear that she couldn't wait to move out, was planning to spend as much time as possible at Simon's once the baby was born, in order to 'help Zoe', and be part of a 'proper family'... Even in her drunken state, Fran recognised that she needed to think this through carefully, use the knowledge she'd gained wisely. If Scarlett was just looking for an excuse to move out altogether, then she wasn't going to hand it to her on a plate.

Simon was hardly likely to carry on paying her so much every month if Scarlett went to live with him...especially now he had another baby on the way...

Though Scarlett had demolished the massive bowl of cereal she'd taken up to her room, she was still hungry. Was it worth risking going back down stairs again to make some toast? Could she really be bothered with the inevitable hassle? She'd learnt from a really young age that it was best, to try and keep out of the way and not draw any attention to her self, when her mum was drinking. She was well practised in the art of being invisible in her own home.

Recently, she'd begun to understand why her dad had always paid the school directly for her dinners while she'd still been at primary. Now she was at The Grange, he always gave the money to her every week. Obviously it was his way of trying to ensure that she got at least one hot meal a day. The school holidays had always been a bit hit and miss though, and social services would have had a field day if they'd known how young she'd been, when she'd fist learnt how to use the toaster and microwave.

At least Zoe's baby (she couldn't help hugging herself every time she took out the secret in private) would have a proper mum and dad, be part of a close family unit like Izzie's, with regular home cooked meals, and lots of laughter round the table.

She sighed to herself as she dreamed yet again about broaching the subject that was never far from her mind lately. She was pretty sure she knew how dad and Zoe would react if she asked if she could live with them permanently, so she could be part of their family full time, but there was just one thing standing in the way of her happiness, as usual... her mother...

20

Before she was even half way down the stairs, Scarlett had a pretty shrewd idea of what she was going to find when she opened the door to the lounge. The familiar staleness in the air alerted her to the fact that her Mum had spent yet another night on the sofa. She wasn't remotely surprised to find her lying here comatose this morning, the lift she'd promised totally forgotten, despite the fact that Scarlett had reminded her again, just before she'd gone up to her room.

Her teen features, still chubby with baby fat, twisted with a bitter resignation that was way beyond her years, as she studied her mother dispassionately for a few moments, while considering her options. There was absolutely no point trying to wake her up, as judging by the amount of empty bottles strewn around the room, she'd be in no fit state to drive anywhere anytime today.

Thinking quickly, Scarlett took the throw from the other sofa and placed it very carefully over the completely oblivious form of her mother. As she shut the door gently behind her, her brain was already working overtime, plotting how to use this situation to her advantage to put the plan she'd come up with into action.

She'd lain there, tossing and turning for hours last night, her growling stomach keeping her awake, until the idea had popped into her head just before she was about to drop off.

Coming down this morning to discover her mother in this state had played straight into her hands, giving her exactly the ammunition she needed to get her dad on side and pave the way towards making everyone's life a little easier- especially hers.

Scarlett took the phone upstairs and closed the door of her room before making the call. The last thing she wanted to do right now was wake her mother up.

"Hi dad....sorry to be such a pain so early in the morning, but I wondered if you or Zoe could give me a lift to Izzie's? I'm supposed to be there for ten as we're all going ice skating, but mum..." she paused deliberately, allowing the silence to convey far more than the carefully selected words that followed, "isn't well enough to take me now."

Knowing just how unreliable her mother's promises of lifts generally turned out to be, Scarlett had got up in plenty of time to catch the bus into town, and then walk to Izzie's house from the station, but she couldn't resist using this golden opportunity to further her cause, and to be fair, as it was currently chucking it down, a lift would save her from getting absolutely soaked.

Cherry Orchard, where Izzie lived, was a really classy leafy residential area, full of big old three storey Victorian houses, but more importantly, it was just a ten minute walk from her dad's house, and that in a nut shell was the vital ingredient of her master plan.

Of course she'd have to talk to Izzie today, make sure they got their stories straight, but essentially, she had no doubt that her best friend would be happy to go along with the idea of inventing an important 'project' that they had to work on together during the summer break.

Once she'd primed Izzie, she would tell her dad all about it and casually suggest it might make life easier if she stayed at his for the first week or so of the holidays, so she wouldn't have to keep asking for lifts or wasting money on busses- genius or what?

She'd already come up with a list of all the ways she could start making herself indispensable around their house- she'd had plenty of practise as she did most of the housework for her mum. If the 'project' just happened to take a little bit longer than expected, one week could turn into two... and then three...once they'd got used to her helping out around the place, realised how useful she could be once the baby arrived, then she would just bide her time, wait for the right moment to suggest making the arrangement permanent...

Scarlett hugged herself with excitement as she imagined waking up every morning in the huge, bright sunny room she'd been allowed to choose all the bedding and furnishings for. When she leaned out of the window, she could actually see the river, and the whole area was always so blissfully quiet.

There would be no more being woken by shrieking neighbours, and better still, she wouldn't have to steel her self to walk past the gang that always seemed to be hanging around by the shops whenever she got off the school bus...

When Scarlett heard her dad's car pulling into the car park just below her bedroom window, she rushed down the stairs to fling both the lounge door, and the front door wide open. She wanted to make absolutely sure her dad got a really good look at what she'd woken up to this morning, exactly why she'd had to ask him for a lift.

She watched her dad's face carefully, but his features so like her own, remained guarded, his expression impassive.

The foul smell had hit Simon as soon as he'd walked through the door, warning him what to expect, so he'd braced him self to show absolutely no emotion as he took in the all too familiar pathetic state of he ex-wife.

He'd trained himself over the years to display complete indifference to Fran's antics, as that seemed to be the only way to deflect the vitriolic resentment she still felt the need to unleash periodically, despite the fact that they had been divorced for many years now.

"You ready to go then love?" He asked simply, feeling absolutely no compulsion to go and check on Fran's wellbeing. He hefted Scarlett's bag over his shoulder without a backward glance, his first priority being to get his daughter out of this place as quickly as possible. Nobody should have to live like this. He was going to have to talk to Fran again... lay down some very firm ground rules...if she wanted to throw her own life away, that was her choice to make, but he couldn't allow her to continue ruining Scarlett's in the process...

21

Fran yanked open the front door and pulled Emily into a fierce hug as soon as she stepped through it. The slept in sourness assaulting her nostrils, made Emily want to recoil, but she endured the awkward embrace, in the tiny speck of floor space at the bottom of the stairs that passed as an entrance hall.

"Thanks for coming over Em. Sorry about the state of the place...I know I probably look like death warmed up, but I didn't get to bed at all last night. I was just too upset..." Unable to follow the garbled sentences and slurred words, Emily prised the mug of neat vodka from Fran's hand. Though she spoke quietly her tone was uncharacteristically firm.

"Why don't you go and have a shower while I make you something to eat and put some coffee on." She was already removing the crumpled throws from the sofa, and opening the French windows to let in some much needed fresh air.

"I don't want coffee I want vodka-"

"Well that is entirely up to you Fran." Emily cut her off even more firmly. "You can go and freshen up while I make you some lunch, or you can carry on drinking and I'll leave right now? "

Emily wasn't quite sure which of them was the most shocked by the stand she had taken, but it had been a long time coming. She'd wasted far too many hours listening to Fran's drunken, maudlin ramblings, and she was really annoyed that she'd been dragged over here so urgently on false pretences.

Fran had been practically incoherent on the phone less than an hour ago, ranting on and on about Scarlett, and how she needed Emily to come and talk some sense into the girl. It had been concern for Scarlett's welfare that had prompted her to drive straight over, but it had been blatantly clear from the moment she'd walked though the door, that Scarlett wasn't here, and equally as obvious that Fran was way past the point of listening to reason.

Clearly her latest 'new leaf' had lasted about as long as they usually did. She'd presumably had some sort of row with her daughter, and typically, Fran was intent on turning it into a great big drama all about her.

As she cleared some space in the kitchen, and began searching the cupboards for something to cook (what on earth did they actually eat in this house?) she remembered how angry she'd been with Fran a couple of years ago, when she'd gone into classic drama queen mode outside the crematorium.

As the hearse came to a standstill, beneath the canopied roof over the entrance, Emily had felt her guts wrench as soon as she saw the raw agony etched into Kath's face as Ben helped her out of the car, his own face equally as gaunt and hollow.

Fran had chosen that exact moment to grab Emily's arm and hiss loudly, "I'm not sure I can go through with this Emily."

Emily remembered how she'd pulled her arm roughly away, practically spitting her reply through clenched teeth, "Just for once this is NOT about you Fran. We're here to support Kath and Ben and if you can't do that then I suggest you go home now."

She'd never spoken to anyone in such a clipped unfeeling tone in her life, but she had been truly disgusted with Fran's histrionics. Kath had Ben had just lost their beautiful daughter Hannah to a tragic road accident, while she'd been out delivering papers on her bike, yet even at a time like that, Fran had still only been thinking about herself...

Blinking rapidly as she pushed aside the images of that dreadful day, Emily began to whisk the eggs she'd found in the fridge, and placed the last two rounds of rather stale bread in the toaster, as soon as she heard Fran coming back down the stairs.

"Better?" She asked, handing her a mug of steaming coffee. Naturally soft hearted, her anger began to fade a little. It was hard not to feel at least some sympathy for the bedraggled looking woman in front of her. Though she brought on a great deal of the stress her self, Fran's life was hardly a bundle of laughs right now, and her unhappiness clearly showed on her bare, puffy face, minus its usual heavy covering of make up, which ordinarily, went some way towards hiding the ravages of her lifestyle.

"Yeah a bit...thanks Em...what would I do without you." Fran pulled Emily into another overly exuberant hug. Though generally tactile by nature, Emily was never particularly comfortable with these effusive shows of affection. She forced herself not to stiffen, as she tentatively returned the embrace.

"So what is the matter with Scarlett then?" Emily cut straight to the chase as soon as Fran started tucking into the fluffy scrambled eggs on toast she'd just put in front of her. She didn't intend to be here any longer than she had to be. She knew the signs well by now, and had learnt the hard way, that there would be very little point in staying to try and 'fix' the situation.

Despite the enormous amount of time and effort she'd put in on previous occasions, she'd achieved precisely nothing- other than draining her self, and delaying the consumption of more alcohol.

Though her presence might stop Fran drinking momentarily, she was under no illusions. The moment she walked out the door the vodka would come out again, so no matter how much thought she put into trying to come up with solutions to Fran's problems, any advice she gave would be consigned to oblivion within seconds of her leaving.

It had been a really hard lesson for Emily to take on board, but so many years of wasting long hours on the phone, or sitting here listening to Fran berating the world, had finally taught her to accept, that it was impossible to help her friend until she reached the point where she wanted to help her self.

"Oh Em...it's such a mess... I'm not supposed to know about any of this, so promise me that you won't breathe a word," Fran paused for dramatic effect before imparting her news, "Zoe is pregnant and Scarlett – to use her own words- wants to go and live with them so they can be a proper family."

"But I thought Simon had had the snip?" Emily stated, looking thoroughly confused...she'd been expecting the standard sort of fall out about curfew times or pocket money...a typical teenage blip, being blown out of all proportion as usual.

"Well yes he has... I haven't actually spoken to him yet obviously... but I suppose he must have had it reversed or something? According to Scarlett's diary, Zoe is due before Christmas but they're not telling anyone until after the twelve week scan on Monday so-"

"Hang on a minute- did you just say Scarlett's diary?" The abject revulsion on Emily's face as she cut across the confusing monologue, made it clear to Fran, that she'd definitely done the right thing by shoving the offending item straight back into her daughters' bag last night, rather than confronting her. "What were you doing reading Scarlett's diary?" Emily's voice had such an icy edge to it now... this was so unfair...she had to make her understand... it wasn't as though she had set out to do it on purpose...if only she could rewind time and make this all go away...

"I didn't plan to read the damn thing..." Fran snapped back, stung into retaliation, "I just caught my foot in the strap of her stupid bag...she'd left it hanging off the table... and everything fell out." Fran went on to explain how it had happened, trying to justify the quick peep she'd intended, as the memories of all the boys named she'd doodled around at the same age, came back to her. Emily's expression didn't alter one iota. She'd broken an unbreakable rule, and deep down she knew it, no matter how hard she tried to pretty it up.

Emily was struggling to follow Fran's garbled version of events as her speech grew faster and faster, the more worked up she became. She'd just had another few weird days this week, when the strange almost flu like virus, that seemed to come from nowhere, just made her want to sleep all the time. Her balance and co-ordination had been really awful this time, and so finally giving in to Tom's nagging, when he'd found her coming down the stairs on her bottom, she'd phoned the surgery. As the intermittent dull ache she'd been getting in her groin was becoming more painful too, she'd decided that it might be worth taking Jess' advice, so she'd made an appointment to see Jane Morgan, the female doctor that her friend obviously held in such high regard.

"I don't understand what I've done to deserve to be treated like this?" Fran's voice was rising dramatically now "After everything I've sacrificed for Scarlie she can't wait to get away from me..." Fran broke off, tears of self pity pouring unheeded down her face as she came to the end of the familiar list of everything she'd apparently forfeited for her daughter. Realising that she'd only been half listening for the last few minutes Emily rallied her thoughts, attempting to be the voice of reason as always.

"Oh come on Fran...whatever you read, you have to take it with a big pinch of salt. Don't all thirteen year old girls exaggerate every word they write in their diary...It's kind of the point of having one." She consoled her confidently.

"But she hates me...you didn't see it..."

"No. And neither should you have." Emily cut in again determinedly. "The whole point of a dairy is you can write down all your most horrible thoughts, safe in the knowledge that no one will ever read them. We've all done it."

"But what am I supposed to do now?" Fran demanded plaintively.

"Absolutely nothing- You can't tell her you've read the thing or you really will loose her respect." Emily kept reiterating the point she was trying to make.

"But I can't let her go and live with Simon Emily." The full use of her name was usually a clear warning that one of Fran's lightening changes of mood was about to take place.

"Try not to make a battle out of it Fran. Remember you are basing all this on something you were never supposed to have seen. Just because she wrote it down doesn't mean she is actually going to do anything about it does it?" Emily wasn't going to back down on this. What Fran had done was wrong and she wasn't about to start letting her pass the buck. She'd gone down that route, taking the easy way out because it tended to be quicker, too many times in the past.

"But she's hardly ever here these days anyway. She's always staying at her friends, or at her dad's." Fran whined miserably.

"Weren't you the same at thirteen? I know it was different for me because I was at boarding school, but I'm sure most girls are learning to spread their wings at this age." Emily pointed out.

"I bet Holly never made you feel as though she hated you and couldn't wait to get away from you." Fran rallied.

Here we go again Emily mouthed silently. It was definitely time to leave. Once Fran started, making comparisons, directing her resentment towards Emily and her apparently gilded life, things always started to get ugly, and right now, Emily was not in the right frame of mind to placate her, in fact, if she stayed much longer, she might just start dishing out a few home truths of her own.

If she couldn't wait to get away from the heavy mantle of depression that filled this house after just an hour or two, was it really any wonder that Scarlett was hankering after a different kind of family life with her dad and her calm, easy going, step-mother, who'd shown her nothing but love and affection over the last few yeas?

22

Once they'd had their cards scanned and made their way through the courtyard at Attingham Park, Emily and Kate quickly realised why the car park had been so full. Judging by the number of families crowding around the cafe tables, the schools had obviously just broken up for the summer. Was it her imagination, or did it seem to get a bit earlier every year Emily wondered?

If they took their usual route through the woods and the walled garden to the deer park, they were going to be surrounded by hoards of excited children heading for the vast play area.

"Shall we walk along the river and then take the short cut back into the deer park?" Emily suggested, desperately in need of a bit of peace. Because their own lives no longer evolved around the school terms, it didn't enter their heads to take the holidays into account before planning a day out.

"If you're sure that's ok?" Though Kath would relish getting away from the crowds around the mansion as much as Emily, she was concerned that the longer walk might be a bit too far for her as she was already leaning on the stick she had brought with her.

"Yeah...honestly Kath...my balance really isn't too bad at the moment. I've just got into the habit of carrying this with me in case I need it." Emily assured her easily, gesturing towards the mahogany stick. "It's probably just physiological, but since I saw Dr Morgan last week, I have been feeling a little bit brighter- I'm not fretting quite so much, now she's checking everything out so thoroughly.

"Well that's good...from what you told me on the phone, it sounds like it was a really positive appointment?" Kath raised an enquiring eyebrow, keen to hear all the details now they had the time and space to discuss Emily's ongoing health issues without being interrupted.

"Mmmm...yeah...definitely... Jess was so right. I just wish I'd gone to see her earlier now. She makes you feel like she has all the time in the world for you, so you don't end up babbling away like a demented idiot, trying to get everything into your ten minute slot." Emily grinned ruefully before turning her head away to drink in her favourite view across the river and the open parkland, towards The Wrekin in the background. The tranquil beauty of this place never failed to restore her sense of well being.

"So presumable, you got a lot further with her than you did with Dr Evanson then?" Kath persisted, knowing how good Emily was at making light of things and then closing the subject down, as she hated to feel like she was burdening you with her problems.

"Totally... You know I was getting worried about this ache in my groin?" Emily paused as Kath nodded. She always found it hard to remember exactly how much she had shared with Kath because she was so good at getting you to spill the beans, share whatever was on your mind... an entirely alien concept to someone as private as Emily. She'd always believed that as you were the only person who could actually live your life, you might as well just get on and do so, without bellyaching about it to anyone who stayed still long enough to listen.

"As soon as I told her what the problem was, she started asking questions about my general health, and then went back over all the tests I've had done this year. Honestly Kath, I must have been there about an hour before she got round to examining me, and all that time I was able to just natter away about all the things that have been bugging me lately."

"So what happens now?" It was all well and good getting on so well with this lady doctor, but Kath was more interested in results. She had become increasingly concerned about Emily lately. She always tried to gloss over her problems, but it had been obvious for some time now that she was really struggling. Apart from the physical ailments, it was as though the vibrancy, the very essence of who she was, had been sucked out of her during these last few months.

They automatically gravitated towards the log that served as a bench, hidden amongst the bracken in a little sun trap, and Emily smiled her thanks as Kath pulled two cartons of apple juice out of her bag. Despite the fact that she was almost ten years older than her, Kath had become her closest friend in recent years, someone she had learnt to trust implicitly, and she knew her well enough to know there was little point in prevaricating now. Kath had been worrying about all her random symptoms for some time now, and had been urging her to go back to the doctor almost as frequently as her mother-in-law did.

"She sent me straight up to the hospital with a card for a chest X-ray, and a whole battery of blood tests. I had a pelvic scan yesterday, and I'm going back to see her next week when she has all the results." Emily filled her in succinctly.

"And...?" Kath nudged her again, instinctively sensing there was something else she wasn't telling her.

"And then we had a brief chat about periods and everything being all right at home." Emily grinned wryly.

"Well there's a surprise." Even now, two years after the death of her daughter, if she went any where near the surgery, with so much as a water infection, she still got that old chestnut thrown at her. She was well aware that there were a lot of unhappy, rather than unhealthy people, clogging up doctors waiting rooms, but she still found the implication incredibly patronising. Her daughter had died suddenly and tragically and no amount of counselling, or antidepressants could ever alter that fact, but she did still get ill now and again.

"The thing was, she wasn't at all patronising about it, and she thinks I am way too young to accept such a rapid decline in my general fitness as hormonal." Emily continued her relief palpable.

"So what is she thinking?" Kath prompted again. Getting personal information out of Emily could be like getting blood out of a stone sometimes- a bit like getting meaningful conversation out of Ben.

Emily swallowed hard. Apart from Tom, she hadn't discussed the end of her appointment with anyone.

As soon as Dr Morgan had finished organising all the tests, and explained that, although she was referring Emily under the two week rule again to eliminate ovarian cancer, she was fully expecting the results to be clear, she'd sat back in her chair with her hands clasped loosely on the desk in front of her.

"So what do you think is going on Emily?" She'd asked softly in her very straight forward manner.

"Honestly? I'm beginning to wonder if it is something degenerative...first my digestive system started breaking down, then my immune system, and now it seems like my nervous system is giving up the ghost too." Having assumed the consultation was over, Emily was caught totally off guard by this last question, so rather than offering Jane Morgan the well rehearsed account she usually brought to an appointment, she answered with completely uncensored candour.

"When you say Degenerative....?" The reassuringly matronly doctor didn't move a muscle, and her expression remained completely neutral as she gently prompted her patient.

"Well I suppose there must be hundreds of other things I've never even heard of, but MS has crossed my mind." As soon as the words left her mouth, Emily realised that this was the first time she'd ever fully admitted the nagging fear, even to her self, but it did explain her growing number of ailments uncomfortably well.

She usually avoided patient web sites like the plague, as she knew how easy it was to convince yourself you had practically anything if you went down that route, but she had done a quick search on Google the other day, and within a few seconds, the parallel between what she was experiencing and the list of symptoms had frightened her so much, she'd logged off again very quickly.

"Obviously I can't speculate at this stage Emily, but I suggest you make another appointment to see me about a week after you've had the pelvic scan. I'd also like you to write down any other changes that have occurred, any concerns at all, whether you think they are relevant or not, and bring that list with you. Once I've got all of the results back, and eliminated everything that I can as a GP, then, I'll decide who I want to refer to you. Is that OK?"

"Umm...yes of course...thank you so much for your time." Emily had felt her legs trembling as she stood up to leave, and she wasn't sure if it was with fear or relief. Someone finally believed her- this dramatic shrinking of her life was not all in her head, and it wasn't just hormones or her age either.

Most people would have rushed straight in with platitudes as soon as Emily finished speaking, but Kath had just studied her silently for a moment or two, before saying very quietly.

"Well whatever it turns out to be, at least it sounds as though you are on the way to getting some answers now."

When Emily got up, Kath took that as her cue to move on too- both physically and conversationally. Until they knew exactly what she was dealing with, she knew her friend well enough to know that Emily wouldn't want to dwell on 'maybes' or mull over the 'what if's'.

If, and when, it was confirmed that her beautiful friends' life was about to change, then she'd do her upmost to stand by her in every way she possibly could.

Kath had had a colleague with M S, and as soon as Emily started mentioning the numbness, the loss of feeling in her hands and feet and the balance issues, alarm bells had began to ring. The recurrent flu like viruses she'd been experiencing recently, coupled with the days she seemed to be stumbling over her words, made the diagnosis look like a pretty open and shut case to her, but right now Emily clearly wasn't ready to hear that.

They'd walked on in a comfortable silence for a few minutes, both quietly processing their thoughts, and then by mutual consent had begun to chat about the inconsequential, everyday patterns of life, and within minutes they were giggling like a pair of school girls over a rather peculiar room request made by one of Emily's clients yesterday.

This was the true beauty of their friendship, the ability to share their innermost fears, and then indulge in the therapeutic power of laughter shortly afterwards. They didn't wallow in misery, or dine out on their troubles, endlessly searching for sympathy or retribution.

When Hannah had been taken away from them so suddenly, part of Kath had died with her, and Emily had been the only friend who'd seemed to grasp the fact that she needed to be treated normally, as Kath, not the mother of that poor tragic girl who'd been killed while out on her bike delivering papers.

Of course people meant to be kind, but it had become so hard to accept the platitudes, the well intentioned awkward expressions of sympathy, when she already knew that no amount of clever words could bring Hannah back to them...that she was gone and they never even got to say goodbye...that the last words she'd spoken to her daughter had been about the state of her room. What she wouldn't give now to see some clutter strewn around the pristine, newly decorated, never used 'guest' room.

Emily had been the one person she'd allowed in during the bleakest weeks following the funeral. Ben had predictably retreated into his cave, dealing with his grief in the only way he knew how, leaving her to cope with the gaping hollow void where her heart used to be.

Thankfully, the five year gap between their children meant that Scott had been able to return to university, and some semblance of normality, been spared the atmosphere in the house as she and Ben increasingly took their frustrations out on each other, as they desperately searched for someone or something to blame...so many lives had been ruined by a moments carelessness.. The driver would get to rebuild his life on his release but they'd been handed a life sentence...

By the time they left the deer park and crossed the bridges over the two weirs, to arrive back at the mansion, Lady Berwicks' tea room looked full to bursting- despite the hefty charge for the dinky little sandwiches, scones, and cakes that adorned the tiered plates they could see being passed around, as they walked past the long sash windows.

"Do you fancy having afternoon tea here as your birthday treat?" Kath suddenly suggested. "It'll be all serene again once the kids are back at school."

"I reckon that could be just what the doctor ordered." Emily quipped, knowing exactly why Kath had put the idea forward. She shared Emily's deep love of this place, understood that the inner peace she drew from being here, would help sustain her while she waited to see what news the next few weeks would bring. "They do offer gluten free bread with their soup, and always have some cakes in the cafe, so I'm sure they can cater for me if we book in advance. Shall we ask Jess and Mel to come too?"

It didn't cross either of their minds to invite Fran as they both knew that a decadent National Trust afternoon tea really wasn't her sort of thing...

23

Llangranog. The name of the village didn't exactly conjure up the most exotic of images, but it looked like the owners of the lodge where Emily and Tom were currently staying, had been spot on again. Berwyn and Gwyneth Pryce had recommended several of these 'off the beaten track' little bays, where it was still possible to escape the crowds, even in August.

Once they'd turned off the main road, the long descent down the twisting switch back lane, offered tantalising glimpses of the bay around each new bend. By the time the picture postcard cottages, and pretty little stream that ran parallel with the road came into view, they really were beginning to feel as though they had stepped back in time.

Their hosts had told them, that it was only when the sea went right out, that the spectacular beauty of this little beach was fully revealed. Only then were you were able to walk through the dramatic black rock formations, to the secret sweep of sand hidden behind the cliffs that was only accessible at low tide.

They spent the morning admiring the stunning coastline, Emily's arm linked through Tom's for support as they meandered along the cliff paths. Then they had eaten an amazingly good fish lunch at 'The Anchor', the rather unimaginatively named little pub right at the waters edge, before making the most of the clear blue sky and spending the rest of afternoon on the beach.

Sheltered from the wind by the rocks, by the time the late afternoon sun began to bathe this magical spot in its golden light, Emily was feeling more at peace than she had for several months.

The decision to book Mill Meadow lodge, which really was located in the proverbial middle of nowhere, had been something of a hasty one, but nothing would be gained by putting their lives on hold for a couple of months while they waited for an appointment with the neurologist.

Emily's second appointment with Dr Morgan couldn't have been any more different than the first- she'd been in and out in a matter of minutes. As soon as she'd sat down, Jane Morgan had assured her that all the test results had come back perfectly normal, including the C25 screening for cancer. She'd studied the list Emily had compiled for a moment or two, making a few notes, before handing the sheet of paper back to her.

"Based on everything you've told me, I think the best thing for me to do now is to refer you to a neurologist Emily." She stated simply, sitting back in her chair and facing Emily directly. "Unfortunately, there in no neurology unit here in Shrewsbury, so the clinics aren't that frequent. You may have a bit of wait, but once you get an appointment, the consultant will want to take a full history, so it would be helpful if you took this list along with you."

"When you say a wait....?" Emily queried.

"I would guess at least a couple of months. After all the checks I have just done, we can be fairly confident that this isn't likely to be something life threatening." The doctor stated reassuringly.

"Just life limiting?" Emily grimaced, her tone half joking.

"Well, as I said before, I can't give you a diagnosis at this stage Emily, but I strongly suspect that the consultant will want to do an MRI of the brain and spine." Jane Morgan had never believed in fudging the issue.

"To look for lesions?" Emily queried, wondering if that was really her own voice sounding so matter of fact.

She'd done a considerable amount of research since her last appointment, and had discovered that the optic neuritis she'd suffered in her twenties was a classic early indicator of MS.

She'd left the surgery with the same peculiar mix of fear and relief. At least if she was diagnosed with MS, she could begin to make some sense of what had been happening to her and get some help. Anything had to be better than living with this unexplained deterioration of her life.

Though she and Tom had decided to be very selective about whom they told at this stage, Emily hadn't been able to put off having a long overdue chat with her manager. Dr Morgan was perfectly happy to sign her off whenever she felt she needed a break, and at least now that her problems were out in the open at work and at home, she wouldn't have to struggle on in shame filled silence.

These few days away had turned out to be exactly what they had both needed, but when Tom first suggested the idea, she hadn't been at all keen. She'd only needed a day or two of licking her wounds to realise that she wasn't being fair as Tom's future was just as much in jeopardy as hers - he'd hardly signed up to be a carer in his mid forties.

In a few weeks, they were very likely to receive confirmation that the gradual shrinking of her life was progressive, that the twilight years they'd envisaged together were now extremely unlikely, so it made sense to start making the very best of every day, while they still could.

Thankfully the well appointed 'autograph collection' lodge had turned out to be everything the web site had promised and more. They'd spent hours sitting in the luxurious hot tub, drinking in the views of the gently rolling Welsh countryside, and would probably go home looking like a pair of prunes.

Armed with their hosts' insider knowledge, they'd managed to find several of these unspoilt little villages, that only the locals seemed to know about. Yesterday they'd visited a really cute little place called Abbey-Cwm-Hyre. They'd found a helpful leaflet about the Abbey and Neo Elizabethan country house, in the drawer packed full of tourist bumph, and decided to make a detour through the village on their way to the Elan Valley.

They'd parked their car by the church, then, set off up the long drive in search of where to pay, but the only sign of any welcome had been from the very friendly black and white border-collie, that had wandered half way down the gravel to meet them.

As they took in the ornate terraces surrounding the house, the dog waited patiently before turning towards some steps constantly glancing back at them, as though urging them to follow. At the top of the steps they came to a path leading down to a pretty little lake, which the dog led them around, before heading to another flight of steps, and once again, turning back towards them.

"She wants us to follow her Tom." Emily had exclaimed, still feeling like an intruder as they roamed the grounds, searching for some other sign of life, as their little fury friend continued to lead the way to each new area.

A couple of hours later, as they were having lunch in the pub in the centre of the village, they'd mentioned their strange experience to the proprietor.

"Oh that'll be Rosie." He'd laughed good-naturedly his accent so strong they struggled to understand half the words. "She gives tours to all the foreigners on the days the house isn't officially open. When you've finished your lunch she'll be waiting outside to take you down to the Abbey."

Emily and Tom had exchanged bemused glances, assuming that they were having their legs pulled, but sure enough, as soon as they'd finished their substantial ploughman's lunches and gone back outside, Rosie had stood up and started to walk towards the narrow lane that led off the back of the pub car park.

They'd spent another peaceful hour or so wandering among the Abbey ruins that bordered the fast flowing river. Their four legged personal guide, had trotted happily along ahead of them the whole time, and then accepted a great big fuss and a gluten free chocolate chip cookie as her tip, when they returned to the car.

Tomorrow they would be heading home, and no doubt the random, completely irrational, worst case scenarios moments would start intruding again, but right now, she was just going to close her eyes and enjoy the last hour of sun. Later they would have a final dip in the hot tub, and then cuddled up in the huge, satin covered four poster bed.

As though reading her mind, Tom shot her a smile of contentment, before settling himself back down on the blanket beside her, using his sweatshirt as a pillow. His hand closed over Emily's as they both shut their eyes and drifted off again...

24

"Oh hi Hol- It's Fran. Is your mum there Hon?"

Holly cringed as the fog-horn voice, that needed no introduction, practically perforated her ear drum. Nobody but Fran ever called her 'Hol' thank goodness, but the 'Hon' tagged on the end was new- presumably she thought it made her sound cool.

"I'm good thank you Fran. How are you?" Holly responded pointedly, fully aware, that her less than subtle lesson in phone etiquette would be totally lost on the older woman. Whenever any of mum's other friends phoned, they generally had the courtesy to at least exchange a word or two with her, before asking for her mum.

"Mum and Dad are away for a few days." Holly continued quickly, conscious of her potential gaffe. She didn't actually want to hear how Fran was, as that invariably involved an awful lot of moaning.

The older she got, the more Holly found herself wondering how her mum and Fran had remained friends for so long. For the life of her she couldn't work out what they could possibly have in common- other than history. When she was little, 'auntie' Fran had always been around, and she'd never thought to question why. It was only in recent years that she'd found her self struggling to understand what on earth her mother gained from a friendship that appeared to be such a one way street- her mum gave and Fran took.

"Oh...Right... She didn't mention that she was going away again. Don't tell me it's another last minute freebie? The jammy mare..." Fran's laughter sounded hollow even to her own ears.

Holly felt her hackles instantly rise in defence. Why did Fran always have to be so abrasive, like she was permanently poised, waiting for the next scrap? She was always so keen to take on the world, fight her corner over every tiny little detail, while seeming to resent, rather than rejoice in anyone else's good fortune. Her mum was not, and never had been a 'jammy mare'. She worked damn hard for a very modest salary, and the perks she received were simply part of that package.

"Mum and Dad have gone to a lodge somewhere in the Welsh hills near Llandrindod Wells." Holly informed her indignantly though gritted teeth. "It was a last minute decision." She added, having no intention of sharing the reason why they had suddenly shot off so quickly.

Holly was pretty certain that she and Josh had been given an edited version of what really lay behind all these hospital appointments, so it was extremely unlikely that mum would have shared any of the details with Fran.

"Ah...Right...That explains why she's not replied to any of my messages over the last few days then." Fran concluded, feeling a little bit relieved.

"Apparently they haven't got any signal at the lodge, so they've just been checking in now and again, whenever they make it back to civilisation." Holly forced a little more warmth into her tone. "Do you want me to give her a message if it's something important?" She asked pleasantly, intent on drawing the call to a close as quickly as possible now.

Fran hung up feeling totally deflated. She'd been relying heavily on being able to talk things through properly with Emily, as she was the only person who actually knew how dire the situation with Scarlett was, the only friend she ever truly confided in.

Pippa and her mates were good company- a lot more fun for a night out- but she'd soon learnt that they were not remotely interested in listening to her problems.

Simon had finally found the guts to tell her about the baby, but that seemed to have made things worse rather than better. Scarlett had gone to stay with him and Zoe for a week at the start of the school holidays. She'd said she needed to be closer to Izzie while they worked on a school project together , but it was now the middle of August and there was still no sign of her coming home.

Though Fran wasn't remotely surprised that Scarlett was spinning it out, she hadn't got a clue how to go about getting her to come back. What she had read in Scarlett's diary left her in absolutely no doubt that her daughter was exactly where she wanted to be right now. If only she could rewind time...shove that stupid diary straight back into her daughters bag without even glancing at it.

Then she wouldn't have to guard every word that came out of her mouth, feel like she was treading on egg shells all the time.

If Emily had managed to contact Holly several times, whenever she was back in phone range, then surely it wouldn't have killed her to answer just one of the many texts Fran had sent? They were supposed to be best friends, yet lately, it seemed as though Emily barely had a moment to spare for her. She'd asked her a few times recently if everything was OK between them, if she'd done something to upset her, but Emily always insisted everything was fine, that it was 'just life', that it was the same for everyone, but Fran still wasn't convinced. Things seemed to have really cooled off between them over the last few months and she really felt as though Emily was starting to drift away from her.

To be fair, she always felt a bit restless, a bit sorry for herself, through the long summer holidays. Everyone else seemed to be away enjoying exotic breaks, while she remained stuck at home on her own. Even James seemed to have no sooner got back from Ireland, before he was preparing to head off again for the South of France.

"We've booked this same villa for years." He'd informed her, casually reaching behind him to pass her a framed picture of him and Sophie, peering over the edge of a huge pool. Noting how substantial the attractive stone villa in the background appeared, Fran had studied the photograph intently as she pondered the likelihood of getting a cheap flight ticket this close to departure...If Scarlett was staying on at Simon's indefinitely then nobody would actually miss her...

"It looks absolutely amazing James. You are so lucky." She gave him her most beguiling smile, before adding wistfully "I've never even been to France..."

The faint glimmer of hope had been short lived, as James had gone on to explain that he was meeting his brother and sister and their partners and kids there, just as he did every summer, in order for Sophie to spend a couple of weeks with her cousins.

It was looking more and more, as though the only offer on the table was the usual unappealing break in rainy Aberystwyth, with her sister.

Chrisse and Ian where only too happy to put her up for a few days at any time of the year, and although, on paper, a few days by the sea, for nothing more than the cost of a tank of petrol, sounded like a good idea, there were two big draw backs and they were called Imogen and Daniel.

Thinking about it, her sister and Emily had a great deal in common- in fact, she could really imagine the two of them being the best of friends. Both women had made it their life's work to ensure that their kids had perfect childhoods, turning this goal into some kind of crusade.

Everyone knew it was wrong to wrap your kids up in cotton wool. Most people recognised that kids needed to take a few knocks in order to learn to survive in the real world, but Emily and Chrissie were both obsessed with giving their offspring everything they felt they had missed out on themselves.

Consequently Fran never got a moment alone with her sister without the perfect little angels demanding their mothers' attention. Watching the four of them playing happy families would just rub salt into her wounds right now, when her own daughter could barely stand to be in the same room as her. She daren't start laying down the law, demanding that Scarlett came home, just in case it back fired and pushed her even further away...

Fran realised that she was spending far too much time on her own again lately, was starting to slip backwards. If she didn't get a break from her own company soon, she knew she was going to be in serious trouble again...

She had listened long and hard, when James had talked about the evils of loneliness and boredom- how they'd become his enemies- and she knew she was on the brink of throwing away all the progress she'd made in the last few weeks.

She couldn't afford to take that risk. Simon had really gone off on one after that last almighty bender, following her fall out with Valerie, and discovery of just how much she featured in her daughters' diary.

Summoning up the very last vestiges of her self will, she pushed a plastic cork into the bottle of wine she'd just opened, and lifted the phone to call her sister- before she had a chance to change her mind.

As Chrissie and Ian were both practically tea total, the most intoxicating thing she was likely to be offered while staying with them was a chocolate-liquor. A few days damage limitation, was exactly what was needed right now.

Ten minutes later and it was all arranged. She would drive over tomorrow afternoon, so all she had to do now was phone Barbara, and explain why she wouldn't be coming into the shop this week. She only needed to embroider the facts a little bit- imply that she was going to help out with some sort of family emergency... and to be fair, that wasn't so far removed from the truth. She actually was going away to avert a potential disaster. She couldn't afford to give Simon anymore ammunition to use against her and risk the current arrangement becoming permanent.

In the last couple of weeks Fran had started to realise that it was no longer just the financial implications that were bothering her either...despite all the struggles she'd faced as a single parent, she was really starting to miss having Scarlie about the place...

25

"So what do you fancy doing for your birthday then Em- it's only a couple of weeks away now?" Fran asked almost as soon as she was settled in the car.

She'd been doing a lot of thinking while she'd been away at her sisters' and managed to get a few things back into perspective. Emily had been having a pretty rough time of it lately, so she could hardly blame her for being a bit on the elusive side. Wasn't she guilty of doing exactly the same thing, hiding herself away whenever she felt low, because she knew she was such rotten company? What Emily needed now was a pick-me-up, a bit of fun, and she was determined to organise it for her.

"I was thinking we could try that new Italian place that's just opened off the square?" She suggested enthusiastically, as she'd been reading rave reviews about the recently opened restaurant, and was keen to give it a whirl- especially as she was able to use her Tesco points at this particular chain.

Emily hesitated, fully aware that she couldn't just keep dodging the issue for ever. It had been difficult enough to get Fran to agree to this bank holiday trip to the cinema, instead of their usual two for one Wednesday arrangement. Even though Emily had offered to pay for the full price tickets, Fran had still taken some convincing. On this occasion though, Emily had stood firm, refusing to be talked into going straight from work.

"I bet the place will be full of kids mucking about all the way through the film and spoiling it." Fran had begrudgingly caved in eventually.

"I can't see many kids being interested in the latest Sandra Bullock Rom Com Fran." Emily's laughter had been placatory as she was well practised in defusing these flash points, and she had actually managed to get her own way for once.

She simply couldn't face the idea of rushing straight round to Fran's after work, just to spend a couple of hours sitting through some pointless drivel she didn't really want to watch. She'd probably just fall asleep half way through the film anyway. She'd been trying to avoid committing herself to anything that wasn't absolutely necessary in the evenings, as she seemed to be in the most discomfort during the last hour or two of the day.

She wasn't sure whether the fatigue and random pains were actually getting progressively worse, or if it was just physiological now that the probability of MS had been raised- a bit like when you cut yourself, and it doesn't hurt until you see the blood- but either way, most days, by the time she walked back up to the car after work, she was so light-headed, she felt like the road was coming up to meet her.

It was over three weeks now since her second appointment with Dr Morgan, and the subsequent weekend away at the lodge, and although she was finding it a little bit easier to cope at work, now that everything was out in the open, she was increasingly aware of just how rapidly her health and fitness seemed to be deteriorating. What sort of future was she going to have if her mobility and concentration continued to decline at this rate? Would she even be capable of holding down a Job by the end of the year?

"Actually Fran, I'm planning to have a very quiet birthday this year with no fuss." Emily replied as she looked for a space in the huge car park that served the cinema, and the adjacent food chains offering the standard fare of Chinese buffet, Portuguese chicken or 'two for ten' pub meals.

"Did I miss something here...did we just fast forward ten years. You'll be forty three Em, not fifty three." Fran laughed, not willing to be put off quite so easily.

Emily took a deep breath. When they'd spoken on the phone, soon after Fran got back from her sisters, she'd told her a little about what had been happening and that she'd been referred for some more tests, but she hadn't gone into any great detail. She and Tom had decided to operate on a strictly need to know basis at this stage, and although Fran definitely wasn't on that list, it was getting harder and harder to hide the problems she was having from her.

"To be honest Fran I feel about seventy three at the moment." She began quietly.

"I thought when they put you on this new medication things had improved a bit?" Fran frowned as she leant forward to pick up her bag.

"My tummy has been much better, but I've been having a lot of other problems too...mainly with my balance and concentration-"

"Welcome to my world. Whenever the doctor decides to try me with a new antidepressant, I feel totally spaced out for a few weeks. You probably just need to stick with it for a bit Em." Fran spouted confidently.

It was always like this. On the rare occasion Emily did try to confide in Fran, she had always experienced the same thing- only ten times worse of course. She was sorely tempted to just leave it there, but she needed Fran to understand that she really wasn't her self at the moment, and she simply didn't have the energy to carry anyone else's problems just now.

"It's not quite that simple. My doctor has referred me to a neurologist as the problems seem to be getting steadily worse." Emily continued.

"A neurologist?" Fran turned towards her in the confined space of the car, leaving Emily with no place to hide.

"Mmmm... she thinks it could be progressive... something like MS."

"MS? Shit Em. Why on earth didn't you tell me before now? I thought we'd fallen out or something, you've been so hard to get hold of lately." Fran practically shouted, grabbing both her hands in hers.

"We're not telling people just yet Fran. I suppose we're still hoping it'll turn out to be a false alarm. The first doctor I saw put it all down to hormones...the change... I've had a shed load of other tests that have all come back clear, so we're not panicking just yet." She reassured her, resisting the urge to pull her hands away now.

"I'm hardly 'people' Emily." The use of her full name indicated that Fran was clearly affronted. "I'm your best friend. I could have been there for you if I'd known what you were going through. You know how much I suffered when I started going through the menopause so early...I bet that's what it'll turn out to be. You probably just need some HRT or something." Fran continued one hundred percent confident in her prognosis, and thinking how typical it was that Emily had been offered a shed load of tests and appointments with specialists, while she'd just been left to get on with it. Her doctor really was useless. She'd been threatening to find a new surgery for years.

Emily tried not to stiffen as Fran predictably pulled her into one of her trademark hugs, promising to stand by her all the way- this was exactly why she had been so reluctant to tell her.

She recalled so clearly the way Kath had thanked her for just treating her normally in those first few weeks after Hannah died. Right now, she was beginning to gain just a tiny insight into what Kath had meant. She didn't want, or need, these great big dollops of sympathy, or effusive promises of unstinting support- she simply wanted her life to go on as normally as possible, at least until they knew exactly what they were dealing with. Even then, if she was diagnosed with MS, or some other degenerative disease, it was going to be life limiting, not life threatening- it wasn't as though she was about to die imminently or anything was it...?

26

As soon as Emily dropped her back home after the film, Fran headed out into the garden. Approaching the end of August, the evenings seemed to be drawing in horribly rapidly, so she was keen to catch the last hour or so of sunshine.

The film had been a huge disappointment, but then, to be fair, she really hadn't been able to concentrate on it after Emily's bomb shell. She had spent most of the time stewing over why Emily had kept her in the dark for so long, but at least now she knew what was going on, she understood why Emily hadn't been exactly sociable lately.

Fran chewed thoughtfully on the end of her pencil, before scribbling down another thought, adding to the list of ways she could show her support and 'be there' for Emily through the tough times ahead.

Pleased with her efforts so far, Fran slipped the straps of her vest top off her shoulders, and sank back down on the sun lounger. The few days she'd just spent at her sisters' had brought her tan up a treat. Another hour or so in the garden this afternoon, and she'd be almost back to the colour she was when she came back from Majorca. She always felt so much more attractive- slimmer even- with a nice golden tan.

The little break in Aberystwyth had proved to be far more beneficial than she'd imagined. Chrissie and Ian's, ritualistic orderly little lives had been as irritating as ever, but at least the weather had been amazingly kind to her, allowing her to spend hours on the beach, or lounging around in their huge south facing garden.

On her last day, Chrissie had really surprised her by suggesting that the two of them go out on their own, as the kids were booked into some sort of summer camp.

"I thought we could do the cliff walk from Clarach Bay to Borth, and then have a bit of lunch there? It's probably just over an hours' walk each way, but the views will be worth the effort on a day like this." She'd proposed enthusiastically.

"That sounds good to me." Fran was more than happy to comply. She'd been doing a fair amount of walking with James over the last couple of months, and although initially she'd just gone along with his suggestions somewhat indifferently, she'd really started to appreciate the fresh air and exercise recently. As well as sleeping better, she was noticeably loosing weight too, and that was a very welcome bonus.

The three and a half year gap, which had always seemed so utterly insurmountable when they were younger, finally started to close as they walked together. They talked to each other in a candid, entirely open way that they had never really adopted before, as they ambled along stopping every now and then, to admire the views and watch the sunlight dancing across the waves.

Plenty of wry humour punctuated their conversations as they recalled their mothers' most spectacularly un-maternal moments, and their fathers' rather ineffectual attempts to maintain some sort of stability. After a light cafe lunch, followed by delicious honey ice cream cones on the beach, the exchanges had become a little more serious as they made their way back.

Fran eventually found herself opening up to Chrissie about the real reason for Scarlett's absence this summer, although she'd deliberately chosen not to mention that flaming diary of course.

"She was only supposed to be staying with Simon for a week or so, in order to be closer to her friend, while they worked on a project together." She concluded, finishing the sorry tale, "but it's been over a month now Chrissie and I don't know how to go about getting her to come home again."

Her sister had studied her silently for a minute or two, in much the same way Emily always did before she offered her thoughts.

"I don't think I would do anything at all yet if I were you Fran." She advised, not appearing to be in the slightest bit phased by her sisters' revelations, as though exchanging their inner most private thoughts was an ordinary everyday occurrence. "I expect it will turn out to be a case of the grass always being greener on the other side. Once the novelty has worn off she'll come home of her own accord."

"Maybe...I suppose you could be right...." Fran pondered on her sisters' words.

"One of my best friends is divorced, and her daughter is just a little bit older than Scarlett. Apparently when Clair's ex and his partner had a baby, Amelia started banging on about how they were going to be a proper family too. I remember Clare feeling so hurt at the time, but the reality of a crying baby soon shattered Amelia's rosy images. I gather that her daughter sees very little of her half brother now." Chrissie had continued confidently.

"I hadn't actually thought about it like that. I don't suppose Zoe is going to have anywhere near as much time for Scarlett once the baby arrives either." Fran felt her spirits starting to lift a little as she digested her younger sisters' words. When had Chrissie become such a wise old owl?

Her little sister had really changed a lot over the last few years. She was no longer such a push over. When they'd been younger, Fran had never been able to resist winding her placid amenable sibling up, enjoying seeing how far she had to push in order to make her retaliate.

It had come as something of a shock when the tables had gradually started to turn, and Fran had found her self being very politely, but firmly, put in her place whenever she stepped on her little sisters' toes.

Chrissie handle disagreements in much the same way as James. She rarely raised her voice or got into an argument with you, she just had this very controlled implacable way of standing her ground and refusing to roll over. Fran had absolutely no doubt that many people underestimated her at their peril, as just like James, she was utterly immovable if she truly believed she had a point to make.

James had been employing exactly the same tactics with her recently, every time she threatened to quit the charity shop again.

"If you can just stay put for another few weeks, I think I can organise a temporary paid position next." He'd encouraged her the other evening, when she'd been having yet another rant about the way Valerie had been treating her.

"At the same shop?" she'd asked warily. She really wasn't interested in staying there, even if they were willing to pay her. The stupid cow was making her days really unbearable now, always poised to have a go at her over the slightest little thing.

"Well no... I wasn't going to say anything until it was all finalised, but one of our receptionists is off to Australia for a couple of months, so we will be getting a temp in. I've suggested to the other partners that you could cover the period while Hilary is away? I was thinking I could take you in on a Sunday, and show you how the system works when the surgery is closed? A receptionist's position would look really good on your C V." He'd finished with a flourish, looking inordinately pleased with himself.

Fran had stared at James speechlessly for a moment or two before offering lamely,

"I don't have a C V." by way of an unintentionally thankless reply.

"Exactly Fran, but voluntary customer service, followed by a stint of paid reception work, will give us exactly the material we need to create one." He'd finished his tone so much more enthusiastic than hers.

Though she'd hugged him, and was genuinely grateful for all the trouble he was going to on her behalf, she couldn't help wondering if she was quite as keen to find herself rejoining the ranks of the gainfully employed as he was.

One thing she had learnt though, over the last couple of months, was that despite his gentle giant persona, there really was no point in arguing with James once he got the bit between his teeth.

It was strange the way things worked out sometimes, as though there was only ever a certain amount of good luck to go around in the world. Just as her life finally seemed to be turning a corner, Emily's was going rapidly downhill.

Fran cast her eye over the list she was compiling again. At least she was going to be ideally placed to offer sympathy and support to her best friend, as she'd gone through absolute hell a couple of years ago when the dreaded menopause had started playing havoc with her own health.

Fran knew exactly how it felt to have people look down on you, treat you as a second class citizen because you failed to function in quite the same way as they did. Depression, the menopause, and even many debilitating conditions, like M S, still carried the stigma of not being considered to be proper physical illnesses by so many ignorant people.

Though she wouldn't wish the misery she'd suffered on anyone else, let alone her best friend, she couldn't help wondering if Emily's problems could possibly bring them closer again as they'd have so much more in common now... their friendship might get back to the way it used to be if she really focussed on repaying Emily for all the years she'd stood so loyally by her...

27

Emily couldn't have been out of the house for more than about ten minutes to pick up her prescription, but the flashing light on the machine indicated she'd missed yet another call. She didn't need to hit play to know who the message would be from either.

Of course she knew that Fran meant well, that she was trying to be supportive in her own inimitable way, but she really was starting to drive Emily round the bend by calling her every day. If she didn't pick up the land line, she could guarantee her mobile would ring, and if she ignored that too, she'd receive a text within a few seconds that always contained the same message.

'Here for you whenever you need to talk hon. Love you to bits xx'

It was almost three weeks now since their trip to the cinema, and although Fran had obviously got the message that she really hadn't got the energy to go out much at the moment, she just couldn't seem to grasp the fact that she really needed some space too. She just wanted to be left in peace, particularly when she got in from work.

It wasn't just Fran's calls she was screening. Tom was checking caller display and asking if she wanted to speak to whoever it was, before he picked up the land line. She wasn't being deliberately evasive it was simply, that after making polite conversation with her clients all day, she'd got nothing left to give. Though this aspect of the job had always come easily to her in the past, it was becoming a major issue now, and she really did need to be left alone by the time she got home.

Customers she'd served for years, whose idiosyncrasies she'd always found mildly amusing, were starting to irritate her beyond belief with their nit picking first world problems. She seemed to be on such a short fuse all the time at the moment, and of course it was Tom who was usually on the sharp end of the majority of these uncharacteristic outbursts.

All she wanted to do when she walked through the door was have something to eat, a long soak in the bath to ease her aches and pains, and then climb into bed. No matter how well intentioned whoever was calling might be, she was getting to the point where she just couldn't face going over and over the same ground. It was getting harder and harder to remember exactly who was privy to what information when she was desperately tired too.

The clumsiness caused by the loss of feeling in her hands and feet, the increasingly frustrating balance issues, combined with such bone weary exhaustion, were all taking their toll, dragging her down. While she was feeling like such a wet blanket, she honestly thought it best to keep herself to her herself.

Some days, the sense of disorientation was so acute, she daren't even risk driving the short distance to work, but if she used the regular number 27 bus service to town, the 'he said, she said' inane drivel that passed for conversation, seemed to reverberate around her head, stretching her already taught nerves to breaking point.

At least now that she finally had an appointment, there was an end in sight to this state of limbo, the period of just worrying and waiting. The hospital had phoned the other evening- one of the few calls Tom had immediately handed over to her- and an appointment had been arranged with a Mr Neil Frobisher, who apparently only held a clinic in Shrewsbury once a month on a Saturday morning. She'd received a letter a day or two later confirming that she was booked in for the fourteenth of October- exactly four weeks today.

As she and Tom couldn't go abroad at the moment, because their annual insurance would not cover her while she was undergoing medical investigations, Emily was taking one day a week as leave, just to take a bit of the pressure off her self.

Glancing at her watch, she realised there was no point in returning Fran's call now, as Kath would be here to pick her up in about ten minutes. She was so looking forward to their afternoon tea, in the grand 'Lady Berwick' room, and at least with the girls she wouldn't have to put on any sort of show.

Kath and Jess had both been absolutely brilliant in their very different ways, and whenever she was with them she didn't have to make an effort to cover the difficulties she was experiencing. It was so liberating to be able to just relax and 'be', as most of the time now, her life felt like one continuous effort to appear as 'normal' as possible.

She smiled to herself as she recalled the exchange she'd had with Jess the other day over coffee, after a short swim. She'd apologised for the fact that she kept loosing her train of thought mid sentence, explaining that it was another of those days when the words seemed to form fine in her head, but just didn't seem to be coming off her tongue in the right order.

"It feels a bit like I've had way too much to drink and have to really slow my speech down so I don't jumble the words." She'd tried to explain.

"You've probably just worn your tongue out." Jess quipped back."I've always had to go up a gear to follow how quickly you talk." She'd grinned cheekily.

Anyone listening to their conversation would have recoiled in horror, thinking that Jess was being egregiously insensitive, but it was these regular exchanges of slightly black humour that had cemented their friendship. Emily never had to guard her tongue remotely with Jess, never worried about offending her sensibilities, she could always just say everything exactly the way it came into her head, just the way she did with Tom, and she knew Jess felt free to do the same.

Never one to sit on the fence, professionally or privately, some of the more controversial views Jess had shared with her over the years, were definitely not for public airing in our politically correctness obsessed society.

Emily often wondered if she'd become so close to Kath and Jess, because of the absence of any female role models in her own family. She'd spent a lot of years banging her head against the proverbial brick wall, trying to fix her fragmented family, doing everything in her power to heal the rifts and draw them closer. Eventually she'd come to realise that all that wasted energy was self destructive, and had taught herself to accept that she could only be responsible for her side of any relationship, that you can't force someone else to care.

To be fair to her older sister, she and Joanna had never really lived as siblings, so although technically related, in reality they were no more than polite strangers. Five years her senior, Joanna had gone straight to boarding school as soon as the Sanderson family arrived in

Germany. Their parents had whole heartedly embraced the better lifestyle afforded to them by the strong Deutschmark back then, so Major Sanderson had opted to extend his original tour of duty many times over. By the time Emily had been sent away to the same school, her sister had already returned to England to start work.

Initially Joanna had lived with a distant aunt in Dorset, before carving out a career for herself in The City. Her sister had never married or stayed in any job for more than a few years. She was currently travelling the world, opening new stores for a high end fashion chain, and was now based in Hong Kong.

Of course there had been the usual noises made about Emily and Tom going out to visit her when she'd first been relocated, but Emily knew from bitter experience that they were just empty words. She'd lay odds on the fact that 'Auntie' Joanna wouldn't even recognise Holly or Josh if she bumped into them out of context. The only input she contributed to her niece and nephew's lives' were the cheques she sent twice a year for birthdays and Christmas.

Emily shook her head, as though trying to physically shake off these maudlin thoughts. What was it about birthdays that always had you doing a bit of naval gazing? She was incredibly lucky that Tom's family had embraced her so fully from the outset, treating her as though she was one of their own. She thought the world of Helen and Mike and was well aware that she couldn't have asked for better in-laws. She had absolutely no reason to be sitting here feeling sorry for herself- other than the fact she might have MS. She grinned ruefully to herself, as a brief spark of her usual wry humour resurfaced...

Today was going to be a good day. Afternoon tea at her favourite place, in this glorious autumn sunshine, with two of the loveliest friends you could have (Mel hadn't been able to make it). Was there a better way to spend an afternoon than that?

A short while later, as though by silent telepathy the three women naturally gravitated towards the flat river walk despite the fact that Emily was walking reasonably well today. They crossed the narrow suspension bridge and turned right to go through the gate, taking the short cut into the bottom of the deer park, which would allow them to follow the river again, on the other side, back towards the mansion.

As their table was reserved for three o'clock, they still had plenty of time to enjoy the autumn sunshine- such a bonus this far into September- so as they came out of the woods they headed towards their favourite bench, which had the most stunning views over the parkland, towards the huge cedars that created a frame around the mansion from this angle.

"So is Fran still bombarding you with calls everyday?" Jess asked broaching the subject they'd all been studiously avoiding so far this afternoon.

"Don't be mean." Emily tried to sound disapproving but she couldn't help grinning. "She does mean well Jess." She added a little more seriously.

Loyal by nature, it wasn't part of Emily's make up to bitch about one friend to another, but over the years, Jess and Kath had both witnessed enough to know the true nature of her relationship with Fran.

"The trouble is, even if her intentions are good, I bet Fran is still spending two seconds asking you about your problems, and then bending your ear for hours about her own list of woes." Kath summarised astutely.

"Mmmm....I suppose so, but I'm pretty much used to that after all these years." Emily conceded ruefully. "I was only thinking the other day, how uncanny it is that you two both seemed to have developed such perfect lives recently. I can't remember the last time either of you had a gripe you needed to share with me." Emily teased, raising an ironic eyebrow at the pair of them.

"Well you've got enough on your plate at the moment haven't you?" Jess stated matter-of-factly, as though it was a given- good friendships should be based on knowing when it was time to support rather than be supported. "Seriously though Emily, I've never understood why you keep the friendship going? You would be the first to admit that you haven't enjoyed Fran's company for years, and you really don't need anyone bleeding you dry right now."

She'd been down this road many times before, with Tom as well as the girls. They just didn't understand though. Everyone thought Fran was as tough as nails, the life and soul of any party, but deep down she was a seething mass of insecurities. Her mother had abandoned her,

her husband had left her, and now her daughter was itching to get away from her too, so how could Emily even think about withdrawing her support? Though it was true that they had very little in common anymore, and Fran really did drive her to distraction at times, she was still inordinately fond of her troubled friend, even if she was a right pain in the butt sometimes.

"It's hard to explain, but we go so far back that I can't just turn my back on her ...especially now that Scarlett is so intent on moving out." Fran had brought her up to date with the latest developments the other evening, wanting her advice on how to handle the situation from here.

As they were now well into the new school term, Scarlett was officially back with Fran, but in reality, she was apparently still spending as many nights as she could get away with at Simon's.

"Perhaps if you weren't there to bale her out all the time, she'd learn to stand on her own two feet like the rest of us have to? You can't be expected to keep propping her up forever Emily." Jess pointed out, concern about Emily's prognosis making her sound far sharper that she'd intended.

"Mmmm...I suppose you could be right..." Emily chewed at her bottom lip, wondering if Jess did actually have a point. If she stopped being Fran's safety blanket all the time, would she rise to the challenge or would she just throw in the towel and drink herself into oblivion?

"It could prove to be the kick up the arse she needs to finally sort her life out?" Jess insisted worried that Emily was far too soft hearted to put her own needs first, even when she faced such an uncertain future herself.

"I reckon it must be about time to go and meet Lady Berwick and eat her outrageously expensive sandwiches." Kath cut in diplomatically. She knew that Jess only had Emily's best interest at heart, and to be honest she agreed with her emphatically, but she could be a bit like a dog with a bone when she believed she was in the right. This afternoon was supposed to be all about treating Emily, making sure that she had some fun, forgot about the cloud that was hanging over her... at least for the next couple of hours...

28

"You are such a spoilt brat Holly Mortimer." Josh teased his younger sister, as he hefted another box of her belongings from the van. "Most fresher's start out in halls and then, if they're really lucky, they get to live in a scuzzy dump like the one I've been in for the last eighteen months."

Emily couldn't help smiling as she compared the light hearted banter being exchanged today, with the gut wrenching sense of abandonment she'd felt, when they'd brought Josh to Bangor two years ago.

Having carefully followed the directions they'd been given, Emily's heart had sunk even further into her boots as they'd pulled up outside the building, in which Josh had been assigned a room. The hideously ugly, archaic grey block looked like it should have been condemned years ago, and bore absolutely no resemblance to the bright modern units they'd been shown on their tour of the university.

Any hopes that things might improve once inside the building had soon been dashed. The long institutional corridors had been about as welcoming as an old Victorian hospital, and the communal bathrooms were beyond disgusting. The only redeeming features of Josh's corner room were the two enormous windows, which let in masses of light, and offered a distant view of the Menai Straits.

Despite Emily's grave misgivings, Josh had appeared to take his new surrounding in his stride, immediately propping his door wide open to encourage other new arrivals to pop their heads in and say hello. Emily had cried throughout the entire journey home, utterly appalled at the thought of him living in such squalid conditions for the next three years.

Though Emily knew Betley End was going to feel pretty desolate without the bubbly presence of their daughter, filling every room with her energy, at least they knew she was going to be safe and comfortable in this house. After all the alterations Tom had done, the property had such a warm welcoming vibe now, and as Josh had come back a few days earlier than he needed to, he'd be on hand to show her the ropes.

Emily was pretty sure that, unlike Josh, Holly would text several times a day, to let them know how she was getting on, rather than just disappearing into the ether for the first couple of weeks, the way her brother had.

When Tom had first mooted the idea of buying a house in Bangor, to avoid paying out two lots of inflated student rent, Emily had had grave reservations. She was concerned that their good intentions might deprive their daughter of a vital part of University life, making it harder for her to fit in. Fran hadn't exactly helped as she had been particularly forthright on the matter, making her opinion crystal clear on numerous occasions.

Gregarious by nature, Holly had been quick to dismiss her mother's fears, assuring Emily that she could have the best of both worlds if she had her own private space to retreat to, and so now, the idea had become reality, and the two of them would be sharing this house for the foreseeable future.

"Do you want to choose which room you want while dad and I finish unloading the last of the boxes?" Josh nonchalantly gave his sister the choice, as he really didn't have the slightest preference. Any of the bedrooms in this bright, airy quietly located house, where he could get his head down and study in peace, would be a massive improvement.

Half way though his first year, when he and five other lads had decided to cram into a three bed-roomed house, in order to save on rent, it had seemed like a fun idea. Eighteen months older and wiser, he couldn't wait to regain some space to call his own again.

"Is it OK if I have this one then?" Holly asked, rushing off down the stairs to find some belongings to start filling it, as soon as Josh offered a casual "Sure..." by way of agreement.

Exactly as he'd predicted, Holly had chosen the room at the back of the house, which although slightly smaller than the main front bedroom, had a virtually uninterrupted view of the coastline and also happened to be closest to the bathroom.

The proximity to the sea at every turn was one of the many things that had drawn Holly to Bangor. The quaint old town, with the various faculties of the university dotted around it, appeared so much more attractive than some of the modern purpose built campuses they'd viewed. The main hall reminded her of Hogwarts, and the grand panelled library had views to die for. She'd visualised herself sitting there lost in the landscape and her own imagination, as she worked on assignments.

As she skipped excitedly from room to room, Holly found it hard to equate this house with the dump they'd viewed a few months ago. The revolting mishmash of dated textured wallpapers, had been replaced by warm buttermilk walls though out, and the dark patterned carpets had all been ripped up and replaced with light laminate flooring. Best of all, there was no longer any trace of the pink '70's' bathroom suite.

Though the kitchen appeared to have had had a complete refit too, dad quickly explained how he'd moved a couple of base units around, replaced the old fashioned cupboard doors and work surfaces, and built some clever shelving to make the most of the awkward corner under the stairwell. The icing on the cake was the neat little shower room he'd managed to shoehorn into what had been a dingy utility area.

Gran's old sofa's covered with a couple of bright throws, purchased in the Dunelm sale, looked great in the open plan lounge/diner. They'd received so many donations from friends and relatives that they'd hardly needed to buy anything in the way of furniture or white goods.

While Tom and the kids spent the rest of the afternoon unpacking boxes- two for Josh and half a van full for Holly- Emily began hanging the curtains she'd kept up in the loft for this very purpose. By five o'clock both the kids were starting to make noises about rumbling tummies.

"Why don't we try that Chinese we passed on the corner- see if it's good enough to become our regular?" Josh suggested. He knew Mum had put a load of food in the cupboards and fridge, and was planning to cook a Bolognese, but she'd been really quiet for the last hour or so and seemed to have gone very pale.

Maybe, it was because he hadn't seen her for a few weeks, but he'd really noticed a difference this time. She'd definitely lost more weight and appeared to be so much frailer all of a sudden.

Half an hour later as they all sat around the table, which had been donated by Rachel and Martin, it soon became apparent that Lee Wong had definitely just gained another two customers.

"Mmmm...Try that duck mum, it's gorgeous." Holly mumbled through a mouthful of peeking sauce.

"These ribs are probably the nicest I've ever had." Tom agreed, sucking the sweet and sour coating off his fingers enthusiastically.

Though Emily appeared to be joining in the feast, she'd actually eaten very little. Everything seemed to taste like cardboard at the moment, so she simply ate to avoid loosing any more weight.

Once they'd finished their meal, they'd head off home pretty soon, and leave the kids to get them selves settled in properly. She had no doubt she'd probably be asleep before they were even back on the A55, as the motion of any vehicle seemed to send her off in minutes these days.

Though the van wasn't as comfortable as the car, she'd still managed to doze off on the way here, despite Holly jabbering away excitedly in the back throughout most of the journey.

"So are you still planning to let us to choose our new housemate then Dad?" Holly asked, cramming another prawn cracker into her mouth.

"Well as the two of you are going have to live with the consequences that seems logical to me." Tom answered confidently. "The details are all in place with the letting agent, so they'll contact you as soon as they get any interest. No matter how nice someone appears, make sure you agree to a trial period though."

"Definitely Dad..." Josh was quick to agree, "I only wish we'd thought of that before we all signed up for Brynteg. We'd have kicked Liam and Mehmet out without a doubt." he assured his father wholeheartedly, knowing there was no chance of him making that mistake again.

"Ideally another fresher, or someone staying on like Josh, would be good, then, if they do fit in, he or she can stay until you two have finished and we sell the place." Tom pointed out.

"The kids have only just moved in and you're already talking about selling." Emily teased her ever practical husband.

"It's a good point though mum. If we get someone nice, it would be great to know that we're all settled for the duration. Do you think it should be another boy or a girl?" Holly mused, not having considered her own preference yet. "I suppose a girl might be more inclined to do her share of the cleaning?" She concluded sombrely. "Perhaps a gay guy would be best option then there would be no chance of either of us falling for our housemate?" Holly's face lit up as she realised she may have just inadvertently stumbled on the perfect solution.

"Most of the gay guys I know are even bigger drama queens than the girls," Josh cut in succinctly. "And to be honest, I really don't fancy being anyone's agony aunt Holly. At least if it's another bloke, he'll only have friends that he actually likes so we won't have to live through the obligatory girly fall outs."

Emily and Holly both opened their mouths to protest, but they're expressions simultaneously acknowledged the truth behind this seemingly ludicrous statement.

"I really want to argue with you but I can't." Holly conceded, punching her brother playfully on the arm as she pulled a face at him.

"I lost count of the number of times Freya started a sentence with 'I love her to bits but....' about one of her friends." Josh went on. Freya had been Josh's long term girlfriend all through sixth form ,and although she'd been a very pretty girl, she'd always struck Emily as incredibly high maintenance, so she hadn't exactly shed any tears when they'd agreed to go their separate ways. "And whenever Fran's number comes up on caller display, you can see mum take a deep breath before she answers it." He pressed his point home, raising a far too knowing eyebrow at his mother before concluding. "Like I said blokes only have friends they like. You wouldn't find dad wasting his time with someone if he didn't enjoy their company would you?"

Emily certainly couldn't disagree with that. Though her husband was one of the most laid back, easy-going people you could meet, if he took a dislike to someone socially, he would make zero effort to cover the fact. He was a typical mans man, and wouldn't give the time of day to the 'networking' types who were simply working the room.

"There is such a thing as loyalty though Josh?" Emily deliberately kept her tone bantering too, but she was very conscious that Josh had just touched a very raw nerve. "You can't just cut someone out of your life because they're going through a difficult time." Especially when you are one of the few people left who they haven't completed alienated, Emily added silently to her self.

"But when was the last time you actually enjoyed Fran's company mum, and I can't remember a time when she hasn't been in need of your help." Josh went on, his tone more serious now.

Even when Mum was so obviously struggling under the weight of her own health issues, according to Holly, Fran was still on the phone most nights, bending her ear about Scarlett. Was it any wonder the poor kid wanted to live with her dad? He'd have been about thirteen him self when he'd started to realise what a total nightmare the woman was. If Fran was his mother, he'd have put him self up for adoption.

As Emily quietly began to clear away the plates, Josh took that as his cue that the conversation was well and truly over. He may be twenty and about a foot taller than his mother, but he still recognised that look, and realised he might have just pushed things a bit too far.

"Did I see some fruit corners in the fridge for pud?" He changed the subject deftly as he had no intention of upsetting his mum, but for the life of him, he'd never be able to understand the complexities of such a demanding friendship.

Emily stood looking out of the kitchen window for a few seconds after she'd rinsed the plates and popped them in the dish washer. Three times now in almost as many days she'd received this same message- was someone up there trying to tell her something?

Tom had lectured her about taking better care of her self after she'd listened to a particularly lengthy phone rant Friday night, then the girls had repeated exactly the same concerns yesterday afternoon, and now even Josh was handing out similar advice.

In a few weeks time, if the neurologist did confirm the diagnosis that she and Dr Morgan were expecting, she'd have to start putting her own needs first...begin setting some much clearer, healthier boundaries, and maybe, just maybe, Fran would benefit from that in the long run...

29

"So how long do you think it will be before dad is back in the office telling Jack what he's doing wrong, or out on site lecturing me?" Tom whispered to his mother. Jack had just finished delivering the short speech they'd prepared, and presented Dad with the holiday gift voucher they'd all clubbed together to buy, to mark his sixty fifth birthday and 'retirement'.

The Corbett Arms in the little village of Uffington, had done them proud as always, allocating them a table at the far end of the conservatory, with a fabulous view over one of the many loops the river Severn made, as it meandered its way through Shropshire. Though they were a group of sixteen, everybody had enjoyed a piping hot meal, and the service had been as faultless and cheerful as ever, with no attempt to hurry them on their way as they lingered over coffee.

Though Ben had been unable to travel all the way back from Edinburgh, all the other children and grandchildren, including Josh and Holly, were gathered together to celebrate the occasion, despite the fact that it was only two weeks since they'd gone to Bangor.

As she studied all the happy smiling faces around the table, Emily's eyes flooded with tears. She couldn't seem to drag her gaze away from her full of life mother-in-law, as she laughed with the twins. The girls were sat either side of their adored grandma, nestled against her, as they giggled away listening to their granddad being ribbed about all the new hobbies he should take up, now he was officially a pensioner.

Emily had always enjoyed being part of this easy affectionate banter. The light hearted teasing glued the family together and was so different from the cruel jibes of her childhood. They had been designed to home in on your weaknesses, seeking out any cracks. Today, she felt isolated from them all, as though she wasn't really part of the celebrations as she censured every word she spoke, and monitored every movement she made.

Helen had been watching her like a hawk these last few weeks, although she was perceptive enough not to push her daughter-in-law for more information than she was willing to share. Emily was determined not to give her any more cause for concern today, as she really didn't want to put any sort of dampener on this special family occasion.

It wasn't as though she and Tom were being deliberately deceitful they had simply come to the conclusion, that it was pointless upsetting the rest of the family, until they knew if there was anything to worry about.

They'd agreed to adopt a 'let's not cross any bridges until we come to them' attitude, but every now and then, despite her best intentions, something random could completely floor her, presenting her with an image of the future that utterly terrified her.

Sitting here now watching Helen, it was hard to ignore the fact that her mother-in-law had been pretty much exactly the same age as she was now, when Josh was born. Helen had been such an absolute God send, seeming to possess a super human supply of energy, when it came to supporting her daughter-in-law through the first few terrifying weeks of motherhood, that no amount of 'new parent' guides ever prepared you for.

By the time Josh and Holly got round to having children, what kind of support was she going to be capable of offering them?

Emily quickly excused herself from the table and headed for the ladies, desperately in need of a moment or two to compose her self. She sat on the closed toilet lid taking in slow deliberate breaths. She couldn't break down here, with Tom's entire family just a few yards away, but it was so hard to block out the thoughts that had been whirling away since her colleague's big announcement yesterday.

As soon as Karen had walked into the office, it was obvious she was itching to tell them something. In the entire fifteen years they had been working together, Emily had never seen the older woman look quite so animated.

"I'm going to be a granny in March..." She'd declared, the words bursting out in a most un-Karen-like fashion. "We've known for about six weeks now, but Megan only had the twelve week scan yesterday, and she didn't want anyone else to know until after that."

Karen was a rather matronly lady who had always kept herself to her herself, but it was impossible not to be drawn in as she continued to regale them with all the details, while continuing to look like the cat that had got the cream.

Naturally Emily had joined in the wave of enthusiastic congratulations, but she'd found herself swallowing bile when an unexpected wave of nausea washed over her. Out of nowhere she'd suddenly conjured up a disturbingly vivid image of herself on a mobility scooter, holding a grandchild of her own. In that split second, it was as though all the subconscious dreams for the future she'd always taken for granted had just been smashed in front of her.

On a practical level, she knew she was being utterly ridiculous, as she had no idea whether Josh or Holly even planned to have children, but the sense of loss she'd experienced had defied that kind of logic, as she'd found herself worrying about carrying a baby up or down a flight of stairs, when she could barely manage to climb them on her own some days?

Thank goodness her appointment was only a couple of weeks away now. She couldn't go on like this- she was driving her self round the bend. One minute she was sitting crying over imaginary grandchildren that might never even exist, and the next she was picturing herself as some sort of benevolent saint, living graciously with her disabilities, the way one of their customers, Sharon Mitchell, did.

Sharon had been a client of Mike's for years and, just like the majority of their regulars, she generally liked to deal with the same travel consultant all the time, as he was familiar with her personal issues and preferences. Until a few days ago, Emily had simply viewed her as that lovely smiley lady on a mobility scooter, but while Mike had been away on compassionate leave recently, she'd found herself dealing with Sharon for the first time. It had been an eye opening experience, terrifying and encouraging in equal measures.

"Sorry Mrs Mitchell...I know Mike probably keeps all your information on file somewhere, but I do have to fill in this special needs form for Thomas Cook." Emily had apologised before opening the long winded document that needed to be completed on line.

"That's absolutely fine Emily but please call me Sharon...I always feel so ancient when people call me Mrs Mitchell." She'd responded warmly.

"I know exactly what you mean, but we were always taught not to use somebody's Christian name unless they invited you to do so." Emily laughed, acknowledging that the old fashioned courtesy did come across as a bit stuffy sometimes.

They'd chatted away easily as she supplied all the information required by the airline, and hotel, and no matter how personal the questions, Sharon had continued to laugh and joke her way through the whole procedure. Having done her usual meticulously detailed research to ensure that both the property and the resort would be suitable for her needs, she'd actually made Emily's job incredibly easy.

"I've done the same sort of home work for a whole list of places we want to see... a kind of bucket list if you like...so we can just choose the next one whenever I'm having a good spell." She'd explained candidly.

"So how long have you had MS?" Emily found her curiosity getting the better of her as Sharon continued to speak so openly about her problems.

"I was actually diagnosed just before my fortieth birthday- a wonderful birthday present- but to be honest I'd suspected that something was wrong for years before that. I just sort of stuck my head in the sand and ignored the symptoms for as long as possible." Sharon confessed.

"Oh I think we can all be pretty good at playing that game." Emily conceded wryly.

"Ummm..." Sharon had studied her quietly for a moment or two before she continued, "Unfortunately my mobility went downhill pretty rapidly for a few years after that, but I seem to have reached a plateau now, which is why we're trying to fit in as much as possible while the going is good."

After Sharon left, Emily had sat quietly in the staff room eating her lunch, processing all she had just learnt. When Sharon had talked about all the help she received from her support group, Emily had begun to suspect she'd probably guessed the reason for Emily's keen interest.

As she'd sat munching on her sandwich, reflecting on how smart Sharon always looked, how cheerful she usually seemed, and how positively she planned for the future, it stuck her for the first time that, even if she was diagnosed with MS, though the way she lived her life might have to start changing, it didn't mean that her life would be over... not unless she chose to view it that way...

Emily took in a long slow breath and pulled her shoulders back before opening the door to the cubicle, and checking her make up in the mirror for any tell tale smudges. If she didn't go and join the others pretty sharply, she'd no doubt have Helen in here, checking if she was O K, and right now she wasn't sure if she was strong enough to evade her mother-in-laws intuitive probing. She'd probably just end up blubbing all over her like a baby....

30

Fran poured herself another hefty slug of vodka and used her sleeve to wipe away the tears of anger and frustration. She was such a moron. She always did this, built her self up for the inevitable fall.

She should never have allowed herself to get caught up in James' fairytale, to start believing that her life was finally on the up. When would she learn to accept, that good luck only ever happened to other people, and stop banging her head against the same brick wall.

What were the odds against the receptionist she was supposed to have been covering, having to cancel her plans at the very last minute? She'd tried to make all the right sympathetic noises when James had explained that the poor woman had just lost her mother unexpectedly- she wasn't completely heartless- but it had been really hard not to feel as though she'd just had the rug pulled out from under her.

She'd had a dirty great big carrot dangled in front of her nose, only to be snatched away again. Common sense told her that of course it wasn't his fault, but right now it really did feel as though James had let her down, in the same way that everybody did in the end.

"You'll just have to stick it out at the shop for a little bit longer until we can come up with another plan." He'd assured her easily, but it wasn't him who had to put up with 'Vile Valerie' being such a vicious cow was it?

There was something about the woman that just seemed to press all her buttons, bringing out the worst in her, and she simply hadn't been able to keep a lid on her frustrations when the old bat had started on at her yet again this morning. As soon as she'd walked through the door, the stuck-up cow had taken a long, pointed, look at her watch.

"I thought you were due in at nine today Frances?" She'd enquired haughtily, arching one of her straggly un-plucked eyebrows at Fran, as though she were a tardy schoolgirl.

"Yeah...the bus didn't turn up again...sorry..." The lie had tripped off her tongue so easily. They could hardly dock her wages for being an hour late if they didn't actually pay her could they, and besides, as she didn't usually work on a Saturday, she was already doing them a massive favour by coming in at all.

"We rely on you to get here on time. I've been on my own for over an hour now, which means I haven't been able to make a start on sorting the new stock." Valerie continued in the same disapproving schoolmarm tones.

"It's just a load of old tat Valerie. We are hardly competing with Debenhams are we?" Fran intended to lighten the mood a little, placate the stupid woman, but she hadn't made allowances for the fact that Valerie was one of those people who seemed to have had a complete sense of humour bypass.

"Well if that is your attitude it's hardly surprising we can't ever rely on you is it? You should be grateful that Barbara is prepared to risk giving someone like you the chance to start again, to try and make-"

"What exactly do you mean by someone like me Valerie?" Fran's voice was deadly as she cut the other woman off. This really was beginning to feel like she was back at school, standing before the dreaded Mrs Baines, who'd taken great delight in informing her that 'someone like her' would never amount to anything.

Valerie's Face blanched as she realised her gaffe. This was, after all, a charity shop, and she was displaying precious little of that virtue at the moment. It was obvious that Fran had some deep seated, major issues, and needed a great deal of help...perhaps she was being a bit too hard on her...

"I just meant someone who is struggling to find their way back into paid employment..."She trailed off awkwardly, the unadulterated fury on Fran's face causing her to step back, as for the first time since leaving the playground, she actually feared she might be in danger of being physically struck.

"I know exactly what you meant you stuck up cow." Fran practically growled, her nose just inches from the other woman's before she turned abruptly, grabbed her bag and coat from the back room, and sailed out of the shop without a backward glance.

She'd tried ringing Emily several times since she'd got home, but as was so often the case at the moment, there had been no answer. She hardly ever seemed to pick up her calls lately, and her texts all seemed to have a slightly dismissive edge that told her absolutely nothing at all

James was still away at some big conference in London, and she'd never been able to get any sympathy from her dad, even at the best of times, and he seemed distinctly off with her right now.

He'd been giving her a really hard time lately, constantly harping on about her being no better than her mother, accusing her of abandoning Scarlett, copping out of her awkward teen years by encouraging her to spend so much time at Simon's. How was she supposed to defend herself against that? Admit to him that it was Scarlett's choice- that she simply didn't want to be, anywhere near her mother these days.

The only comfort available to her right now was the bottle of vodka that would take her to oblivion for a little while... blot out the utter nightmare her life seemed to have become again, at least for a few blessed hours...

31

Tom had never been the sort of bloke who sat around feeling sorry for him self. He was pragmatic enough to accept that shit happened to everyone. When it was his turn, he generally just took it on the chin, but even he had to admit that he was pretty hacked off right now.

In the past, whenever life had thrown them a curved ball, he and Emily had worked through the problem together, but over the last few months, she'd become so withdrawn, had cut herself off physically and emotionally, leaving him feeling so alone.

As Emily tended to be in bed by about nine most evenings, he'd resorted to sleeping in the spare room, so as not to disturb her when he came up later. Watching telly on his own every evening, then climbing into a cold empty bed, was not what he was used to, and he was desperately missing her company. It wasn't just the lack of sex- though, God knows, that was getting tough enough- he was pining for the woman he'd married.

The majority of the time now, it was like living with a polite stranger who bore little resemblance to his vibrant, funny, sexy, affectionate wife. Emily seemed to be permanently on edge, snapping at him over the slightest thing, and she had completely lost her sense of humour.

Whenever he tried to inject a little of the easy banter that had become an integral part of their relationship, the humour came across as stilted and awkward as he trod on eggshells, wary of upsetting her again.

Though she hadn't actually withdrawn her hand from his as they sat, on the hard plastic chairs, waiting to see the neurologist, he might as well not be here for all the connection there was between them. He just didn't seem to be able to reach her anymore and that hurt like hell.

The anxiety radiating from her this morning was a tangible force, and he was actually beginning to wonder if maybe Dr Evanson had been right all along. Perhaps this neurologist was going to take one look at her, and agree that it was all down to hormones or some kind of depression- he'd been doing a lot of reading while he was sat downstairs on his own every night, and had been shocked to discover that, one in three women used antidepressants at some point in their lives.

A few months ago he'd have laughed in the face of the mere suggestion that his Emily would ever suffer from any form of mental illness, but now he was no longer quite so sure...

"Mr & Mrs Mortimer..." They were simultaneously jolted out of their isolating bubbles of introspection as the consultant popped his head around the corner. "Would you like to come through now?"

As they entered the consulting room, the reassuringly mature bespectacled gentleman remained standing, shaking hands with them both, before indicating the two chairs placed close to his desk.

"I'm Neil Frobisher, and I'm part of the neurology team based in Birmingham." He paused, gazing over the top of his glasses at Emily, his slightly rumpled, kindly professor persona, instantly reminding her of Elliot Hope from Holby. "So Emily...is it OK if I call you Emily?" He paused again as she nodded consent, remembering her conversation with Sharon Mitchell on this very subject a few weeks ago. "I've read the report from Dr Morgan, so what I'd like to do today is to take a much more detailed history from you, and then we'll run through a few cognitive tests if that's OK?"

Emily nodded again swallowing hard before she spoke.

"This is a copy of the list Dr Morgan asked me to make for her. She suggested it might help if I brought it with me today." She fidgeted nervously as he began to scan the typed sheet.

"This is a great help Emily thank you." He glanced up, offering her another reassuring smile, before continuing to work meticulously down the page, underlining several items which he then questioned her about in more detail, making copious notes, whilst also seeking Tom's input on several occasions.

"Some of the tests I'm going to do now may seem a bit strange, childish even, but their designed to rule out a whole set of neurological problems, so just bare with me OK?"

Having been stressing about this day for the last couple of months, dreading the thought of the consultant dismissing her problems in the same offhand manner that Dr Evanson had, Emily felt herself finally begin to relax a little. They had already been here over half an hour, and Mr Frobisher could not be doing more to reassure her, that he was taking every one of the symptoms she'd flagged up seriously.

"Do you want me to wait outside?" Tom stood up at the same time as Emily and the consultant.

"No need to leave on my account." Neil Frobisher assured him easily.

The next fifteen minutes or so, did indeed involve a series of tests that were pretty strange to say the least, including following his finger with her eyes, pushing against his hands, moving her finger back and to between her nose and his hand, and walking across the room with her eyes closed.

By the time she'd put her shoes back on and sat down again at his desk, the sheet of notes he'd been making seemed to have lengthened considerably.

"OK." Forming a Steeple with his fingers the consultant appeared to be marshalling his thoughts before he spoke again. "A neurological diagnosis is generally reached by a process of elimination Emily. The test's we've just done were to rule out the likelihood of early onset dementia, so what I'd like to arrange next is an MRI of the brain and spine."

"To look for lesions?" She asked very quietly.

"Exactly. I gather Dr Morgan has already explained that a lot of your symptoms are what we would expect to see in the early stages of MS, but there are of course numerous other possibilities too." He turned the piece of paper he'd been writing on towards her, before working through a brief explanation of his thoughts so far.

Many of the long, unfamiliar words meant nothing at all to her but at the top of the first group he'd written MS and ME, Followed by vitamin B12 or D deficiencies.

"If the MRI comes back clear, then we will start working through this list of other likely causes. Are you a vegetarian by any chance?" He paused, carrying on as soon as Emily had shaken her head, looking somewhat bemused. "A B12 deficiency can be the result of a diet lacking in red meat, but it can also be caused by something called pernicious anaemia, which is an autoimmune disease that stops the body absorbing vitamins properly. The early signs of deficiency tend to mimic the symptoms of MS very closely."

The next group was headed with something called fibromyalgia, and contained several other equally unpronounceable conditions which were all degenerative. The final group, which needed no explanation at all, included things like chronic fatigue and anxiety issues.

"I'll organise the MRI today, so you should receive an appointment within a couple of weeks, and I'll send a full report of my findings so far to Dr Morgan OK? Have you got any other questions you'd like to ask me at this stage?"

Just as he had been though the entire hour they'd been with him, Neil Frobisher remained relaxed, unhurried, appearing to have all the time in the world for them.

"I don't suppose I could have a copy of that list...It's just I know I'll forget half of what you have just said as soon as I walk out the door." Emily laughed, a glimmer of her usual self deprecating humour emerging.

"Of course- though you may struggle to decipher my dreadful writing." He turned and ran the sheet of A4 through the scanner behind him before handing it to Emily, then stood and walked them to the door shaking hands with them both again, before turning back towards to his desk.

As soon as they stepped out into the corridor, Emily linked her arm through Tom's, smiling up at him as she let out a huge sigh of relief.

"Thank goodness that is over. I've been working myself up into a right old state, imagining some arrogant, up his own backside consultant, granting me two minutes of his precious time, before dismissing me in much the same manner that Dr Evanson did, but he couldn't have been more thorough could he?" Her bright eyes actually looked a bit more like Emily's again, as they met and held Tom's gaze without sliding away, as she waited for him to reply.

"He certainly seemed to examine you very thoroughly." Tom agreed, feeling a bit sheepish now, over the unsupportive thoughts he'd been having earlier on, when they'd been in the waiting room.

"I just hope he gets this MRI sorted out quickly, and then we can really start getting some answers."

"It's all the waiting that is so hard isn't it? The thing is Tom I really want this scan to come back clear now, because he has given us so many other possibilities." Tom stared at her strangely, his expression clearly indicating that he thought that that was a given.

Emily hurried on quickly, trying to explain, to get Tom to understand what had been whirling away in her head for the last few weeks. "It's really hard to put this into words and it probably sounds a bit barmy, but before we spoke to him today, I kind of assumed that if the consultant decided it wasn't MS, I'd be pretty much left to just get on with it again, like I was after the doctor did the first load of blood tests and chest x-rays. At least if I get a diagnosis I can get some help, and be sure that I'm not just going round the twist."

"Why didn't you tell me any of this before Em?" Tom asked quietly.

"To be honest Tom, I've been tying myself up in so many knots lately, that I don't think I could have explained what has been going on inside my head to my self, let alone to you." She answered honestly.

"Well whatever happens from here on, it'll be a whole lot easier for me to understand if you talk to me Em." His words were really soft, but his tone was deadly serious before he suddenly changed tack. "Look... I know it seems a bit daft because we don't actually know anymore than we did this morning, but why don't we just bunk off for the rest of the day... maybe head to Llangollen and take a trip on the canal... get a meal by the river or something...I reckon we both deserve a few treats right now don't you?"

"Aren't you supposed to be going back to work?" Emily pointed out sensibly, though he could see by the grin on her face that she wasn't going to take much persuading.

"Bugger work. What's the point of being my own boss if I can't skive off once in a blue moon and spend the day spoiling my gorgeous wife?" he laughed, before pulling Emily in close for a long overdue hug...

32

Fran read the text from Emily again, then hurled the phone onto the bed in a fit of hurt and frustration. This really was getting beyond a joke now. It was almost two weeks since she'd left the shop following her row with Valerie, yet she still hadn't had a chance to talk to Emily about the situation properly, and now, to add insult to injury she'd just sent what was obviously a bland round robin message.

'Appointment went well... consultant really thorough... he's ruled out dementia so at least I know I'm not going round the bend just yet.... MRI in a couple of weeks... Ta so much for all the support.'

Fran hadn't spoken to Emily at all this week since receiving a ticking off from Tom the other evening.

"She's having a long soak in the bath right now Fran, and to be honest with you I think Emily would really appreciate it if you didn't ring on the days she's been at work, because she comes home absolutely exhausted and doesn't want to talk to anyone."

Tom didn't use that clipped tone with her very often, but when he did, Fran knew there was absolutely no point in arguing with him, pointing out that she was only trying to be supportive. If Emily was really struggling so much that she couldn't manage to exchange a few words on the phone, then why the hell was she still going into work for goodness sake?

Fran snatched the discarded phone from the bed and reread the text again, examining every word this time. This was the first contact she'd had with Emily in days, and it was blatantly obvious that she hadn't even bothered to personalise one single word of the generic message before sending it.

To be fair, Fran had to admit that she hadn't really had much contact with anyone all week, as she'd been lying low licking her wounds. In the past though, whenever she'd gone to ground for a bit, Emily had always seemed to sense when it was time to be a bit pushy, to come round and give her a much needed kick up the backside.

She totally got the fact that Emily was going through a pretty rough patch too right now, but surely that ought to be bringing them closer not driving a wedge between them? Emily was only dealing with the same sort of issues that Fran had been coping with for years, but nobody had suggested arranging a shed of load of tests for her, or referring her to some top notch consultant...she'd just been left to plod on alone...

She really was starting to get concerned about the mole on her right arm. It had changed shape and colour since she'd got back from Majorca in May, but she kept putting off making an appointment at the surgery because Doctor Young always made her feel like she was just making a fuss. You could clearly see the 'not her again' expression on his face before she'd even opened her mouth to say what was troubling her.

She'd checked out her symptoms on line and was growing ever more convinced it was skin cancer. Life was so unfair. She had always been so scrupulously careful about slathering cream all over her, whether sunbathing in this country or abroad. One of the few free pleasures available to her was a good dollop of sunshine, so it would be just typical of her luck if she had to stay in the shade for the rest of her life now.

She reached for the phone, deciding to try and call Emily again, but then quickly changed her mind. She'd been hitting the vodka pretty steadily since lunch time, and Emily always seemed to get really snitty with her lately if she called her when she'd been drinking. Perhaps it would be better to just send another text...she really did need to talk to her...get her advice about where to go from here...

'Really glad the appointment went well for you. Have phoned you several times and left messages as I'm not too good my self at the moment and could really use some company. Love you to bits. Fran X'.

Emily bit her lip as she read Fran's reply, the tone of which was in such stark contrast to the encouraging messages she'd just received from Kate, Jess and Mel.

She and Tom had had such a fabulous afternoon in Llangollen. Bunking off like a pair of school kids had been a brilliant idea. A bit of spontaneous fun was exactly what they'd needed to start getting themselves back on track, an element that had been sorely missing from their lives recently.

Thankfully, as it was midweek and so late in the season, Llangollen had been lovely and quiet, so, mindful of the fact that Emily wasn't exactly walking miles at the moment, they'd opted for the 'afternoon tea' canal cruise. Despite the nip in the air, they'd sat outside on the front of the boat, enjoying the autumn sunshine and peace as they glided through the scenic Welsh countryside. The highlight of the two hour cruise had been crossing the Pontcysyllte aqueduct, with the beautiful Ceiriog Valley spread out as far as the eye could see beneath them.

They had drawn steadily closer, at ease in each others company again by the time they got home. With only a handful of people on the boat, it had been an idyllic way to spend the afternoon.

Tom had just gone down to The Parade, to fetch an Indian and a bottle of wine to round the day off nicely, so the last thing Emily wanted to do right now was spoil the mood by picking up the phone and listening to an hour of Fran whinging ...whatever it was she wanted to bend her ear about was just going to have to wait until tomorrow now...

33

It only took a few minutes to complete the review of her medication and set up a repeat prescription, as the Ranitidine definitely seemed to be suiting her better than the proton pump inhibitors. Emily was just wondering how to broach the subject of the research she had been doing, when Doctor Morgan gave her the perfect opening.

"Have you had your appointment through for the MRI yet Emily?" She enquired as soon as she had finished entering the required information on the computer.

"Mmmm...It's a week today." Conscious of the waiting room full of patients, she wasn't sure if this was the right time to discuss her ongoing issues, or if she was supposed to make another appointment.

"And how did you get on with Neil Frobisher?"

"Brilliantly...He makes you feel as though he has all in the time in the world for you." Emily scrambled in her bag, quickly producing several sheets of paper. "I'm not sure what he put in his report to you but he let me have a copy of his notes." Emily turned the sheet of A4 at an angle so that they could both read the three columns.

"His report said pretty much the same- just in a rather more legible form." Dr Morgan smiled. She'd realised that Emily would probably have to wait a little longer to see him, but Neil was such a lovely, gentle guy, who always took the time to put his patients at ease, and seemed to possess a real gift for distinguishing between anxiety being caused by debilitating symptoms, and symptoms being caused by anxiety.

"He talked for quite a while about the two vitamin deficiencies, and to be honest, at the time, I was pretty dismissive, as I've always eaten a good varied diet, but I've been doing a bit of research since and it has been a real eye opener." Emily watched Dr Morgan's face carefully as she unfolded the relevant paragraphs she'd printed off.

The last thing she wanted to do now was step on the toes of this very thorough doctor, by telling her how to do her job, but the reading she'd been doing had been truly terrifying. This deficiency thing, which she had never even heard of, if left unchecked, wreaked absolute havoc in peoples' lives.

"This really isn't my area of expertise Emily, but I am aware that there is a great deal or research being done at the moment about the possible link between low B12 levels and dementia." Dr Morgan leaned forward, creating a steeple with her fingers as she read the facts and figures that Emily had so carefully produced.

"I've been reading case after case, of patients who have been fobbed off for years, told that they had some form of anxiety or depression, and then, by the time they eventually get a diagnosis, irreparable nerve damage has already been done, leaving them practically incontinent or using a mobility scooter."

"... and of course this would be so easy to treat too..." Dr Morgan mused as though speaking to her self, before she glanced up from the sheet of statistics and gave Emily a wry smile as she caught her eye. The two women laughed together simultaneously, realising that it was highly unusual for a doctor to actually be wishing a condition on to one of their patients.

Emily understood her thinking perfectly though. Compared to everything else on the list, a B12 deficiency would be a very welcome outcome as far as she was concerned.

"If the phlebotomist is still here, we could do a blood test today." Jane Morgan picked up her phone and had a brief conversation on an internal line, before she addressed Emily again.

"If you take a seat in the waiting room, Eileen will squeeze you in before she goes." She confirmed.

Emily was just on the point of standing to leave the room, but decided that as she'd got this far, she may as well finish what she'd started. She pointed to the last paragraph in which she'd highlighted some more figures.

"Apparently, in this country the accepted range is anywhere between 900 and 200, so you are not considered to be deficient unless you register below that. In Japan and many European countries, it is recognised that people can suffer from neurological problems when they register in the two or even three hundreds so they are now recommending four or five hundred as the minimum."

"Don't worry Emily. If your results come back the low end of normal, I will still contact Mr Frobisher and we'll go from there. I should get the results back in a couple of days- probably before you have the MRI- but please bear in mind that even if you are deficient that wouldn't automatically rule out M S, so please do keep an open mind for the time being." Doctor Morgan cautioned her patient not wanting to give any false hope.

Emily was sitting reading the paper while having her lunch, on her day off, when she got the phone call.
"Hi Emily. It's Jane Morgan from the surgery." Emily sat further back in her chair and took a deep breath. She'd never had a phone call from a doctor in her life before. What on earth had they found in her blood this time?
"I've had your results back this morning and you're reading is 195." The doctor paused, allowing the fact that her levels were officially under the recommended guide lines, even in this country, to fully sink in. "I've just spoken to Neil Frobisher, and as I suspected, he still wants you to go ahead with the MRI. He also wants you to start eating as much red meat, eggs, marmite, liver etc as you can for the next few weeks, and then we'll test you again, by which time, we should have your scan results back as well."
"Right...Ok...thank you so much...." Emily's head was reeling. Could it really be that simple, was the worrying finally over?
"Like I said before Emily, we have to keep an open mind until we have the MRI results." Doctor Morgan reiterated, "But Mr Frobisher was 'cautiously optimistic.' at this stage."
"Well that sounds good to me" Emily's voice was full of gratitude. "I'd better get down to Sainsbury's and buy up all their steak and liver then." she laughed, "Thank you so much for getting back to me so quickly... bye...bye-bye now...."
Emily sat staring up the garden for a full five minutes after she'd put the phone down. Of course she'd taken on board the fact that the consultant still wanted her to have the scan, so he obviously didn't considered her to be out of the woods just yet, but her gut instinct urged her to celebrate, to shout the news from the roof tops.

Of course she couldn't be sure that this meant she was actually going to get her life back on track, but, whatever the scan did or didn't reveal, the one thing today's results had proved beyond any doubt, was that she was NOT just loosing the plot.

Now she knew for certain that there really was a specific physical, underlying medical condition causing her mind and body to fail so badly ...Thank God for Jane Morgan and Neil Frobisher...who knew how much irreparable nerve damage she might have suffered if she'd just been left to plod on for much longer...

34

Emily sat patiently waiting in yet another hospital reception area, but at least this time, with a little bit of luck, today's procedure would provide the final piece of the puzzle.

Tom had really wanted to come with her this morning but she'd remained adamant that it would just be a waste of half a day. She'd been warned that the MRI itself was going to take about forty five minutes, so, by the time she'd changed, and the necessary paperwork had been double checked, he'd have been sitting here for at least an hour- assuming that her appointment ran to time. It wasn't as though they were likely to tell her anything today anyway...

Emily would much rather have him with her when she went to see Doctor Morgan for the results. She had been making a real effort to share her thoughts with Tom lately, good and bad, to include him as much as possible, as she'd come to realise that her attempts to protect him over the last few months had back fired somewhat spectacularly.

The afternoon they'd spent in Llangollen, had brought home to her just how deeply she was damaging their marriage by retreating into an isolation of her own making.

After Jane Morgan had called with her B12 results, she'd decided to pop and see Tom on her way to Sainsbury's, as he was currently working on an extension just down the road in Meole village. She'd wanted to share the brilliant news with him in person, rather than over the phone, but his reaction had actually been something of a wet blanket, deflating her sense of euphoria, as he'd cautioned her to wait for the scan results before pinning all her hopes on this one test.

Kath and Jess had both been equally as cautious when she'd shared the good news with them too. She understood where they were all coming from, that they only had her best interests at heart, were worried that she might just be building her self up for an almighty fall, but they simply didn't understand. None of them had spent the number of hours she had researching the numerous forums, reading story after story about the devastation this silent epidemic was causing in peoples lives. The more she had read the more certain she had become, that as soon as she was able to start the injections, she'd be as right as rain again, could start to get her old life back.

"Emily Mortimer?" The soft Irish lilt brought her out of her introspection and back to the matter in hand- to this last hurdle, which, from what she'd been told, was a far from pleasant one, especially for someone who dreaded being shut in a confined space as much as she did.

Emily couldn't help smiling as she followed the bustling middle aged lady through the double doors into the MRI suite. With her strong accent and classic Celtic colouring, she looked like she could have just stepped straight out of a Maeve Binchy novel, and the name displayed on her badge would have lent itself perfectly to such a character too.

Sheila Flaherty handed Emily a small plastic key, accompanied by a well practised reassuring smile, as she indicated the curtained cubicles behind them "If you'd like to put all your things in the locker and slip into one our designer gowns I'll be waiting for you right out here." She nodded towards the desk, upon which sat Emily's open file.

Sheila had been a radiographers' assistant for more years than she cared to remember, and particularly enjoyed being part of the close knit MRI team here in Shrewsbury. She'd learnt decades ago that there was nought as queer as folk, and never to judge a book by its cover in this job.

They had patients that wandered in looking like they were in the best of health and hadn't a care in the world, yet almost as soon she'd set them up correctly and the machinery began producing images, they'd discover a tumour the size of a melon. Others would come in full of woe, already preparing to meet their maker yet they wouldn't find a single thing wrong with them.

As she went through all the familiar checks with Emily, it was hard not to notice how much this bubbly smiley lady favoured her right leg when she walked, or how carefully she seemed to turn her head to avoid the disorientation that any sudden movement obviously caused her, and how awkwardly she nursed her left arm, so though she always offered up a little prayer for all her patients, Sheila had a strong feeling that the outcome of this scan was pretty much already preordained.

"Did you bring a CD with you love?" She asked Emily cheerfully.

"Oh yes... sorry I forgot...I've left it in my bag in the locker." Emily immediately jumped to her feet, conscious of wasting precious hospital time.

"No hurry. Do you want to get it for me now and then you can come on through- we do have a few here, but to be honest the choice is pretty dire." When Emily handed her 'Glimpses of Glory' a moment of two later Sheila's round florid face lit up with pleasure. "Ooh...this is one of my all time favourites- I brought it at a Christian festival in Minehead about ten years ago." She smiled remembering the event fondly.

"Spring harvest?" Emily guessed correctly, the instant connection allowing the two women to jabber away quite animatedly, comparing their favourite tracks and worship leaders while Sheila continued her preparations.

"OK Emily. Can you have a good wiggle for me now, and make sure I've got the pillow in the right place for you, and that you are perfectly comfortable." Emily gingerly did as she was bid.

"That feels fine." She assured the older woman quietly.

"Because you are going to be on your back, you will be more aware of the machinery clanking around you. Would you like me to put the blindfold on, or would you be happier just closing your eyes?" Sheila asked gently.

Emily swallowed hard. This lovely lady had been a real God send, brilliant at getting her to relax and almost forget about the cylinder behind her that the table was about to slide into. She had to lie, without moving, for about thirty minutes while they scanned her brain. Sheila would then come back and change her position, and she would need to lie still for another fifteen minutes while they scanned her spine. Wouldn't a blindfold just make her feel even more trapped and hemmed in?

"I think I'll try without if that's OK." She replied hesitantly her face suddenly blanching.

"Remember you can speak to me any time if you need a break, and I can talk to you through the headphones too. I will be interrupting your music every now and then just to check you are still OK Emily"

She touched her hand briefly, before she pressed the button and the table started to glide backwards. This was the point at which some patients actually flipped out completely and they couldn't continue, but as she watched Emily close her eyes, she had absolutely no doubt that this pretty little woman's prayers were winging their way heavenwards, alongside her own...

35

Emily watched Josh and Holly wolfing down the mound of lasagne she'd just put in front of them through narrowed eyes. Her pleasure at having them home for the weekend was tinged with anxiety. The way they were shovelling their food down, it looked as though they hadn't eaten for days, which immediately caused Emily to start fretting over whether they were feeding themselves' properly.

"So how is Michelle settling in then?" She asked warily, broaching her other major topic of concern- what did any of them really know about this stranger who had moved in with her children? She might have the morals of an alley cat for all they knew.

"Mmmm...Yeah... really well..." Josh mumbled, through an enormous mouthful of pasta. "We hardly even notice she's there most of the time to be honest. She goes home pretty much every weekend, and we don't see that much of her in the week either, as she works at a bistro most evenings. I don't think we could have asked for an easier person to share with Mum."

"We've already told her we're happy to make the arrangement permanent, even though the trial period isn't up for a few weeks yet." Holly chipped in, while sprinkling more parmesan liberally over what was left on her plate, "She's in her first year, the same as me, but because she's twenty five she's classed as a mature student. Apparently she was married at twenty, and divorced at twenty four, so she's decided she wants to make a completely fresh start as a teacher. She's not remotely interested in the social side of university life, and as she has her own car she drives back to Whitchurch most Fridays, which means we get the house to ourselves over the weekend. She's already offered to give us a lift as far as her house, but unfortunately, at the moment, our timetables don't really tally. She hasn't got any lectures on a Friday afternoon or a Monday morning, so she gets a much longer weekend break than either of us two."

Tom smiled indulgently enjoying having his daughters' rapid babble filling the kitchen again. Much like her mother, Holly barely seemed to draw breath whenever she spoke. He was relieved to hear that it was working out so well with the young woman they'd chosen though, as this had been the one area in which he and Emily had disagreed.

Because he'd interviewed so many potential employees over the years, and had learnt to spot the difference between somebody telling you what they actually thought, and someone just telling you what they thought you wanted to hear, Emily had been really keen for him to sit in on the interviews. He didn't dig his heels in very often, but he had been unmovable on this point. As they were already making life considerably easier for the kids for the next few years, he felt very strongly that they ought to make this crucial decision for them selves. Selecting the right person from the handful that had applied was a vital part of the learning curve as far as he was concerned, especially as they were the ones who would be living with the consequences- literally!

"And how is your course work going Holly?" Tom asked his daughter pointedly. She'd been waxing lyrical about how well she was settling in and all the friends she was making, but just like when she'd been at school and college, the academic side barely got a mention.

Josh had always worked really hard to maintain pretty much straight A's, but Holly, being more of a social butterfly, had done just enough to get by and settled for B's and C's. Not particularly academic themselves he and Emily had never been pushy parents. They'd agreed years ago that they'd rather have happy rounded popular kids, than a couple of A* geeks, but, he didn't want Holly to throw away this chance to give herself opportunities in the future.

"So far so good dad- I'm really enjoying the tutorials and the few assignments I've completed have received pretty good grades. Josh has been giving me a few pointers about what actually gets the marks up, and even though I know very little of what we do this year will actually count towards my degree, it's still all good practice." She replied.

Tom reeled back in his chair, more surprised by her studious tone than the actual words. Was this really the same girl who'd spent most of her A-level revision time topping up her tan in the garden? She'd been away barely two months, yet the changes were already blatantly clear, and her next words only confirmed her growing maturity as far as he was concerned.

"So how are you getting on with the new medication then mum?" This more adult version of their daughter shifted the conversation deftly, just as she'd been itching to do from the moment she'd walked through the front door an hour ago.

Mum had phoned them the evening she'd received her results, emphatically assuring them that there was absolutely nothing to worry about now, as the scan had been clear. She'd gone on to explain about the vitamin deficiency that had been diagnosed, making it sound as though it was really easy to treat, but she and Josh had done a bit of research of their own since then.

Though they accepted that the outcome was undeniably good news when compared with the alternatives, they had found it really hard to get their heads around this whole B12 thing, struggling to comprehend how such an innocuous sounding condition could cause so much damage.

Though Mum had been making light of her symptoms and all the various tests she'd been having, neither of them had been remotely fooled. You didn't have to be a brain surgeon to work out the most likely cause of their mothers' rapid decline in health, especially when it was superseded by a neurological appointment and then a swift MRI Scan.

They'd been pretty much steeling themselves for an MS diagnosis, despite their parents' best efforts to protect them, so consequently, they were in need of a great deal of reassurance that they were actually being told the whole truth now.

"I can't believe how much things have improved already." Emily answered truthfully, still finding it hard to credit that the tablets could have made such a difference after just two weeks. She could see that the kids were not entirely convinced, that they wondered if she was still being a little economical with the truth, and it was a reaction Emily was getting used to...Everybody seemed to be sceptical about this diagnosis, as they questioned the feasibility of something as simple as a vitamin deficiency causing so much damage.

As soon as Jane Morgan had summoned her and Tom through from the waiting room, it had been obvious from her expression that she had good news for them. She hadn't kept them waiting a moment longer than necessary, beginning to speak as soon as they had followed her into the consulting room.

"I won't get the written report for a week or two yet, but Mr Frobisher has confirmed that the MRI was clear. We've also had the second blood test back and the reading has gone up very slightly to 205, which is actually very significant." She informed them, looking incredibly pleased.

"I assume the second test was to see if it was worth trying me with oral supplements rather than injections?" Emily asked, trying hard to concentrate on following the doctors' words about treatment, rather than just giving in to the sense of utter relief that was coursing through her as Tom tightened his grip on her hand.

"You have been doing your research." Jane Morgan acknowledged happily. "As you've no doubt read, the usual course of treatment would be to start you on injections, every other day for a couple of weeks, and then once we have your levels back up to normal, you would continue with injections every three months for the rest of your life." She paused for a moment to allow this information to sink in. "The only disadvantage of this treatment, is that towards the end of the three month period, as your levels drop again, the symptoms tend to return. Mr Frobisher has had a lot of success trialling patients with very high oral doses and, as long as you agree Emily, that is what we would like to try."

Jane Morgan had gone on to explain that although the suggested dose was a staggering forty thousand times the RDA, Emily would only be able to absorb a tiny amount, and because it was soluble, the rest would simply pass through.

Every morning for the past two weeks, as she swallowed the tiny little pink tablet, she thanked God that she had been so incredibly fortunate, compared to so many of the people she'd read about on line who had suffered for years.

Within days she'd felt her head starting to clear a little, as though it was slowly being reconnected to her body again. Her thoughts no longer seemed to be swimming in fog and her stomach felt entirely different too. It was hard to explain, but the constant churning sensation- like a washing machine on final spin- had completely gone now.

She was still having issues with her balance and the numbness in her hands and feet was still causing co-ordination problems, but not as acutely as before. Best of all, the heavy mantle of fear had been completely lifted from her shoulders. She was gradually going to get her life back...she and Tom had a future to plan for again...

36

As soon as James stepped through the unlocked French windows, he knew he was in way over his head. He cursed himself for being so naive- bloody arrogant actually. He had truly believed that he could pull Fran back from the brink, before she hit the self destruct button, just because he had been there himself.

He had never turned up at her house on speck before, but he'd been unable to shake the feeling that something was desperately wrong during his drive home. This sense of unease had been growing steadily more urgent over the last few days, as Fran continued to ignore his calls, so he'd decided to trust his instincts...

He'd honestly had no idea that her drinking had become so bad. Clearly her problems were not going to be solved by the 'band aids' he'd been so glibly applying. She needed professional help, but how was he supposed to convince her to reach out to other recovering alcoholics for support, when he'd let her down so spectacularly.

He'd genuinely believed that when Fran had listened to his own fall from grace so intently, agreed to take the job at the shop, and started joining him for days out that didn't evolve around drink, she was taking the first all important steps in the right direction. He'd been so sure that all she needed was somebody to show a bit of faith in her, to lend her a hand in getting her life back on track, offer her a bit of a 'leg up' ...

"A leg up..." Fran spat back at him now, looking like a rabbit caught in headlights. "And what do you get in return James? A leg over..."

James recoiled from the white hot fury. Her tone was pure venom, making him instantly regret the unfortunate phrase he'd chosen while trying to justify his unannounced, and obviously unwelcome presence in her house- to explain why he'd continued knocking for a good ten minutes, before eventually letting himself in around the back.

As soon as he'd seen the pathetic state of her and the diabolic mess the house was in, he'd been transported back to a place he'd done his level best to erase from his memory.

He knew exactly what she was trying to do now. He'd done the same thing himself often enough. If you pushed hard enough, most people eventually went away, allowing you to carry on drinking. He was obviously going to have to dig very deep, push aside his own emotions.

"I think we both know that is never going to happen Fran..." He tried to keep his tone light to ease the heavy atmosphere in the room, but it was desperately hard when she'd inadvertently hit a very raw nerve.

Fran stared at him intently for a few seconds without blinking, before she slowly began to undo the buttons of her stained shirt.

"Isn't this what you really want though James...what all men want in the end..?" She rasped a look of abject misery clouding her eyes, as she stepped forward pushing her full breasts up against him.

Every fibre of his being clamoured to just hold her, to comfort her, to teach her that it doesn't always have to be about sex, that, if she could just learn to value her self, then other people would start to follow suit. What he actually did was turn away abruptly, so that she couldn't see the raw emotion in his own eyes. His voice sounded so much harsher than he'd intended when he eventually spoke.

"I'm going to go and make some coffee while you have a shower Fran." He stated emphatically, his tone brooking no room for argument.

With one of the mercurial mood swings that he was growing accustomed to, the palpable aggression that had been filling the room from the moment he'd stepped in through the French window, suddenly dissolved into hysterical laughter.

"I've just offered to go to bed with you, and you're basically turning me down because I stink!" She slurred, before eventually making her way up the stairs, like a recalcitrant child doing as she was told.

Hand on heart, James could honestly say his motives had been one hundred percent altruistic when he'd first ridden in on his white charger- obviously a woman like Fran would never look at someone like him twice. He'd recognised that Fran was in serious trouble when they'd met at Tom's birthday party a few months ago, and simply thought he might be able to help. Socially ex-drinkers could be even more of a pain in the arse than ex-smokers, always monitoring other peoples' relationships with the demon drink.

Initially, he had been motivated by nothing more than the desire to prevent someone else from tipping over the edge. Over the last few weeks, as he'd got to know the funny, spontaneous, vulnerable, self deprecating mix that was the real Fran- the Fran that was kept very well hidden behind the rather scary persona she presented to the world- he'd found himself really looking forward to the time they spent together.

He'd realised he was in deep trouble, in danger of crossing the line a couple of weeks ago. They'd had one of those classic clichéd, mills and boons scenes- the moment when the beautiful heroin suddenly sees the ordinary dependable bloke in a new light.

He'd just been putting the finishing touches to the C.V. he was trying to create for her, and her face had lit up like a little girls' at Christmas, when she'd read the finished article.

"Is that really me? She'd laughed looking slightly incredulous, "I think someone should snap me up immediately." She'd been kneeling on the floor, smiling up at him, her face just inches from his own as he lent over the lap top.

It wasn't just gratitude that he'd seen in her eyes, and he'd known with absolute certainty, that if he'd leant forward just a fraction, she'd have welcomed his kiss.

Thank God he'd followed his head and not his heart, standing up quickly to diffuse the mood. The last thing she needed right now was someone else abandoning her, and James knew full well, that if he ever blurred the lines he would no longer be in a position to help her. All Fran could cope with in her life right now was a friend... someone she could depend on who demanded nothing from her...

37

Before she even opened her eyes, Fran was aware of the weight of another body beside her. Though this was hardly the first time she'd woken up with a stranger in her bed, it was the first time she couldn't even remember having left the house. Where the hell had she gone? What on earth had she got up to last night?

She rolled onto her back very cautiously, partly because every movement aggravated the clogs dancing in her head, and also because she was in no particular hurry to discover just how low she might have sunk this time.

Finding James snoring away next to her was a huge relief, though it took a moment or two to register, that, as he was lying on top of the duvet fully clothed it was highly unlikely that they'd shared a night of unbridled passion. She wasn't quite sure if that pleased or disappointed her?

Sipping gingerly, from the pint of water that had been placed on the cabinet beside her, she waited a moment or two for the nausea to pass, before slumping back down onto the pillows.

She had no idea of the time as neither her watch, or her phone, seemed to be anywhere in sight. To be honest, she'd had very little concept of day or night since the weekend as she hadn't left the house or bothered to draw the curtains.

Generally, at this time of year, if she stayed in bed till lunchtime, it hardly seemed worth getting dressed when it would be dark again by four. Snuggled on the sofa, wrapped in a duvet, was the only place to be when she felt this low. There came a point beyond which she could no longer plaster on her best smile, and pretend to the world that she was 'fine'.

As always, it had been an amalgamation of little things that had dragged her down, but it was seeing Simon making such an almighty fuss over Zoe that had finally pushed her over the edge, stirred up all the old resentments, the comparisons that inevitably sucked her back into the pit of despair.

She'd had high blood pressure when she'd been pregnant with Scarlett, but of course she'd just been told to rest and get on with it, unlike his precious Zoe, who'd been admitted to hospital and had everyone running round like headless chickens.

Simon had looked as white as a sheet, with huge dark circles under his eyes, when he'd dropped Scarlett off on Sunday so that he could spend the day at the hospital with Zoe. Throughout the years that they'd been married, and bearing in mind everything she had gone through, he'd never looked so utterly distraught about her well being.

All the old familiar feelings of rejection had immediately started clamouring to be heard, the humiliation rising to the fore again, as acute as though it were yesterday. It had been hard enough to come to terms with the fact that sensible dependable Simon was having an affair, let alone that, when confronted and given an ultimatum, he'd chosen someone as mousey and boring as Zoe over her.

Fran cast a shy, sideways glance at James's reassuring bulk on the bed beside her, cringing as the vivid images of being wrapped tightly in his arms, flooded her befuddled brain.

'Oh God' she mouthed silently as the hazy memories continued to take shape. He must have lain beside her for hours, listening to the endless tirade, as she purged herself of the pent up, long buried string of rejections she'd suffered. Once she'd started, it was like a damn bursting and she hadn't been able to stop. She'd spewed it all out, starting with the way her mum had abandoned her and Chrissie, how her dad had pushed her away as she became more like Angie, and then finally, Simon deserting her and Scarlett to shack up with Zoe. She'd gone on to explain that her own daughter no longer wanted to live with her, and her best friend seemed to have abandoned her now she had her own health issues to deal with.

She closed her eyes again feeling utterly mortified, as though, like a young child playing hide and seek, the action would make her invisible. She was beginning to wish that this had been one of those binges when the blackout was so severe that she didn't have to face the shame of recalling her actions.

She cringed again as remembered sharing every minute detail of her last phone call with Emily, ranting about how hurt she'd been that, because her kids were home for the weekend, her best friend couldn't make a little bit of time for her. Though she'd done her level best to be there for Emily during these last few months, it would seem that she wasn't prepared to return the favour and offer Fran a little bit of support when she so desperately needed it.

"I'm going to let you go now Fran, otherwise we're just going to fall out." She'd stated firmly, cutting Fran off when she'd tried to point out that Josh and Holly would be there all weekend, and that she was merely asking for an hour or two of her oldest friends' time because she was really struggling right now and had nobody else to turn to.

James had simply listened to her hysterical ramblings. He hadn't tried to rationalise or offer solutions, the way Emily always felt compelled to do, yet she could clearly recall the words he'd spoken, just before she'd finally given in to exhaustion and drifted off to sleep in his arms.

"When you're looking at the world through the end of a bottle, it does feel as though everyone else is living the high life, while you're wading about in the brown stuff doesn't it." There had been no trace of judgement, no censure in his tone. He'd simply been there before her and knew how it felt.

Had James just fallen asleep too she wondered, or had he stayed to keep an eye on her- make sure she didn't start drinking again? Either way, she felt strangely nervous about facing him when he woke up. She'd never been held like that in her life, never felt so safe, so unthreatened in any man's arms, almost as though she belonged there, but how on earth was she supposed to treat him now, having bared her soul to him so unreservedly.

Should she simply carry on as normal, handle this the way she usually did, by pretending that nothing had happened, studiously ignoring the consequences of one of her binges?

Right from the beginning she had been struggling with the nature of this relationship- with being James' 'friend'. It was so alien to her, and just a week or two ago, when they'd been working on her CV, she'd been so sure that he was going to kiss her. Fat chance of that now! He was hardly likely to want to get involved with a complete and utter basket case was he? She'd be lucky if he still wanted to know her at all after last night.

She felt the heat suffusing her face again, her humiliation complete, as she recalled the way she'd spoken to him when he'd first pushed his way in, lashing out at him in shame at having been found in such squalor.

She'd practically thrown herself at him, behaved like some sort of cheap lap dancer, rubbing herself up against him as she started to undress. The way he'd turned away in disgust, instructing her to go and have a shower, would be indelibly carved on her memory for ever... yet another rejection... but this time she knew that she'd undoubtedly asked for it.

38

Like the majority of lads his age, Josh hadn't been particularly keen on the idea of a twenty first birthday party when the idea was first mooted. He'd never really seen the point of the whole 'well done for having lived x amount of years thing.'

To be honest, he would far rather have had a night out with his mates, and a simple family meal, but celebrating this 'milestone' birthday seemed to mean a great deal to his mum so he'd just gone along with it.

After all the crap she'd been through lately, he'd been more than happy to fall in with her wishes, as in reality, all that had been required of him so far, was to turn up and pretend to be impressed with a load of naff presents- did anyone his age actually need an engraved tankard, let alone three of them.

The stack of cards, containing cheques or cash, was a real bonus though. He'd bought all the books he needed this year second hand, but they were still costing him a small fortune.

Of course he'd had to endure the obligatory cringe-worthy greetings from relatives, and friends of his parents, who he hadn't seen for years. By the time the third bottle of bud had been placed in his hand, without him having made a single trip to the bar, it had become a whole lot easier to welcome the late arrivals- he even managed not to recoil too obviously when Fran pulled him into one of the totally inappropriate, bone crushing hugs, he'd done anything to avoid in his teens.

"I've put a cheque in the card for you Josh, as I thought you'd probably prefer that." She yelled over the music, which the DJ had just cranked up in a bid to get the first brave souls onto the little dance floor.

"All right Josh?" The guy standing next to Fran extending his hand did seem vaguely familiar, but Josh couldn't quite place him. As though reading his mind, James tactfully filled in the blanks for the young lad.

"James Marsden, I used to take care of the menagerie you guys had when you were kids." He reminded him easily.

"Oh right...yeah...of course." Josh recalled his mum describing how compassionate James had been, when they had to have Molly put to sleep not long after he left for Uni. He also remembered the time they'd phoned the practice, laughing about the fact that 'Honey'- Holly's rabbit- was staggering around the garden as though she'd been on the beers.

They'd been told to bring the poor thing down to the surgery immediately, and after James had finished gently explaining how serious a middle ear infection could be for a rabbit, he'd prescribed a strong course of antibiotics. Mum and Holly had stayed up all night, attempting to dribble water and antibiotics into the rolling bundle of fluff, and somehow, Honey had defied the odds and pulled though.

Compared to a lot of his Uni mates, he and his sister had had such a charmed idyllic childhood, which typically, they'd just taken for granted when they was younger. It was only now that they appreciated, that, having parents who still actually seemed to like each other was something of a rarity amongst theirs piers.

Because they'd both attended just one primary, and then one secondary school, they were still in touch with friends they'd known all their lives- unlike their mother.

Although Mum never really talked about her own childhood, unless pushed, it was pretty evident that it had been the polar opposite of his. She'd been moved from pillar to post so many times, that Josh had actually asked her to count how many schools she'd been to once. He couldn't remember the exact figure now, but it had definitely run into double digits. He'd never heard his mother bad mouthing her parents, but the facts did kind of speak for themselves.

As a kid he'd never really given any thought to the fact that he usually saw his Nan and Granddad a couple of times a week, whereas he only saw his 'other grandparents'- as he and Holly called them- about twice a year. He wondered if mum had even bothered mentioning this party to them, as the usual bland card had arrived this morning- a day late- with the standard ten pound note in it...Auntie Joanna's card had arrived on the day, and though the message inside was as impersonal as always, she had included a far more generous cheque than usual...

"Good to see you James...How're you doing?" Emily waited for Tom to stop enthusiastically pumping James's hand before she stepped forward to give him a warm embrace.

After hugging them both herself, Fran stood back a little, watching Emily and Tom chatting away to James as the three of them did a quick catch up. She kept studiously avoiding the curious glances that Emily kept darting her way, obviously keen to get the story behind her choice of 'plus one'.

"I hope you don't mind me tagging along," James dropped in casually, as though reading her mind, "Fran has been keeping me company at school events lately, so I don't turn up looking like Billy-no-mates, and I offered to return the complement this evening."

How did he manage to do that, Fran wondered? He always made everything sound so uncomplicated, so above board. She would have got all defensive, insisting far too vehemently that they were 'just friends', and thereby giving Emily the entirely wrong impression. To be blunt though, whatever direction their relationship was or wasn't heading, it was no one's business but their own...

She was really glad that she'd eventually decided to mention this party to James now. There was nothing worse than arriving at this type of event on your own, and though she didn't intend to stay for very long, at least now she'd be able to say she'd shown her face. She always had every intention of coming when she accepted the invitation, but would then spend the entire day worrying about what to wear and who she was going to talk to, until eventually she cried off at the last minute claiming a sudden illness.

As they headed over to speak to another cluster of friends that James clearly knew very well, Fran began to realise just how much his social life must have been interwoven with Tom and Emily's, before his divorce.

She felt the usual dread sweeping over her as they approached the group, and took a huge gulp of red wine to steady her nerves. She always found it hard to make small talk in this kind of setting, as she had so little of worth to contribute. She always felt as though these professional types were looking down their noses at her, just waiting for her to trip up, and she didn't have to wait long before the inevitable question, that she'd come to hate with a vengeance, was aimed in her direction.

"So what do you do Frances?" With her mouth full of wine as she'd just drained her glass, Fran felt the gaze of the entire group resting on her, as she faced the classic ice-breaker that was guaranteed to reduce her to nothing in their eyes.

"Fran has been a full time mum for a few years, but she's recently done some voluntary work to refresh her C V." James cut in smoothly, giving her a moment to compose herself, and a way into the conversation. His answer appeared to have created a general air of admiration, rather than the haughty dismissal that usually occurred at this point.

Just as he had done while creating her CV, he seemed to have this uncanny knack of turning around every thing she saw as negative in her life, and presenting it as a positive- just like on Saturday morning.

When he'd eventually woken up-after her spectacular demonstration of just how low she could sink- instead of running for the hills at the earliest opportunity, he'd stayed the entire weekend- sleeping in Scarlet's room, of course. Fran had well and truly got the message that he had no interest in being anything more than her friend now, so she definitely wouldn't be making that mistake again...

James had popped out to the local Co-op and brought a whole pile of food, as though it was the most natural thing in the world. He'd then disappeared into her tiny kitchen and produced an impressive brunch for the pair of them. If he'd asked her before he started cooking, she'd have said it was the last thing she wanted, but actually as soon as they began to demolish the mounds of food he'd prepared, she'd started to feel a whole lot better.

He'd been so matter of fact, sharing the humiliations of his own downfall with her in such an open manner, she'd felt incredibly humbled by his honesty. Simon had always been so stoic, such a closed book who shared very little of him self, and her previous boyfriends had all tended to be such Neanderthals they'd hardly been into deep-and-meaningful exchanges either. James was the only person who actually seemed to get it, who understood that she didn't consciously choose to live like this.

He'd talked a great deal about the period in which he'd continued resisting any professional help, still hanging on to the belief that he wasn't some sad old wino- that he could stop drinking whenever he chose to- he simply didn't want to just yet.

She'd listened intently when he'd gone on to describe how he'd eventually been persuaded to attend an 'open' meeting, explaining exactly what that meant, and how shocked he'd been by the amount of 'normal' people from all walks of life that had been there. As soon as he'd began to describe his shame, his fear that he'd be exposed by someone he knew, she understood the point of an open meeting, a meeting that could be attended by anyone with an interest in learning about AA, rather than a closed meeting, which was purely for alcoholics.

If you were able to convince yourself that you were only attending out of curiosity, if you passed yourself off as a relative of someone with a problem, or maybe a professional attending for research purposes, then you wouldn't have to admit to anyone- even yourself- that you had a problem...

Fran and James made their excuses and left the party with all the oldies, almost as soon as Tom's short speech was over and the cake had been cut. As she watched them go, Emily had a very perplexed expression on her face, which fully reflected her less than charitable take on the situation.

"So what do you make of that then?" She asked Tom looking up at him expectantly.

"Ummm?" he blinked back at her somewhat blankly, having just sunk another pint.

"Fran and James?" Emily prompted him, exasperatedly.

"Well like he said...it sounds as though they're just keeping each other company now and again...don't tell me you're matchmaking already... you'll be planning to invite them round for a meal next?" Tom teased.

That was the last thing Emily intended to do. She actually felt decidedly put out that Fran hadn't even told her she was bringing James to the party. Presumably he was also the mystery friend who'd been helping with the decorating, and found her that job in the charity shop? She honestly couldn't put a name to the emotions that the idea of them sharing any sort of relationship stirred up in her, but she did know she wouldn't be fanning the flames any time soon.

What on earth was James doing...it was a classic case of out of the frying pan into the fire! Grace had been pretty high maintenance, but life with her would have been a stroll in the park, compared to the prospect of sharing his days with someone as volatile as Fran.

When it all went wrong- which inevitably it would- no doubt, she'd be the one expected to answer the phone at all hours of the day or night, listening to the same old self pitying ramblings. She'd been doing a great deal of thinking in the last few weeks and the bottom line was, she was no longer prepared to be Fran's whipping boy...things were going to change...

Of course every woman knew the rules. It might be considered OK to dump a boyfriend, or even divorce a husband, when you realised you'd outgrown the relationship, but friends were a different kettle of fish altogether. Unless they moved away, or emigrated, you were pretty much stuck with them, no matter how much of a trial the friendship might have become. The only solution in a situation like this was to gradually scale down the unhealthy dependency, and that was exactly what Emily needed to start doing now...for both their sakes...

Encouraged by her close friends and family- the people who genuinely cared about her- Emily had had to give priority to her own health issues recently. Consequently, there had been a rather abrupt withdrawal of the support she usually gave to Fran.

She'd finally stopped dancing to her friend's tune, had no longer been at her beck and call 24/7, and the world hadn't come to an end so far had it? If she wasn't around to pick up the pieces all the time, then inevitably Fran would have to learn to fend for herself a little more.

Now that she was starting to get her life back on track again, she was absolutely determined not to just let things slide back to the way they had been. She wasn't about to pick up the mantle of responsibility again and allow a friendship that had become little more than a burden most of the time, to bleed her dry.

Of course they'd stay in touch, see each other from time to time. There was no need for any big dramatic bust up, but her twenty one year old son had been right- what was the point of spending a huge percentage of her free time in the company of someone she no longer enjoyed being with?

The last few months had taught Emily that life was extremely precious, far too short to waste propping up somebody who took you for granted, treated you with a total lack of respect, and sapped the life blood out of you...it was time to let go...to lay down the burden that she had been carrying for far too many years...

39

Emily was feeling really pleased with her self as she waved goodbye to Fran, and turned her attention to reversing out of one of the ridiculously narrow spaces in Dobbies car park. She was still wearing the same slightly smug expression as she merged into the heavy traffic on the bypass and headed down to the Retail Park. She was determined to tick off the last few awkward Christmas presents remaining on her list- the one's for all the men in her life, naturally.

If she just stuck to her guns, in exactly the same way as she had today, then lessening Fran's unhealthy dependency on her was going to prove a lot more straightforward than she'd imagined. In the last couple of weeks, the only responses she'd made to Fran's frequent calls had been a couple of short practical text. Emily simply wasn't allowing herself to get embroiled in Fran's issues, and she was proud of how neatly she'd managed to side-step the histrionics so far.

Zoe had apparently had the baby a few weeks early, and Scarlett had moved back in with her dad 'to help', but typically, Fran still came first, last and in the middle. Despite Fran's considerable efforts to get her to go over 'to relax', Emily had stuck rigidly to the suggestion of meeting for a coffee.

"Why don't you come over this way and make it lunch instead?" Fran had urged yet again this morning, just an hour or so before they were due to meet. "We haven't had a proper catch up in ages and I've loads to tell you." She'd whined, but still Emily hadn't faltered for a moment.

"To be honest Fran I've got loads of Christmas shopping to finish off today, so I've only really got an hour or so. It would be pretty stupid to spend most of that driving so I'll meet you in the foyer at eleven OK?" Her take it or it leave it tone had brooked no argument. To be truthful she didn't really care that much whether Fran showed up or not. If she took offence and suddenly developed 'car trouble' (it was a bit too late to be ill even by Fran's standards.) Emily would be quite happy, as it would mean she'd have more time to get her last minute presents finished.

It was as though someone had finally flicked a switch in her head, allowing Emily to see that Fran could only weigh her down by transferring responsibility onto her shoulders if she allowed her to. She'd had a similar 'light bulb' moment with regard to her parents many years ago, suddenly realising that they could only hurt her by their lack of involvement, if she gave them the power to do so.

Having banged her head against that particular brick wall for way too long, she'd eventually learnt to accept that the 'out of sight out of mind' approach they'd always adopted with their daughters, was obviously going to be carried over into the next generation too, and there was absolutely nothing she could do to change that.

She'd had to make a choice back then, just as she was doing now, to mentally shift someone to a place where they could no longer hurt her. She stopped building her self up for the inevitable let downs that had punctuated every milestone in the first few years of the children's lives. If you expected absolutely nothing from someone, then they couldn't disappoint you could they?

She'd learnt the hard way that you can only be responsible for your side of any relationship. You can't fundamentally change someone, make them into the person you would like them to be, and you only cause yourself a great deal of heartache when you try.

The whole point of this morning had been to break the pattern, to have a short causal meeting in a public place to establish a very different, much lighter tone. Every time the conversation had been in danger of veering off down the familiar, heavy,' me-me-me' path, Emily had simply changed the subject...

"Damn...Damn...Damn.". Fran banged the flat of her hand against the steering wheel in frustration, as she saw the blue lights flashing in her rear view mirror. Could today possibly get any worse?

She'd been so engrossed in analysing what had just taken place with Emily, that she had absolutely no idea how long the police car might have been following her. Surely she couldn't have been doing that much over the speed limit? If she hadn't been so stressed out about Emily, wondering why on earth she'd been acting so weirdly this morning, she'd have had her mind on her driving.

She plastered on her best smile as soon as she saw it was a middle aged male officer approaching the car. A bit of charm had dug her out of no end of scrapes in the past. She moistened her lips and ran her fingers through her hair, widening her eyes appealingly before she climbed out of the car.

"I'm so sorry officer." She purred. "Was I going a little over the limit? I've just come from a hospital appointment so my mind might not have been on my driving quite as much as it should have been." She improvised, fixing him with a doleful look from the big almond eyes that she'd always been told were her best feature.

"Oh right...I hope it wasn't anything too serious." He responded pleasantly enough, giving her a fleeting moments hope that she could talk her way out of a fine.

"I've been following you since the Abbey Foregate junction." He went on studying her intently. "You were in the wrong lane and didn't indicate before you pulled over." He informed her, already busy checking the vehicle and seemingly impervious to her sultry smile. "In the weeks before Christmas we pull over anyone who is driving erratically." He went on before calmly informing her that he required her to blow into the machine that he was about to retrieve from the car.

Fran was still pondering on the irony of being pulled over, on one of the few occasions when she genuinely had only been for a coffee, when the light on the machine changed colour and she found herself being issued with a caution on the side of the road in full view of every passing vehicle...

40

Emily couldn't wait to get the kettle on as she unloaded the boot and opened the front door. The crowds had been absolutely horrendous, so the brief shopping trip she'd been planning had turned into a mammoth expedition.

Feeling like a pack horse as she made her way down the hall juggling all her purchases, she was more than ready to put her feet up with a well earned cuppa. She'd no sooner dumped the bags on the kitchen table and picked up the kettle, when the land line began to ring. A quick glance at caller display was enough to reassure her she didn't need to pick up the call, but she'd barely managed to fill the kettle, before her mobile started vibrating in her bag.

She sighed heavily, wondering what on earth could have happened in the few short hours since she'd left Fran, to warrant a string of missed calls and text messages.

So much for her smug self congratulations earlier, she thought to herself as she took a deep breath and dug deep before accepting the call...it was all well and good taking this tougher stance, but she'd never forgive herself if she ignored a genuine cry for help...

"So now, on top of everything else it looks like I'm going to loose my licence..." Fran made no attempt to disguise her anger as she gave Emily chapter and verse. The accusatory edge to her voice made it more than obvious, that she was trying to blame Emily for the fact that she'd been arrested and carted off to the police station. The implication was crystal clear. If Emily had gone over for lunch as Fran had suggested, she wouldn't be in this mess now, wouldn't have been treated like a common criminal, and released on bale to appear in court in a few weeks.

Emily had just listened without interrupting, until the self pitying tirade eventually came to an end. She bit back her initial confusion over the fact that they'd only been drinking coffee. This was Fran she was speaking to, not one of her more conventional friends and for all she knew, she was probably washing her cornflakes down with vodka these days.

"Maybe it will turn out to be a blessing in disguise." Emily improvised, clutching at straws, knowing she was obliged to throw something into the deafening silence now echoing down the line.

What she was really thinking was that, if Fran had tested positive at such a random time of the day, then surely it was in everyone's best interest if she was off the road, but she was pretty sure this was hardly the right time to be sharing that particular nugget of wisdom.

"You've been saying for ages that your car is totally unreliable and you can't afford to run it. If you take it off the road, think of all the money you'll save from the tax and insurance." She threw in a bit desperately.

"Oh that's a great help Emily. I'll be playing right into Scarlett's hands then won't I? She hasn't come home once since the baby was born. If I haven't got the car to give her lifts, then that will be just another excuse she can throw at me to justify moving in with her dad permanently. Simon really is going to start questioning what he's actually paying maintenance for soon, especially now that he has another mouth to feed...."

Emily was struggling to follow Fran's garbled logic, let alone her slurred delivery, and she knew she would just be wasting her time trying to come up with any solutions when Fran was in this mood. It was obvious she'd been drinking heavily, despite the nature of her arrest this morning.

"Simon has always been very good about supporting you and Scarlett..." Emily began firmly "I don't think he would-

"You really don't get it do you?" Fran snapped at her. "Zoe has given him the son that I couldn't." She snarled, her voice rising to a screech by the end of the sentence.

Here we go. Emily gritted her teeth as she half listened to the warped, self centred familiar diatribe that followed. She continued calmly sipping her tea while settling herself into the recliner chair that was placed right by the window, drinking in her favourite view across the length of the garden.

"I suppose I was hoping that when they actually had the baby, Scarlett might get her nose pushed out of joint a bit and want to come home." Fran whaled "but now she says she's going to spend Christmas there too. James is in Ireland, and if I can't even drive to my sister's I'll probably just end up sitting here on my own with a microwave meal."

From her new position of detachment, Emily actually struggled not to laugh at the melodramatics, let alone the less than subtle angling for an invitation to be picked up and brought over to their house for Christmas dinner. There was absolutely no way she was going to ask Tom to be out on the road ferrying Fran back and to on Christmas day, besides which, it was one of the few years that it was just going to be the four of them, as they weren't going over to Helen and Mike's until boxing day.

Emily was not going to allow anyone to intrude on this precious family time. Fran had her dad, her sister and supposedly a shed load of other friends, so, though, it did not come naturally to her to be so harsh, she was determined not to get suckered in- besides which, what sort of mother would actually want her own child's 'nose pushed out of joint' in favour of a new baby, just so that she wasn't left on her own on Christmas day?

"You should be pleased that Simon and Zoe are still as keen to have Scarlett there." Emily pointed out, doing her best to completely side step the whole Christmas day thing. "She would have been devastated if Simon and Zoe hadn't wanted her around as much now that Jack has arrived." She pointed out reasonably.

"That's easy for you to say, you've always had Tom to take care of you and the kids, you're not the one who was left on her own to cope, the one who had to put her whole life on hold to-"

"That was a long time ago now Fran. We all go through phases when life is tough, and we just have to get through it the best way we can." Emily cut in, sensing the need to bring this call to an end as soon as possible now.

"God Emily.... You've really changed lately...You're supposed to my best friend. A little support wouldn't go amiss right now."

The white hot fury that coursed though Emily was so alien that she had to bite down hard on her lower lip, and then take a very deep breath, in order to prevent herself from spewing out the pent up frustrations that had been buried for too many years. Fran may be on familiar ground here, but this confrontational kind of exchange was simply not the way that Emily operated.

She may no longer be the push over she used to be when she was younger, but she was used to making her points quietly, trading views in a dignified manner, agreeing to disagree if necessary out of respect for the other person's point of view. Fran had used Emily as her vocal punch bag once too often though, and she simply wasn't prepared to stand for it any longer.

"Yes I have changed Fran." She stated coldly through gritted teeth. "Being confronted by the reality of a very different future than the one you had planned tends to bring you up short...make you take stock."

"Oh please... spare me one of your religious lectures about counting my blessings. I don't actually see very many of those at the moment. It's all right for you. As always, everything has turned out just fine for Princess Emily while I'm left to struggle on with no-one to fight my corner...

"Would you rather it HAD turned out to be MS then Fran? Is that the problem here? You would have been able to carry on wallowing in the misery with me then wouldn't you?" The brutal words seemed to leave Emily's mouth of their own volition, stunning them both into silence.

Every one else had been nothing short of thrilled when they heard the good news (especially Helen and Mike who'd clucked around her beaming from ear to ear all day) but ever since she'd had the all clear, she'd sensed this undercurrent of jealously from Fran- almost as though she resented the fact that Emily was going to get her life back on track again. The very idea seemed utterly ludicrous of course, yet now that she'd put the thought into words, it did make sense. The pity party that Fran had been envisaging was over.

"What the hell has got into you Emily? I was there for you the whole time you were ill, but you can't even be bothered to answer the phone half the time now when I need you..." Fran countered, floundering a bit. She was not used to being the one on the receiving end.

"There for me? You were an absolute pain in the arse. Kath and Jess both understood that I needed some space, a bit of peace and quiet when I got home from work, but you were on the phone every bloody night giving me grief-"

"I was trying to support you...I-"

"No Fran. You spent two minutes asking me how I was, then the rest of the call expecting me to listen to all you're crap as usual." Unlike Fran, Emily's voice had grown quieter, her words becoming more clipped as the argument went on.

"So what exactly DO you want from me then Emily, You know I love you to pieces, I just want things to be like they used to be. I really miss-"

"And that in a nutshell is the problem." Emily's voice was dangerously low now. "It's time to grow up, move on- you can't keep harking back almost thirty years to when we were kids Fran. We've both changed, want different things from life" Emily cringed, realising this was starting to sound awfully like a 'you're dumped' speech- minus the bit about remaining friends of course.

"Well I'm so glad I called my oldest friend for a bit of moral support after my ordeal." Fran spat back sarcastically. "I was hoping for a bit of sympathy, not a lecture about all my apparent shortcomings."

"And what exactly am I supposed to be feeling sorry for you about? If you were driving when you'd been drinking then you deserve to have the book thrown at you." Emily stated flatly.

"I wouldn't have been driving if you'd come over as I asked you to though would I?" Fran trumped her, always used to having the last word.

"So it's my fault you got arrested then is it Fran?" Emily queried her tone one of utter bemusement now.

"If the cap fits..." Fran trilled, totally oblivious to the intended sarcasm.

"I think we should end this call right now because if we carry on we really are going to fall out." Emily warned Fran, her voice cracking slightly as her fury evaporated as quickly as it had arrived, leaving her feeling slightly nauseous.

"You know something Emily, I think I did prefer you when you were ill, at least then I got to see you now and again and you didn't jump down my throat when I asked for a bit of support-"

"I'm going to stop you right there Fran. I've listened to enough of your self pity, and more than enough of you constantly trying to pass the buck. I'm utterly sick of the complete lack of respect you show me, so until you are ready to start behaving like an adult and assume responsibility for your own actions, I really don't want to be around you anymore."

As soon as she had replaced the phone very carefully back on its stand, Emily began to shake violently. The tears pouring down her face were a complicated mix- relief that she'd finally found the courage to deliver a few long overdue home truths, and deep sorrow that almost thirty years of friendship had just ended in such a vitriolic manner.

Before today, she could honestly say, that, hand on heart she had never considered severing the tie with Fran as a viable option, but maybe this clean break would prove to be the best thing for them both in the long run? Fran was so incredibly thick skinned, that in reality, all the plans that Emily had been so confidently making recently to down grade the friendship, had probably been little more than pie in the sky... wishful thinking.

Now that she'd finally had her say, given vent to the seething mass of resentment that had been churning away inside her for so many years, there was to be absolutely no turning back. She was well aware that she was going to have to really steel herself not to give in to the inevitable niggling of her conscience, but effectively, her days of mollifying Fran, being bled dry by her constant demands for attention, were well and truly over....

41

Fran had worked her way through just about every expletive known to man, by the time she started on the bottle of rank liquor that had been lurking at the back of the cupboard since last Christmas. She'd already drained what was left of the vodka, and that had barely touched the sides. After the first few mouthfuls she stopped noticing the cloying consistency of the sweet coffee flavoured gloop.

The initial ranting and railing that spewed out of her mouth, as soon as she realised that Emily had hung up on her again, soon gave way to sobbing. After the indignity of being arrested at the side of the road for anyone to see, then being carted off to the police station, having Emily turn on her so uncharacteristically really had been the final straw.

What the hell was going on? All she'd done was ask for a bit of sympathy, a bit of support, from her oldest friend. Fran had gone over and over the conversation, analysing and reanalysing every single word, trying to work out what had caused Emily to lash out at her in such an uncalled for manner. Falling out with Simon, having a row with her dad, or a spat with one of the neighbours, had become an everyday occurrence in recent years, but Emily had always been different. She'd remained her constant ally since their teens, the one person she could always call on at any time, the voice of reason, the dependable friend who'd always had her back- until recently that is.

Fran had been absolutely frantic by the time she'd finally got hold of Emily, yet thinking about it now, her friend had seemed distant from the moment she'd picked up the call, as though her mind was elsewhere and she really wasn't all that interested in listening to the indignity Fran had been subjected to.

She had had the same air of detachment about her when they'd met for coffee this morning, not remotely appearing to grasp why Zoe having giving birth to a boy was such a catastrophe.

Simon had never made any secret of the fact that he wanted a big family, especially sons to play footie with as he'd had no siblings of his own. It had taken all her considerable powers of persuasion to convince him to have the vasectomy. She'd eventually resorted to black-mail; the classic ban in the bedroom tactic, because there had been absolutely no way she was going to risk putting herself through such utter hell for a second time.

Mother earth types like Emily, who sailed through their pregnancies, hadn't got a clue what it was like to feel as though your life was gradually spiralling out of control, and no matter how desperately Simon had pleaded with her, promised that they'd be much better prepared the second time, she hadn't been willing to risk being sucked back into that all encompassing vortex of despair again.

No doubt, now she'd given Simon his precious son, Zoe would take to motherhood in the same way she'd slipped into her role as his second wife- Scarlett's step-mother. Nothing ever seemed to faze the bloody woman, and Fran deeply resented the way Scarlett put her up on some kind of pedestal. It was so unfair.

Zoe was the one who had been in the wrong, the cow who had taken their comfortable lifestyle away from them, yet she always appeared to come up smelling of roses, while Fran was painted as the wicked witch. She'd been the one who'd had to make all the sacrifices, tried to hold all the pieces together as best she could.

Fran's chaotic thoughts continued to race around in ever decreasing circles, as she desperately searched for somewhere to park the blame for all that had gone wrong with her life.

Emily had a lot in common with Zoe now she came to think about it. They were both married to blokes who wrapped them up in cotton wool, treating them like spoilt little princesses, making a fuss over every little thing that happened to them, while nobody ever seemed to give a damn about what she had to endure every day just to survive.

She still couldn't believe that Emily had flung such an utterly despicable accusation at her, when she'd simply been pointing out, perfectly correctly, how much she'd changed lately.

Why was she even having such ugly thoughts, let alone verbalising them? Admittedly, it HAD felt as though the two of them were drawing a little closer again when Emily had been ill. She'd been given a little taste of what it was like to live in Fran's world, struggling to get out of bed some days to do the things that other people simply took for granted, but to accuse her of wishing that Emily had been diagnosed with MS... Where the hell had that heinous thought come from?

She could honestly say, she'd bent over backwards to try and support Emily, and all the thanks she'd got was to be compared unfavourably to Kath and Jess. Maybe that was the reason why Emily had become such a kill joy all of a sudden ... She was spending so much time with that pair of stuck-up boring old farts that perhaps their fuddy-duddy ways were beginning to rub off on her?

The more she thought about it though, the more she began to wonder if it was something to do with the medication she was on. Emily had mentioned how worried she was about the dose she was taking being so high, thousands of time the RDA. Perhaps her strange behaviour today had all been down to some sort of chemical imbalance? She was probably just going through a period of adjustment which would explain why she'd lashed out so uncharacteristically?

It was so unlike Emily not to have picked up on the fact that Fran was likely to be spending Christmas day all on her own either. The Emily that she knew- her oldest friend- would never have allowed that in a million years...her thoughts spun on as she warmed to her theme...

When they had met for coffee this morning it had felt really awkward, as though the real Emily wasn't there at all, as though she had been replaced by a polite stranger. Every time Fran had tried to talk about something that actually mattered, Emily had changed the subject to something really inane like the presents she intended to buy later, or the bloody weather for goodness sake.

The more she thought about it, the more convinced she became that she was on to something here. Though initially, she'd been really distraught over the way Emily had finished the call so coldly, making it sound as though she never wanted to hear from her again, it was obvious to Fran now that she'd just been sounding off in the heat of the moment.

No doubt, she'd be bitterly regretting it already...sitting at home wondering how she could put things right between them, atone for her irrational outburst...she'd probably be on the phone first thing tomorrow morning desperate to make amends...

Fran imagined herself magnanimously accepting Emily's apology, assuring her best mate that their friendship was strong enough to survive the odd blip, that she was more than willing to overlook any odd behaviour while her body adjusted to the medication...she'd been through the same thing enough times herself...

By the time she'd polished off the last few drops of the sickly liquor, Fran had convinced herself that this would all blow over tomorrow...and better still, when Emily rang her all contrite, it was going to be an absolute doddle to wangle an invitation for Christmas day.

As she settled herself down on the sofa, and drew the throw around her, Fran started to recall how she and Scarlett had spent their first Christmas with them after Simon left. Tom and Emily had made them so welcome, and having Holly running around after her daughter all day had been a bit like having her own personal nanny.

Just before she finally passed out, Fran envisaged herself spending the big day at Emily's house again, being waited on hand and foot by her very penitent friend...

42

The phone had been ringing every couple of hours, like clockwork, for the last few days, and Tom was finding it increasingly hard to ignore.

Despite Emily's valiant efforts to feign a nonchalance she was far from feeling, he knew exactly what this was costing her. He saw her tense as she checked caller display, watched her body stiffen as she walked away, betraying her soft heart. He knew it was just a question of time now. She would give in and pick up Fran's call eventually.

Though Tom had never been one of those sad insecure blokes, who felt threatened by his wife's close friendships, this particular parting of the ways was long overdue as far as he was concerned, but the timing could have been better.

He only had a few days off while the kids were back, and he really wasn't prepared to allow Fran to go on ruining the rest of their Christmas break.

Fran had never abided by any normal sort of phone etiquette, never grasped the basic concept of when it was considered acceptable to call, other than in an emergency. When the phone rang yet again, at about half past ten last night, Tom had been more than ready to put an end to this fiasco, but Emily had insisted that if they just kept ignoring her calls, even someone as thick skinned as Fran would get the message eventually.

Josh was currently sprawled on the sofa watching reruns of scrubs, while Tom was engrossed in the annual ritual of untangling the lights, so that Emily and Holly could start decorating the tree together, exactly as they had been doing every year since Holly was about four. Right on cue, the phone broke into this content domesticity again.

Because the calls had been coming so regularly all morning, nobody even paused in what they were doing this time, and that was what really got to Tom. Clearly they were all just assuming that it would be Fran now. How long was Emily going to let this drag on for?

"Let me deal with her love." Tom issued the words as more of a statement than a question as he held his wife's gaze, immediately striding across the room and grabbing the phone when she didn't put up any objections.

"Oh hi Tom...where have you two been hiding yourselves." Tom wasn't exactly sure what he'd been expecting, but Fran's casual greeting, her assumption that everything could just carry on as usual, wiped the civility from his tongue. He was way past being straight-jacketed by good old British politeness, so he allowed the deafening silence that hung between them to speak for him.

"Is Emily about?" Though her tone was still just as bright and breezy, he clearly detected a dip in confidence.

"Yes she is here." Tom stated simply, his tone absolutely neutral.

"Right...can I have a word then...." Fran faltered.

"No." Tom paused to make sure she'd fully absorbed the single word response, before he continued. "I believe Emily made her position perfectly clear on Wednesday Fran. She has nothing more to add." For a moment or two there was nothing but her sharp intake of breath, but she'd soon shown her true colours, just as he'd expected her to.

"Since when did you start speaking for your wife Tom? You have no right to try and come between-"

"Please don't call this number again." The way he cut her off had a finality to it that was deliberately brutal...sometimes in life you had to be cruel to be kind, and the stance Emily had taken was undoubtedly the right one for both their sakes. He'd sensed a long time ago that Emily would need to step back completely, if Fran was ever going to learn to start taking responsibility for her mistakes. She wasn't a young woman anymore, and shouldn't expect to keep foisting her troubles onto Emily's shoulders indefinitely, the way she had for the last two decades. The problem was he seriously doubted whether his soft hearted wife actually had it in her to see this through to the end...

For the second time in as many days, Fran stared unseeingly into space as the dead phone line hummed in her ear.

She had absolutely no idea what she was supposed to do now? She'd always got on pretty well with Tom, or so she had thought. He'd always been pretty easy going- apart from the odd occasion when she'd inadvertently trodden on his toes- but the vibe that had just radiated from him so strongly, even over the phone, had smacked of pure hatred.

Had be just been hiding his jealousy all these years, suppressing how much he resented the fact that she was his wife's closest friend, had known Emily for longer than he had? Until she actually heard it from Emily herself, Fran refused to believe that their friendship could possibly be over. The very idea was completely ludicrous...

She knew deep down that Emily would never turn her back on her, particularly now, when she was in such a rubbish place...on and on her thoughts whirled, becoming more and more obsessive as the level of the bottle beside her went down. She could barely focus on the letters on the screen by the time she got round to sending a text.

'I'm really sorry for whatever it is I've done to upset you. We have to talk about it though mate so call me. Love you to bits X'

As soon as the text arrived, Tom quietly left the room and came back a few minutes later clutching a lopsidedly wrapped package.

"I think it might be a good idea if you open this a few days early love." He suggested wryly. He and the kids had decided it was about time Emily joined the rest of the world with a decent contract phone, instead of the basic little 'pay as you go' thing she'd had for years.

It was already registered and charged, so all they needed to do now was switch over all her contacts- minus one obvious one of course- and she'd be good to go with her new number...

43

Simon's features were set in an implacably mask of steely determination, as he used the key he'd had cut for use in emergencies, for the second time in less than twenty four hours.

This was hardly the way he'd envisaged spending Jack's first Christmas morning, he acknowledged wryly, as he opened the door to 10 Amber Mews, praying that what he'd find this morning, would be far removed from the appalling scene he'd walked into yesterday.

"Can you wait here a moment love?" He cautioned his daughter, not entirely convinced that Fran had taken on board how serious he had been yesterday evening when he'd laid down the law, issuing his ex-wife with an ultimatum regarding their daughter's future.

If Fran had not followed those instructions to the letter, then he would turn around, walk straight back out the door, and apply for sole custody just as soon as the holiday season was over.

He wasn't quite sure which of them had been the most shocked by the stand he'd taken last night, but the wake up call had been long overdue.

After knocking repeatedly on the front door, he'd let himself in to find her soaked in her own urine and vomit. Operating on automatic pilot, he'd suppressed all emotion and concentrated solely on the practicalities.

Somehow he'd managed to manhandle her dead weight up the narrow staircase and un-ceremoniously plonk her in the bath. A blast of stone cold water had seemed like the quickest way to sober her up and deal with the worst of the filth.

He'd schooled himself to feel absolutely nothing as she'd floundered around, yelling abuse at him as he began peeling off the soiled garments. Eventually he'd turned the temperature of the water up a little, once her teeth had begun to chatter.

As soon as he'd felt she was remotely coherent enough to listen to him, he'd taken her back downstairs, wrapped in a towelling robe that had been hanging on the back of the bathroom door. He'd poured several glasses of water down her before starting to outline the ground rules for their daughter's future from here on in.

"I only came round because Zoe was getting increasingly concerned when you wouldn't answer my calls." He began ironically. "The woman you have been so utterly vile to for the last eight years, was worried about you being on your own so much over the holidays." his mouth twisted wryly, acknowledging that his wife's intuitive sense of unease had been spot on as usual- God only knows what sort of state Fran would have been in if she'd been left to her own devices much longer. "Zoe thought it would be a good idea for me to bring Scarlett over for a couple of hours in the morning-"

"Oh how very gracious of her." Fran had spat back at him sarcastically, Zoe's extreme generosity, under the circumstances, completely lost on her. "Who the hell does she think she is granting me time with my own daughter?"

"I told Zoe that that was probably the way you'd react, that you wouldn't show an atom of gratitude for the fact that she is prepared to put your-"

"Gratitude.-you expect me to be grateful to the woman who stole my husband, and is currently doing her best to turn my daughter against me too?" Fran shouted back at him, attempting to restore a shred of dignity and claw back a little control.

This cool detached Simon, who kept telling her what to do, was not the man she was used to dealing with. He'd always been a soft touch and she'd always been able to twist him around her little finger- especially where Scarlett was concerned. She honestly didn't know how to handle him right now.

"Zoe didn't 'steal' me Fran. Our marriage had been over in all but name for a long time, and the only person driving Scarlett away right now is you. Look at the state of this place. A dosser would refuse to stay here." He had never spoken to her like this before, and his clipped tone merely served to remind Fran of the icy way Tom had cut her off mid sentence just a couple of days ago...

"That's not fair...I've had a really bad week... things have just got on top of me..." She'd gone on to explain the indignity of being arrested in full view of anyone passing, and then, how Emily had suddenly turned against her when she'd been in dire need of some support. Just to cap it all off, her sister had launched into a lecture about taking responsibility for her own actions, when she'd phoned her looking for a little sympathy.

Chrissie had been her last hope. She'd really been expecting an invitation to spend Christmas there, but as soon as she'd mentioned the subject, Chrissie had told her that they were going up to Scotland for a week to spend the holidays with Ian's family.

Chrissie had gone on to suggest that Fran should ring their dad. When she'd replied that she'd rather eat her own eyeballs than face the prospect of eating her turkey looking at Sarah's miserable face, Chrissie had given her yet another lecture about giving their stepmother a fair chance.

"It sounds to me as though Emily and Chrissie are spot on Fran." Simon had stated astutely, snuffing out any last vestige of hope of anyone actually seeing her side of things. He handed her a steaming mug of coffee, and some buttered toast, before adding his own sermon. "It really is time to grow up and stop blaming everyone else for the mess you have made of your life. You need to face up to the fact that you're an alcoholic and get some help."

Under different circumstances, the way her draw had dropped, leaving her mouth gaping open, might have been comical. The words seemed to have left his mouth of their own volition. Though stating the stark truth had been completely unpremeditated, once the elephant that had been lurking in the room for so long was out, there was no brushing it back under the carpet again.

Fran had reached the end of the line, and Simon was no longer prepared to turn a blind eye, not when their daughter's future was at stake here. At thirteen, Scarlett was at such an impressionable age, and goodness knows what sort of messages she was picking up while her mother's behaviour continued to careen so totally out of control.

It was impossible not to notice how much his daughter seemed to have blossomed lately. She was so much more confident, had become visibly more outgoing since spending most of her time with him and Zoe. She'd been an absolute star helping them out with Jack, and seemed to be totally besotted with her half brother. The thought that it could have been Scarlett walking in to find her mother in such a pitiful state, sickened him to his core.

Simon had taken a deep breath before going on to lay down the ground rules for this short, supervised visit this morning, making it crystal clear to Fran that if she wanted to continue having any contact at all with her daughter, then things were going to have to change...

As soon as Fran came into the hall to meet them, he could see that it was going to be OK to let Scarlett come in and exchange presents with her mother as arranged.

Condition one, the most important criteria of all, was that Fran had to be sober. Condition two was that she would be showered and presentable, and condition three the house had to be reasonably tidy, and no longer smelling like the back alley of a club on a Saturday night.

The smell of croissants warming in the oven was the strongest indication of just how seriously Fran had taken his threat, to apply for sole custody if she didn't get help and clean herself up immediately.

Simon watched Fran as she crouched on the floor with their daughter taking turns to open their gifts. With their heads just inches apart, Fran was enthusing over each parcel. Her face lit up with pleasure at the treats Zoe had helped Scarlett to choose for her, and Simon caught a tiny glimpse of the funny, vivacious, mercurial woman he'd fallen in love with... from now on, he was determined to ensure that this was the only version of her mother Scarlett spent any time with...

44

Before sitting down to the traditional Marsden family gargantuan Christmas dinner, James had spent most of the morning on the phone, monitoring Fran's progress. He'd definitely made the right choice when he'd turned to Gayle Humphreys for help yesterday evening.

Initially, he'd been frustrated by the fact that that he couldn't go to her, when a very subdued broken Fran, had called him on Christmas Eve begging for help. In hind-sight, he'd quickly realised that it was probably healthier for both of them this way.

One of the first things you were taught as a sponsor was the importance of setting clear boundaries. If you got too closely involved, particularly if you already had any kind of personal connection with the new member, then inevitably you were much less effective.

Feeling the way he did about Fran, it had been incredibly hard to back off over the last few weeks, but he'd sensed that it was the right thing to do. He'd known that she was about to hit rock bottom, and accepted that she had to do that if she was ever going to admit that she needed help, and ask for support.

Now that she had done precisely that, it was imperative to ensure that she got the right sort of guidance from someone who could remain totally objective and detached. Fran was going to be incredibly vulnerable over the next few weeks, months even, and she was going to need a whole network of people she could turn to, not someone who was far too close for his own good and could so easily cross the line, whenever she was in need of comfort.

He was in absolutely no doubt now, that Fran would welcome that kind of shift in their relationship, that she was confused by the mixed messages he had unconsciously been giving out recently. Until she was in a place where she was able to make that kind of decision rationally, he had no intention of taking advantage of the fact that she needed to be loved right now, and just about anybody would do.

It sounded as though Gayle had sprung into action in her usual forthright manner. She'd apparently taken Fran to the twenty four hour Tesco store, padding out the paltry gift she'd ordered for Scarlett on line, by purchasing an I-tune voucher, some cute pyjamas, a set of nail varnishes and some pretty knickers.

As soon as they'd got back they'd set about cleaning up the house together, and then Gayle had stayed with Fran until she was ready to go to bed. No doubt she would have shattered any image the younger woman might have formed of her by then, by sharing the concise, but brutal version, of her own downfall.

Her story never failed to shock when delivered from the lips of such an archetypical pillar of society- a former vicar's wife for almost twenty years.

As he tucked into his plate full of turkey with all the usual trimmings, a wry smile hovered around James' mouth as he tried to picture Fran, working alongside Gayle right now, as they served a rather more modest version of the same dinner, at the homeless shelter where Gayle had been volunteering every Christmas Day for the last few years.

He had arranged to cut his own break short and travel back the day after tomorrow, in order to be able to accompany Fran to her first meeting on Tuesday evening. He had no doubt there would be a quite a few new faces.

It was the same every year. AA groups, like health clubs, always tended to get a big influx of new members after the excesses of the season of good will.

Every last one of the honeyed parsnips, floury roast potatoes and peppered sprouts had been polished off by Josh, the human dustbin, and the Christmas pudding and rocky road cheesecake had both been pretty much demolished too. Tom and the kids were in the kitchen clearing everything away and loading the dishwasher, just as they did every year, allowing Emily to put her feet up for a few minutes.

In a little while, when order had been restored, no doubt the daft games that came out every Christmas, would be fetched from the cupboard under the stairs. Josh could always be relied on to download the usual pub quiz for them to play later too. It was a tradition they'd started years ago- no telly on Christmas day- and she knew how lucky she and Tom were that at twenty one and eighteen, Josh and Holly didn't just go along with this ritual to humour their parents, they actively looked forward to this part of the day.

As Emily sat quietly in the lounge, able to relax now that the meal had been served without mishap, she felt the growing sense of disquiet that had been washing over her periodically since yesterday afternoon, niggling again. No matter how hard she tried to ignore the sense of unease, it simply wouldn't go away, and she was getting increasingly annoyed with herself for allowing her concerns to blight this special family day, just as they had done so many times in the past.

That old adage about being careful what you wished for sprang to mind. Wasn't this exactly what she'd wanted? A Christmas day that had only been punctuated with thoughtful texts from family and friends, rather than several ill-timed inebriated calls from Fran, one of which usually always managed to come just as she was in the middle of serving the dinner.

Her new phone had been blissfully quiet over the last couple of days, and yet, a number of times she'd found herself on the verge of calling John or Simon, just to put her mind at ease and assure herself that Fran was OK, that she hadn't done anything stupid...

Though she genuinely believed that a clean break would prove to be the best thing in the long run, it was certainly coming at a price. The guilt had been eating away at her ever since their bitter row. Why couldn't she have just held her tongue for a little longer, gradually easing herself away from Fran's unhealthy dependency, rather than ending the friendship on such an unnecessarily harsh note- especially at this time of year?

She'd been really close to Laura Mathews for three of four years when the kids were little, but as soon as they'd both gone back to work, there had been a gradual dwindling of contact between them. They still sent each other birthday and Christmas cards, had a good old catch up if they met at the shops, or on the park-and-ride bus, but they'd both accepted that the close friendship they'd once shared had been for a period of time only. There is only so much us to go round, so the bigger our circle of friends, the less quality time we got to spend with any of them.

Of course it would have been a great deal harder to arrive at a similarly amicable arrangement with Fran- she was a different kettle of fish altogether- but Emily had genuinely hoped that in time, they could have reached some sort of mutually acceptable downgrading of their relationship, rather than this hostile cut off.

What if Scarlett was with Simon and Fran was spending the entire day on her own? Christmas was renowned for being the worst possible time of the year to be alone- she might have shut herself away since their row and been drinking steadily for days now...what if-

"Do you want another glass of bubbly mum?" Holly cut into her mothers' dire ruminations as she popped her head round the lounge door, brandishing what was left of the bottle of pink fizz they'd been drinking with their lunch.

"Mmmm....?" Emily blinked vacantly at her daughter before making a quick recovery. "Actually I think I'm all right for the moment love." She smiled at her daughter fondly before adding, "You know what a light weight I am. I'd better leave a bit of a gap- at least until after the quiz- or I won't be able to answer any of Josh's questions."

Emily took a deep breath and pulled her shoulders back as her family re-entered the room. She was just going to have to make a concerted effort to push these nagging concerns aside, allow herself to be drawn into the easy banter that had been drifting through from the kitchen for the last half hour.

This was a special family day and she wasn't about to ruin it with morbid conjecture. It was time to let go, to finally embrace the fact that Frances Carrington was no longer a part of her life... no longer her responsibility...

45

Fran's mouth had gone so dry it felt as though her tongue had been welded to the roof of her mouth. Her legs had turned to jelly too, causing her to cling tightly to the railings as she climbed the narrow stairs. St Nicholas hall was on the very top floor of the United Reformed Church, which was located directly opposite the English bridge. She'd passed this beautiful old building, right by the river, so many times, yet had no idea of the range of services this church provided.

If it hadn't been for James' confident strides ringing out behind her, she would probably have turned tail right about now and made a run for it. Despite everything James had told her about the format of this meeting, all the common myths he'd tried to dispel in his attempts to reassure her, she couldn't overcome her fear of actually walking into the room. She was still balking at the idea of being surrounded by a bunch of 'helpful' do-gooders, all intent on prising her miserable story out of her.

Though James had reiterated many times, that she wasn't obliged to do, say, or take part in anything that made her remotely uncomfortable, the thought of a group of complete strangers all staring at her, waiting for the new girl to introduce herself by her first name, before adding the classic 'I am an alcoholic' to rapturous applause, was totally freaking her out.

Would it be considered really bad form if she didn't join in with the prayers? What if they expected her to take part in group hugs? She glanced around furtively as she slipped into the room as unobtrusively as possible, keeping her gaze lowered to the floor in order to avoid making eye contact.

Fran was relieved to see that although the majority of people were in groups chatting away, there were others sitting alone looking as anxious as she felt. She took a seat close to the door, so she could escape easily if she really couldn't cope, and simply nodded at anyone who said hello to James, hoping fervently that they wouldn't linger or try and introduce themselves.

As the room began to fill up- there must have been at least forty people here by now- Fran was struck again, just as she had been when helping Gayle serve the Christmas lunch, by the diversity in age, intellect and appearance of everyone present. Rather than the dregs of society her imagination had been conjuring up, ever since she'd agreed to attend this meeting, she now found herself surrounded by such a bunch of 'normal' looking people, that, this could easily pass as a meeting of the congregation of the church.

The possibility that they'd inadvertently wandered into the wrong room crossed her mind, until the person in the middle- the chairperson- began to read the preamble, before leading the group in a prayer, which at least two thirds of those present seemed to recite with her.

The chairperson then asked if their were any first timers, who would like to introduce themselves, and as a few hands went up Fran stared intently at a mark on the carpet, painfully aware that the colour suffusing her face was flagging her up as a newcomer, just as surely as if she'd stood on her chair and announced who she was with a loud speaker.

Much to her surprise, Fran soon found herself totally engrossed in the softly spoken words of the pretty young woman who was leading the meeting, studying her closely when she went on to announce the 'step' they were working on this evening . Once she'd finished reading the chapter, she then opened the floor to anyone who wanted to share their relevant experiences.

Fran was profoundly touched by the candid honesty, the total lack of embarrassment, with which people were prepared to share their stories- many of which resonated deeply with her own feelings of always having been on the outside looking in, of never truly having belonged anywhere. The warmth of the genuine gratitude shown by the whole group, towards each person as they finished speaking, was deeply moving.

Fran had intended to be out of her seat and back down the stairs, the moment the meeting was formally closed, but she actually found herself lingering for just a little while longer, as one or two people came over to introduce themselves, almost immediately proffering their phone numbers, in much the same way that Gayle had done on Christmas eve, when James had still been in Ireland.

By the time they finally did leave the room, Fran's emotions were all over the place, her preconceived perceptions of how the evening would unfold having been completely blown out of the water. She felt in awe of some of the speakers, a deep sense of relief that she'd actually got through this first meeting relatively unscathed, and an overwhelming sense of shame about the superior air with which she'd arrived.

Just because some people had sunk a lot lower before seeking help, did that really make them any worse a person than her? Fran was under no illusions about what had brought her here tonight.

If she hadn't met James a few months ago, if Emily hadn't finally run out of patience with her and Simon hadn't issued his stark ultimatum, could she honestly say that she would have sought help of her own volition? Not a chance- she'd probably be lying in a gutter somewhere by now, having alienated just about every last person who had ever cared about her.

As Fran climbed back into James' car, it was with the certain knowledge that she would definitely be coming back again next week...and the week after that...and the week after that...because, unless she wanted to loose her daughter permanently, she really didn't have any other choice now....

46

Though Fran would begrudgingly have to admit, that her resolutely atheistic stance had been severely challenged over the last eight weeks, she was still a very long way away from fully accepting some of the spiritual aspects of the testimonies she listened to every Tuesday night.

Despite this deeply routed scepticism, she couldn't deny that knowing so many people were praying for her this morning was proving to be a real comfort, as it created an almost tangible force of protection around her. She could just imagine Gayle smiling serenely at her, if she shared that particular little nugget of information with the group later this evening.

Comparing the way she felt today as she made her way up the steps to the magistrates court, to the way she'd felt a couple of months ago as she'd climbed the stairs to her first AA meeting, made her appreciate how far she'd come in such a relatively short time.

The difference in just a few weeks was actually quite amazing and that, without a shadow of doubt, was all down to the unwavering support she'd received every time she was in the slightest danger of falling off the wagon- and she'd been sorely tempted many, many times.

Initially, when she'd been formally charged on that bleak day, just before Christmas, she'd seen very little point in seeking legal advice, as she was clearly guilty. However, once she'd met David Yates, her legal aid accredited solicitor, he'd very quickly managed to change her mind.

David had gone into infinite detail, so she knew exactly what to expect this morning from her arrival through to the sentencing. He'd listed everyone who would be present in the court, and explained their individual roles. He'd also made it very clear that a well constructed plea of mitigation could make an enormous difference to the length of disqualification, and the amount of fine imposed.

Gayle had marched her around all the charity shops- tactfully avoiding the heart foundation shop of course- until they'd come across a smart tailored suit and pale blue blouse. This outfit would also be ideal for any interviews that arose as a result of the job applications she'd been sending off recently.

Just as David had warned her, there had been a lengthy wait between making her self known at the reception desk and finally being called through by the court usher. Following exactly the same sequence as when David had walked her through it, once she'd confirmed her name and address and pleaded guilty, she was asked to sit down again and took no further part in the proceedings, which were all over in a matter of minutes.

Once the prosecuting solicitor had put forward the statements and police evidence, it was David's turn, and although Fran knew the course he was going to take, it was still incredibly hard to just sit there, feeling as though all eyes were upon her, as he explained that his client was an alcoholic, who was now in recovery.

The clever wording made it sound as though being arrested had been the wake up call she'd needed, that it was remorse that had galvanised her into attending AA meetings- there was, of course, no mention of the ultimatum her ex-husband had issued her with.

David had gone on to explain that his client had now been dry for over two months, was receiving counselling to help her find better strategies to cope with her problems, and had been holding down a front of house position in the hospitality industry, for several weeks, on a voluntary basis, as a means to getting back into paid employment.

He actually managed to make her sound like a victim of circumstances rather than a criminal. The 'front of house' position that he made sound so grand was actually just helping out in a coffee shop that a 'friend of a friend' of Gayle's owned.

Fran had learnt very quickly, that whatever you needed, someone always 'knew someone who knew someone' when you became part of the AA network.

Naturally David was just doing his job, and doing it very well by embellishing the facts a little, and thanks to him the magistrates had taken only a few minutes to reach their decision. She'd been handed the minimum twelve month driving ban, with the option of reducing this further by completing a drink driving rehabilitation course, and the fine imposed had been fairly lenient too.

Though it was one hundred percent true that she was doing her level best to turn her life around, Fran was deeply conscious of the fact that her motivations weren't quite as altruistic as David had painted them.

Whatever had initially prompted her to seek help though, there was absolutely no denying that attending the meetings every week for the last two months, had really opened her eyes in so many ways. For the first time in her life she was actually starting to listen, to accept other peoples' points of view, rather than just shouting over them the moment they paused to take a breath. She'd read somewhere in one of the many self help manuals she'd been given, that God had deliberately created us with two ears and one mouth, as we were supposed to do twice as much listening.

Fran could now appreciate just how much of her life she had spent swimming up stream, constantly raging against the unfair hand she felt fate had dealt her. She'd believed that she was somehow different, deserved more than the boring nine to five grind that most people seemed to settle for. In her mind, everything she'd been through, was always so much more intense than the minor little hiccups that life seemed to throw at her friends- especially friends like Emily.

She was slowly beginning to recognise the pattern that had developed throughout her life. Running away and making excuses, never stopping to try and learn from her mistakes, was a habit that had started to form as soon as she'd placed the blame for her teenage angst on her mothers' shoulders. She'd been far too keen to assume the role of the poor abandoned daughter.

She'd carried on transferring blame, in much the same way, every time another job, or relationship, didn't work out the way she'd expected it to. For all these years since their divorce, she'd been holding Simon solely responsible for the breakdown of their marriage. In her mind, Sarah had caused all the difficulties between her and her father, and Zoe was totally to blame for the gulf that had been opening up between her and Scarlett recently.

If her daughter hadn't chosen to practically leave home, and Emily and Simon hadn't both run out of their seemingly endless supplies of patience, within days of each other, she would no doubt have viewed loosing her licence in exactly the same way as all her other problems- just another demonstration of how unfair life had always been to her.

Rather than accepting any responsibility for being behind the wheel of a car when she had been way over the limit, she still wouldn't have been able to see that it was her fault in any way. She'd have somehow managed to twist it all around in her head, until she'd genuinely believed she was only in such a mess because Emily had refused to come over when she'd asked her to.

She could just imagine the way her thoughts would have run. If Emily hadn't been fobbing her off for months, if her best friend had been able to spare just a little more of her precious time so that they could have had a proper catch up over lunch, then Fran wouldn't have been driving at all...

It was amazing how easy it was to shift the blame for practically anything, when you'd been practising the art for as long as Fran had...she could only hope it wouldn't take her as long to convince her family and friends that she really was trying to change, that she was doing her level best to start taking responsibility for all those mistakes she'd made.

She was really keen to try and start making amends, to attempt to undo some of the damage she'd inflicted... She wondered how many of the people she had hurt over and over again, would be willing to meet her half way.

47

Fran sighed heavily, as she despaired of ever finding the right words. She crumpled up yet another sheet of paper and tossed it into the wastepaper basket beside her. Though she'd been jotting down her thoughts all week, and had pages and pages of hastily scrawled notes, she was still no closer to composing an opening to this all important letter.

Chewing on the end of the pen, she gazed out of the French windows, hoping for a flash of inspiration. Where exactly was she supposed to start? How could she even begin to express just how deeply ashamed of her behaviour she was?

It wasn't seven o'clock yet, but the sun was already dipping out of sight behind the garden fence. The days seemed to be drawing in rapidly as they approached mid September, yet Fran didn't feel the usual dread at the thought of the dark winter evenings ahead. Now that she was surrounded by people all day at work, for the first time in her life she actually relished a bit of peace when she got home. She was steadily growing more and more comfortable in her own company.

The voluntary work in the coffee shop, organised by Gayle, had soon led to a paid position at the rather old fashioned, aptly named 'Poppy's Pantry', situated in one of the many little cobbled passageways off the High Street in Shrewsbury.

Poppy herself was a really eccentric character who had a hugely loyal following of lunch-break customers, many of whom returned almost daily because of the huge range of gluten free food on offer. Fran added that thought to the list, then immediately slashed a line through the words.

She was quite sure that Emily would appreciate knowing about all the homemade quiches and cakes on offer at Poppy's Pantry, but that sort of chit chat was hardly the way to get this letter of apology off the ground.

The eighth, of the twelve steps alcoholics anonymous used, consisted of making a list of all the people you had harmed. The ninth concentrated on making direct amends, wherever it was possible to do so, without causing further hurt. A considerable number of people in the group had found that, the most effective way to do this was to write a letter, acknowledging all the ways you had wronged the person, and asking for their forgiveness.

The first letter she had written had of course, been to Scarlett. Once she had begun jotting down her thoughts, her pen had simply flown across the paper. She'd filled pages and pages, most of which had not been remotely suitable for a thirteen year old to read. It had been a deeply cathartic exercise. She'd felt a real sense of purging as she acknowledged each and every one of her many failings as a mother.

The heavily censored version, she eventually gave to her daughter a week or two later, focussed on one undeniable fact. Though she hadn't physically left the country like Angie, she'd still effectively abandoned her daughter just at the age when she'd needed her mother's guidance the most.

Fran had realised that somebody of her fathers' character and generation would be uncomfortable with any sort of emotional outpouring. Consequently, the letter she'd written to her dad had been concise and factual- much briefer than the one she'd sent to Sarah, on the same day, but in a separate envelope.

Though they'd made it crystal clear that they didn't go in for any of this Americanised bearing of the soul stuff, she'd received a rather stiff phone call thanking her for the letters, and inviting her for Sunday dinner. Progress was very slow as they obviously thought it was just a matter of time before she would fall off the wagon again. Understandably, they were going to take some convincing that this 'new Fran' was actually here to stay.

Chrissie had written her a beautiful, deeply encouraging letter, by return of post, which she would treasure for the rest of her life. Simon and Zoe had surprised her the most, offering their forgiveness with more grace than could possibly have imagined.

Fran had been incredibly humbled by Zoe's unbelievably generous heart as the three of them, accompanied by Jack's gurgling in the background, had sat down to discuss the arrangements for Scarlett's future- assuming Fran remained dry of course.

It was over nine months now since she'd had a drink, and her relationship with Scarlett, had gone from strength to strength- as had her 'friendship' with James.

Just thinking about the big bear of a man, who had been instrumental in helping her to turn her life around, brought a wide grin to her lips. What she felt for James went way beyond gratitude...cheesy as it sounded, she'd finally found her soul mate...

It was the first time in her life that she'd ever really got to know someone, inside out, before jumping into bed with them, and boy, had the wait been worth it. Instead of her usual alcohol fuelled performance, where she faked her own enjoyment in order to hasten her partners, she'd revelled in their slow sensuous mutual exploration of each others bodies. They were connected on every level, mentally and physically.

She'd soon realised that James possessed more actual strength; the kind that really mattered, than all her previous partners put together. Apart from Simon, she'd always been attracted to the strutting alpha male types, making the same mistakes over and over again. She'd never understood, that, the competitive, aggressive edge, she'd admired as strength, was actually just a sign of weakness, fuelled by insecurity.

Though they were spending a great deal of time together, and she regularly stayed over at his house when Scarlett was at Simon's, neither of them were in the slightest hurry to take things to the next level.

Fran had spent her entire life hurtling from one failed relationship to the next, rushing headlong into new friendships, or different jobs, in a desperate bid to find someone who could fix her. For the first time in her life, she was involved in an honest uncomplicated relationship, in which she shared her true self, warts and all. She had finally learnt that happiness, or peace of mind, was something you had to find inside yourself, not something that somebody else could give you.

She was really enjoying the feeling of independence that earning a modest living, in a job she enjoyed doing, was giving her. Though she was still receiving a top up of benefits, she finally understood what Emily had been trying to get her to grasp for years. She wasn't any better off financially, but she'd regained those two priceless things called pride and a sense of purpose.

Perhaps that would be a good place to place start this letter? She'd written so much down but was finding it almost impossible to form any sort of logical beginning or end.

The letters she'd sent to each of her relatives had dealt with the specific hurts she'd caused them, but it had always been Emily that she'd turned to afterwards. Dumping her warped view of events on her friend, she'd regularly railed at her when the tongue lashing had really been intended for someone else.

How did she even begin to apologise for treating her friend so appallingly for all these years. She cringed as she recalled all the times she'd phoned Emily at any old time of the day or night, taking her soft heart for granted, as she'd offloaded her latest round of troubles onto her friends' shoulders.

She was acutely aware that this letter was proving the hardest to write, because she had no idea how it was going to be received.

To some extent, her family were pretty much stuck with her, obliged to meet her request for a fresh start with at least some degree of acceptance. Maybe that old adage about being able to choose your friends, but not your family, was about to be proved true.

Emily had finally walked away, given up on her quest to try and sort out Fran's life. Frankly, when she looked back over the years and the contemptuous way she had treated her, Fran could only marvel at the fact that it had taken Emily so long to reach the end of the line...

48

Helen was humming away to herself as she put the finishing touches to the enormous family sized cheesecake- raspberry of course as that was Emily's favourite.

She only ever really let rip, singing along to the familiar old tunes on the local radio station, when Mike was out of the house. She'd learned to accept the sad reality that her ability fell way short of her enthusiasm when it came to holding a tune.

Helen had finished icing the surprise birthday cake last night, and she could honestly say she was absolutely thrilled with the results. More often than not, any design Helen came up with in her head had to be adapted to cover the inevitable wonky bits. She'd grown accustomed to improvising as she went along, because although she could always guarantee that any cake she made would taste good, icing them had never exactly been her forte.

"What do you think?" She'd asked Mike, offering him a wide grin as he wandered into the kitchen, looking to see if there was any sign of his supper yet, as the hands of the old fashioned carriage clock on the mantelpiece had moved past nine o'clock a little while ago.

"Emily will love it Helen." He assured his wife heartily, realising just how much this meant to her. Knowing Emily the way he did, even if it the cake had been a complete botch job, she would still have been grateful for all the time and effort Helen had put into it, rather than just grabbing something from the supermarket shelf.

He sat contentedly at the big oak table, watching as Helen bustled around the enormous kitchen, cutting them both a thick wedge of home made fruit loaf, slathered with a generous layer of proper butter- they'd tried several of those low fat healthy spreads that were all the rage, but they always ended up coming back to their usual brand.

As he stirred his mug of hot chocolate his thoughts began to run ahead to the party tomorrow. With all the fuss that was being made, anyone would think that Emily was about to celebrate a big, significant, milestone birthday. The whole family had been in cahoots for days, exchanging hush-hush phone calls about presents, party-poppers, balloons and banners. Helen seemed to have been preparing enough food to feed an army over the last few days.

They were all keen to mark the occasion, to celebrate the fact that Emily seemed to be back to her usual vibrant self.

Only last weekend, he'd been standing here in the kitchen watching his daughter-in-law jabbering away to Helen, with her hands flailing around everywhere as she spoke. Suddenly he'd had to turn away for a moment, claiming to have got something in his eye.

 He must be having some sort of mid life crisis or something. Men like him didn't blub like some big girl's blouse, but he'd been forcibly struck with just how different the future might have turned out for Emily and Tom...

It had been such a relief to learn that this lovely young woman, this girl they'd both adored as though she were one of their own, for over twenty years, was not about to be robbed of the best years of her life.

Emily and Tom had been totally dedicated parents, and he and Helen couldn't be prouder of the fine young people their eldest grandchildren were shaping up to be. They had earned the right to be able to focus on them selves for a few years now while the kids were away at university. He hoped they'd really make the most of the next couple of decades, in much the same way that he and Helen had always tried to.

Now that the twins had started school and their services would only be required during the holidays, they had finally got round to planning some really long extended breaks in the caravan. They were going to take off for several weeks at a time next year, to explore Scotland, Ireland, and all the beautiful counties they had never reached before- just as they'd been promising themselves they would for ages.

 Life was far too short, much too precious, to waste. Their fifties seemed to have flown by, and he was already halfway towards the next big milestone- his seventieth birthday. That really didn't bear thinking about.

Compared to some of their friends, he and Helen were both in rude health. They had their fare share of aches and pains of course, but they really couldn't grumble... They considered themselves to be incredibly fortunate to still have all the family living so close... A few of their friends had kids and grandkids at the other end of the country, or abroad, so they were lucky if they saw them a couple of times a year.

Naturally everybody made all the right encouraging noises about cheap airfares and the beauty of Skype, but you could hardly put your hands into the screen and have a cuddle, or inhale that unique smell of a new born baby....

Mike stood up abruptly, swilling his cup in the sink before placing it very precisely in the dishwasher- he really must be starting to go a bit soft in his old age. It was definitely time to start the nightly rituals, check that everything had been switched off, that the curtains had all been drawn, and that the central heating had been set properly, before he and Helen made their way up to bed together...

49

Emily paused before stepping through the patio doors, taking a moment just to savour the scene before her. All her family, friends and colleagues; the people that really mattered to her, were jabbering away on the crowded lawn, bathed in the unparalleled golden light of this glorious autumn afternoon.

She'd had so many of these 'good to be alive' instances in the last few months, ephemeral moments when she chose to take just a few seconds out to acknowledge how content she was, how good life could be.

If there was one lesson that the trials and tribulations of the last eighteen months had taught Emily, it was not to take her health or her good fortune for granted. Life was for living, so if there was something she wanted to do, she was damn well going to get on and do it- while she still could.

Forty four- it was hardly a special 'milestone' birthday, yet as soon as she'd mooted the idea of a party, the little gathering she'd had in mind had quickly snowballed into a major event. It was as though everyone who knew her had instantly understood. Today, wasn't really about marking the day that she was born at all, it was more to do with celebrating the fact that she had been given her life back.

Doctor Morgan was absolutely thrilled with the progress she was making so far. She had been having her B12 level checked every three months, and it had been climbing, slowly but surely, every time.

Emily was positively euphoric. She had to metaphorically pinch herself every now and again, and still found it incredibly hard to get her head around the fact, that taking such a tiny little speck of a tablet every morning, could make such an enormous difference to her health. She didn't just feel like she'd been handed her old life back, she actually felt like she'd turned the clock back a few years.

It wasn't just the physical change in her that was so obvious. She felt much more clear-headed, able to focus and get on with things so much more efficiently. She was packing so much more into her days again, now that her energy levels where back to where they used to be. Even more importantly though, she felt as though she had her enthusiasm back- her zest for life- and that was probably the thing that had troubled her the most while she'd been ill. She'd hated the idea of turning into a miserable old fart who didn't want to go anywhere or do anything.

She and Tom were certainly making up for that now though.

Emily could still hardly believe that she had actually pressed the buttons and confirmed all the elements of their once in a lifetime amazing trip. In just a few short weeks they'd be leaving the grey November skies behind, to cruise around the South Pacific islands, before spending a couple of weeks in New Zealand. The itinerary she'd created involved driving the length of both islands, as they worked their way down from Bay of Islands in the extreme north, to Milford Sound, before flying back from Christchurch.

Emily had actually been looking at a deal for a client, when she'd come across the exotic cruise itinerary from Napier to Auckland at a ridiculously reduced price. Doing some rough calculations of the cost of flights, and a couple of weeks in New Zealand, she'd taken the idea home, half expecting Tom to dismiss the pipe dream.

"I've never even heard of half these islands." He'd laughed, his eyes lighting up at the possibility of them actually being there in a few weeks as he drooled over the pictures.

"Mmmm...they're the sort of places that only really come up in pub quizzes or on 'Pointless'" She'd grinned back at him, doing her best to suppress the urge to babble on about what a fantastic, once in a lifetime opportunity this was, to emphasise again the value of the low priced flights she'd found on the Travel Industry Staff web site.

This was huge, and she had to let Tom draw his own conclusions about whether or not the trip was remotely viable. It may be greatly reduced, but it was still a hell of a lot of money to them, and of course Tom would need to take a whole month off work to do everything she'd outlined.

"We could shorten the time in New Zealand if you think it's too long to be away from work?" She pointed out tentatively, watching the almost permanent groove between his eyebrows deepening as he studied the Transalpine rail journey, the glacier walks, whale watching and fjord cruising she'd highlighted in the brochure.

"It would be a bit daft to go all that way and not do as much as we can." Tom had stated simply, causing her heart to flip. He clearly wasn't about to dismiss the idea out of hand, even though it was the type of trip they'd only ever vaguely discussed as something they might do in the future- probably when they retired.

"I know it's still an awful lot of money to spend on a holiday...." she continued seriously, "but we didn't go anywhere last year and we could do something really modest next year...?"

"Well we can't take it with us can we Em, so we might as well start enjoying some of our savings before we get too decrepit." Tom cut in.

The look that passed between them, articulated so much more than what was actually being put into words. They'd both just had an enormous kick up the backside, realised that their health was a very precious commodity that was not to be taken for granted. Things really shouldn't be put off for a rainy day, because that rainy day might not actually come.

"Why don't I give Jack a ring and see how he and Dad would feel about me being away that long. I take it you've already asked your boss?" Though his dad was officially retired, not a great deal had really changed- except that he and Mum went off in the caravan for longer periods now.

Emily had jumped up at that point and hugged Tom exuberantly. Even if they weren't able to go, because too many other factors got in the way, the fact that, having had this sprung on him out of the blue, Tom was still willing to try and grab the opportunity with both hands, meant the world to her.

With an almost imperceptible shake of her head, Emily stopped dreaming about exotic islands and went back outside to join the throng. One or two of their guests were starting to round up their families, obviously getting ready to leave, and Helen was already circling the garden, clearing up discarded plates and glasses, and throwing rubbish into a black bin liner.

"It's been such a lovely day Emily..."

"Great to see you looking so well again..."

"Thanks so much for inviting us...."

As soon as one or two couples began to say their goodbyes, it wasn't long before the others started to drift away too, and peace was restored. Emily immediately took a much needed cuppa down to 'her' bench at the bottom of the garden.

Tom had built the small area of decking that filled the narrow, almost triangular space, right at the far end of the garden, years ago. Hedged on three sides, the little suntrap got the very last of the evening sun, so, whenever they'd had a fine day, Emily tended to take a piece of fruit or yoghurt down to this little spot after her tea- especially when she'd been cooped up at work all day.

In a few minutes she'd go back inside and start opening the huge pile of cards and presents that were waiting for her, watched by her precious family. Right now though, while Tom and the kids were still busy tidying up, she was going to take advantage of the privacy and open the thick cream envelope that had dropped through the letterbox earlier, along with a few other cards from people who hadn't been able to make it to the party...

This particular envelope, the one that had been addressed in a very distinct, immediately recognisable loopy scrawl, was one that Emily had subconsciously been waiting for ever since she'd heard that Fran was in recovery...

Printed in Great Britain
by Amazon